THE BOOK OF ZOG

ALEC HUTSON

The Book of Zog © 2022 by Alec Hutson
Published by Alec Hutson

Cover Art by Armand Cabrera
Cover Design by Christian Bentulan

Edited by Taya Latham, Editing by Taya

ISBN: 978-1-7342574-7-2 (paperback)
978-1-7342574-6-5 (ebook)

Please visit Alec's website at
www.authoralechutson.com

1

Deep in the cold dark, far beyond the frayed reach of the stars, a consciousness unfurled.

It was not, and then it was. The emergence was sudden, violent, a wrenching shuddering spasm in the fabric of the universe. Something appeared from nothing, slicked by cosmic afterbirth.

The void swaddled this inchoate awareness as it drifted through the black. A thought came, but if this formed in an instant or an aeon, it did not know. Time had little meaning in this place.

Zogrusz.

The entity had no mouth to shape this word – indeed, nothing to make any sort of sound. But this was its name, though it knew not what had bestowed such knowledge.

Perhaps it had been one of the Others.

For Zogrusz was not alone. It – no, he, Zogrusz knew that as well – could sense them floating out there, in the dark. Vast and terrible and oh, so ancient – the penumbra surrounding these presences was heavy with the weight of unfathomable time. They dreamed of universes long dead and ages yet to be, shifting and grumbling in their sleep, thoughts spilling out in a flood of images and sensations he could not comprehend.

Zogrusz felt something like kinship with these Others, these Old Ones, though he realized he was but an inconsequential mote when compared to those slumbering leviathans.

A child.

He extended a pseudopod of his understanding, hungry to know more. With infinite care, so as not to wake the Other closest to him, he mapped its shape, his perception skittering along coiled tendrils, sharp scales, cold pebbled skin, and its membrane-filmed eyes that stared at nothing and everything. Still, the Other shivered at his gossamer touch, murmuring as it turned away. A wash of whatever filled this place buffeted Zogrusz, sending him tumbling.

But when he finally came to rest, he knew what this Other looked like.

And so he bent to the task of forming himself.

He fashioned a body that was like and yet unlike what he had sensed, the void's chill licking his solidifying flesh. Limbs unfolded, flexed. Stunted wings fluttered. Eyes slid open and peered into the endless dark.

He *existed*. Zogrusz reveled in simply *being*.

Excitement overwhelmed him. He surged once more towards the Other whose shape he had appropriated.

I am here! he crowed into the void, sending this thought hurtling out with reckless gloating joy. *Welcome me! Show me what we are, what this place is. Tell me our purpose!*

The Other muttered, slapping in its sleep at this buzzing annoyance. Space and time rippled as an immense tentacle struck Zogrusz, obliterating the clarity of his thoughts and sending him spinning away, every pore of his newly-crafted body erupting with a novel and terrible sensation.

Pain.

Zogrusz's jaw unhinged for the first time, and he howled into the dark . . . and then fell silent when he sensed the nearest Other lurching towards awareness.

The heart he had so recently given himself thundered in his chest until the Old One gradually sank once more into its dreams.

Zogrusz considered what had just happened. Since his birth he had felt joy, and then pain, and now he thrummed with fear that he might be obliterated accidentally by these uncaring giants as they slept.

It would be like he had never been . . . and this was something he could not accept.

Chastened, Zogrusz turned, staring away from the Others. The void was different in this direction. At the very edge of his perception, he sensed a lightening. The black was not seamless.

Something was out there.

A new emotion stirred in him.

Following his burgeoning curiosity, he swam towards the distant stars.

THE JOURNEY across this dark sea was long and tiring.

At first he explored his new body, marveling at all the intricate systems that when bound together made up the whole of him. He counted his scales, measured the lengths of his claws, sent his perception winding through the pathways sunk beneath his flesh, the veins and nerves and arteries. Zogrusz forced his heart to stop beating, then made it resume when he realized he preferred the feeling of flowing blood. He flapped his ungainly wings to see if this might increase his speed (it did not). He practiced creating noises like he had heard the Old Ones make in their sleep.

When he knew everything that could be known about his physical form, he turned inwards, ruminating on what he was and the nature of this realm he was now traversing. Had he existed before his birth? Sometimes he felt like he had, that there was a great store of memories and knowledge sequestered deep within his mind . . . but in other moments he believed that these glimpses of other places – and those strange pangs of nostalgia – had seeped into his consciousness from the dreamers in the first darkness, those slumbering Old Ones.

He certainly knew some things that he had no right to know. When the first glimmering points of light emerged from the black, he realized he had been expecting their appearance.

Stars.

The remains of a fire that had blazed long ago, a failed attempt to push back the endless void. Embers slowly fading in the dark, around which huddled . . . what? Something. Something important, even for his kind.

How did he know this?

What was he?

IT BEGAN AS A FAINT ACHE, barely noticeable, but since there was little else to do, Zogrusz brought his full focus to bear in an effort to understand this new feeling. There was an emptiness inside him, he realized, and it seemed far too large for the actual dimensions of his flesh-formed body. It was from this gaping hollow that pain was radiating. *You hunger* murmured the ancient memories that he suspected were not his own. *You must eat.*

Eat what?

The blackness he traveled through lapped against his scales, but when he opened his mouth and let his tongue slip out from between his fangs, he tasted nothing.

Not the void. He would get no sustenance there.

His gaze returned to the stars that had quickly proliferated and now filled the black in every direction. One seemed larger and brighter than its brethren, and this he decided to make his destination.

THE SUN AWED HIM. It hung huge and bloated and red, far larger even than the sleeping Old Ones he had left far behind in the void. Despite its size, Zogrusz could sense the star was sick, dying, the ember in its core on the verge of guttering out. It had spilled forth from its shell long ago and swallowed whatever else had once existed in this place, save for a small dark speck that hovered just outside its ravenous boundaries. Zogrusz surged towards this anomaly, his curiosity rising.

A world, the voice inside him whispered.

His feet settled on the empty surface, raising a cloud of gray dust. He bent and scooped up a handful of this regolith, watching as it sifted through his claws and slowly drifted down again. The swollen star encompassed nearly everything above him, its sullen red veined by black fissures. He felt warmth for the first time, heating his scales and making the tips of his mouth-tendrils tingle.

He preferred the cold.

Dead. This place was dead; there was nothing for him here. The hollowness inside him twisted.

ZOGRUSZ WANDERED BETWEEN THE STARS, searching for something he could not describe.

He sank into the depths of a world formed from swirling gases and stood upon its churning molten core. He ran his tongue along the flowing metal, but this did not assuage the ache inside him. Elsewhere he explored pockmarked surfaces and ammonia seas and moons scoured by flensing solar winds, but he found nothing, and during this long and empty time his strength began to seep away.

On a frozen world, he felt a stab of hope that his long search was finally over. As the ice surged and clashed around him, he sensed something strange beneath his taloned feet. A dim awareness unlike anything he had encountered before. Then the ice cracked and shattered, and through this gap emerged a blunt, eyeless head. It swung back and forth as if trying to understand the nature of this new interloper in its domain. Zogrusz also extended his perception – he sensed a great sinuous length, its coils studded with shards used to break through the icy crust. He lingered in its rudimentary mind, tried to make sense of the worm's stunted consciousness, but in the end decided there was not enough there to try communication.

The creature seemed to arrive at a similar conclusion, as after snuffling around his legs it dove once more into the ice and was gone.

Zogrusz was briefly tempted to pursue it and attempt to fill the emptiness inside him with whatever he could take from the worm, but somehow he knew he would find no satisfaction there. This thing did not have what he needed.

So with a sigh, he lifted from the ice and resumed his quest.

HIS BODY CONTINUED TO WEAKEN, his thoughts clotting and growing slower, and when he found the next world he briefly wondered whether its strangeness might be the result of hunger-induced delirium. It was blue and green and banded with white clouds, and as he approached, Zogrusz could sense something different enveloping this planet, protecting it from the ravages of its star and holding tight a rich and fragrant mix of gases. He breathed deep as he descended through this atmosphere, savoring these new smells, and his mouth-tendrils writhed in excitement as he burst from the clouds and beheld a great sweep of verdant forest.

It thronged with life, the sheer overwhelming fecundity of this world making Zogrusz dizzy. Countless tiny consciousnesses infringed upon his thoughts, many of these far more complicated than the ice-worm he had encountered in the frozen waste. None were as deep as the baroque, fathomless minds of the Old Ones, but this was almost a relief. As far beyond the worm as he had been, the gap between him and the dreamers in darkness had been even greater. But perhaps here, among this panoply of shrieking chittering buzzing life, he might find something to communicate with.

And then he would no longer be alone.

THE FADING day trickled down through the thick canopy, painting the jungle in striations of shadow. Zogrusz wandered through a maze of gnarled trunks and knotted roots, his head brushing branches heavy with blue-veined leaves and pendulous red fruit. He sensed tiny creatures huddled in dens and burrows watching him in mute terror, while the larger animals hastened away as he approached, unwilling to challenge what they did not know. The raucous sounds he'd heard from above had quieted after his descent, as if the forest itself was holding its breath. Still, the smells and colors and even the humidity that sheathed his skin and the hissing crackle of the detritus beneath his feet were all overwhelming after so many barren worlds and the stark silence of the black between the stars.

But he found nothing to sate his hunger. He tried – he plucked a swollen fruit and swallowed it whole. Then he plunged his claws into a towering nest of insects and ate as many of the scurrying multitudes as he could catch. He even shoved his head into a stagnant pond and sucked in great mouthfuls of the murky water, wriggling fish and cold mud sliding down his throat to settle in his stomach.

The ache did not diminish. If anything, it grew stronger, and Zogrusz was forced to steady himself by sinking his claws into the bark of the trees as he passed to keep from sprawling among the roots.

He was dying.

This realization brought a welter of new emotions – anger, outrage, indignation. Was this his fate? To be vomited forth by the universe, only to slowly wither away? Even the wilting flowers clinging to the vines that wrapped these trees had some purpose – with their deaths, the seeds of the next generation would be spread, their legacy assured. What would happen when he finally collapsed here in the forest?

His would have been a meaningless existence. All he had seen, all he had experienced would be lost forever.

Night fell as he stumbled along, his movements growing more sluggish. His eyes easily pierced this darkness, since they had been created to function in the blackness of the void, and through the gaps in the forest canopy he glimpsed stars. He wondered which of those glittering points he had visited in his wanderings. His memories were growing hazy as his thoughts calcified. What would happen to the body he had shaped from the void's substance after he perished here? Would some strange new flower grow from his rotting flesh? He hoped so –

Wait.

Zogrusz came to an abrupt stop, the mist in his mind suddenly clearing. Through the tangle in front of him, he saw a flicker of light, and new sounds drifted to him that rose and fell with a far different cadence than the jungle's other noises.

Slowly, he crept forward.

A large clearing had been hacked from the forest and filled with crude structures fashioned from fallen trees lashed together with vines. A different animal skull was perched atop each of these buildings, gleaming in the moonlight, and a freshly butchered beast was splayed out in the grass, much of its flesh already stripped from its bones. Meat was turning on a spit over the fire where the creatures of this little community were clustered. They were making gabbling noises – loud, cheerful sounds – that suggested they did not fear the darkness their flame was pressing back.

Zogrusz hovered among the trees fringing their camp and drank deep of their thoughts. These were not simple creatures – their internal lives were nearly as rich as his own. He learned of this place, of the beasts in the forest and the fruit that was good to eat and the way to catch fish barehanded while sunk waist-deep in the river. He learned of the People and the great skull their chief wore when he was inhabited by the Spirit and of the drought that had chased them from the grasslands last summer and that their tribe had been blessed with five births so far this spring, three boys and two girls, all miraculously healthy and strong.

These were not worms or insects or animals slaved to base instincts.

They *thought*. They *dreamed*. They *desired*.

For so long, he had sought companionship. And finally, after a journey that had spanned the cosmos, he had found it.

He stepped into the light.

A woman feeding an infant turned towards him, and in her mind, he saw she was expecting to see her brother returning from his hunt.

"Hello!" Zogrusz exclaimed, raising his hands in this tribe's gesture of peace. "I am Zogrusz!"

She screamed, shielding her babe with her body. Every face in the clearing whirled at the sound.

Zogrusz's mouth-tendrils twitched nervously. "Hello?" he tried again as an avalanche of thoughts and emotions rushed over him.

Surprise. Confusion. Fear.

He rocked back on his heels, momentarily stunned by the raw intensity of the feelings erupting from these creatures. Scattered images assailed him – a great shadow looming from the forest, yellow eyes glowing, firelight glinting on wickedly curving claws. Shrieking noises emanated from it, vaguely word-like but far too harsh and grating to be understood.

Him. He was staring at himself, as seen and experienced by these strange thinking animals.

More screams, sparks exploding as the creatures scrambled away from the fire. A long piece of wood with a sharpened end bounced harmlessly off his shoulder. A spear, the knowledge he had drunk earlier from their flayed minds told him.

A weapon.

"Why are you frightened?" Zogrusz asked, trying to speak more clearly as he strode farther into the clearing. "I mean you no harm! I am Zogrusz! I only wish to feed and grow strong again!" He hesitated, realizing how poorly he had phrased this last statement. "But not on you! None of you look very appetizing, to be honest."

Another spear shattered against his scales.

The creatures were fleeing, tumbling over each other in their haste to escape. Even the few that had briefly thought to challenge him were now retreating, having seen their attacks fail. Zogrusz wanted to chase after them and give assurances that he was no threat, but from the panic he felt swirling in this clearing, he knew such actions would be misunderstood.

Also, something was different now.

As he watched the last of the animals vanish into the forest, he turned inwards, exploring this strange new sensation.

Full. He was sated. The gnawing ache inside him had disappeared with the last of these animals. Something had filled the emptiness. His tongue flickered out, tasting the humid air. It was . . . delicious. Thick with the sweet taste of terror. The panic his appearance had created, the fear . . . it was flowing into him, pooling in his gullet.

Dizzied, he stumbled into the fire, raising another scattering of sparks. His head was swimming, his own thoughts difficult to parse. He felt gorged, bloated, and he had the sudden overwhelming desire to rest.

But not here. Not in the ruins of this camp, with the bravest of the animals out there in the trees watching.

No, he needed somewhere dark and quiet. Zogrusz lifted his head, to where the shadow of a mountain loomed over the jungle. He imagined the deepness beneath, utterly bereft of light, not so different from the void of his birth. A place to sleep and slowly digest what had filled him to the brim and brought him near to bursting.

Mouth-tendrils quivering, Zogrusz staggered into the forest.

2

Zogrusz dreamed of floating in an endless black sea, but when he woke, he found himself curled on stone. He yawned as he sat up, his jaw clicking. His body felt stiff, unresponsive, and he wondered how long he had slept. He remembered dragging himself into a cave, wending his way deeper and deeper under the mountain until he had found this cavern. It was surprisingly large, stone teeth dripping from a ceiling so tall that most of the trees he'd seen in the forest could have stood here without their tops brushing rock. There was also a pool of dark water, phosphorescent fish flickering in its depths, and many-legged insects that scurried along the walls in a continuous clicking patter.

Zogrusz heaved himself to his feet and stretched. He ran his tongue over his jagged teeth and flexed his stunted wings. He felt . . . different. He had been worried that the hunger would return after he rested, but in truth, he felt even better than when he'd thrown himself down among the boulders to sleep. From his foray into the minds of the animals around the fire, he knew he had experienced something like when they celebrated and drank the fermented juice of certain fruits. Drunk. He'd grown drunk on whatever he'd consumed as the animals had run screaming from him.

The People, they had called themselves, though from their pilfered memories he also knew that they were not the only tribe. They had wandered all over these lands, from the plains to the hills to the jungle, and everywhere they had encountered others like themselves to fight and trade and mate with.

He must find them again. His hunger had vanished in those chaotic moments after he'd tried to introduce himself, and Zogrusz savored the memory of the delicious sweetness he'd tasted in the air. Had he truly feasted on their fear? He wasn't sure what he thought of that. It was certainly good that he'd learned how to fill the emptiness inside himself . . . but it did not bode well for making any sort of connection with these creatures. And he had yearned for so long to communicate with something else in the universe.

Zogrusz's eyes drifted to the tunnel where he'd entered this cavern. There were yet more things to discover in this world, he was sure of it.

HE EMERGED BLINKING into the day. The star around which this planet circled was yellow, young and vibrant. It would be many billions of years before it burst forth from its shell and swelled to consume this world. Zogrusz found this thought comforting, as the riot of life here would have ages yet to flourish.

The sun drenched the mountainside sloping down away from him in golden light. A few scraggly trees grew among the boulders, but mostly the view was unobstructed all the way to where the mountain merged with the plains below.

Plains?

Zogrusz frowned in confusion. He distinctly remembered slogging through the thick jungle right until reaching the mountain's stony flank, but now he could only see a few scattered patches of trees, not the great green expanse that had spread below him when he'd first descended from the stars. Strange. He narrowed his eyes, focusing on these colored flat patches of land where once trees had been. On some, huge herds of four-legged animals roamed, while others were divided into neat rows of plants, almost as if there was some intelligence behind their order. And in the far distance, he could make out what looked like heaps of stone, smoke rising from several of these piles to stain the sky.

The world had changed as he slept. He had not been curled under the mountain for a month or a year – he guessed that this world had journeyed around its star hundreds of times since last he'd stood on this slope. But if that was true, why had his hunger not returned? In fact, he could sense a trickle of sustenance entering him right now, and as he followed this stream back to its source, he realized it was coming from the collection of stone buildings beyond where the great herds milled on the plains below.

How was that possible?

He needed to investigate. But the memory of those animals scrambling away from the fire was seared into Zogrusz's mind. If he wandered down into that village as he was now, he suspected the response would be much the same.

But there was something different. He had changed after the hole within himself had been filled. He had grown larger . . . and new things were fluttering inside him. Powers he did not have before, and he sensed that one of them was the ability to alter his appearance like he had in the hazy time long ago when he had first emerged from the void. He thought back to the night in the clearing, the image of that animal's sibling that had been in her thoughts when she had first turned to Zogrusz as he stepped from the trees. A young . . . man. Yes, that was what these creatures called the male half of their species. Olive-skinned with dark curly hair, dressed in the cured hides of other creatures, brandishing a spear. That was who she had been expecting to see. Keeping that memory firmly fixed in his mind, Zogrusz began to change his form – he felt himself dwindling, his scales growing smooth and soft, his mouth-tendrils and wings receding. With his newly fashioned fingers he traced his lips and nose, tugged on his shoulder-length curls.

He now looked like one of these animals. One of the People.

It was time to go introduce himself again.

THE TREK across the grasslands was frustratingly slow on these stumpy little legs, and more than once Zogrusz considered reverting to his true form to hurry the journey. He quashed this idea, though, when a man watching a herd of four-legged animals graze straightened from where he had been leaning against a crooked staff and waved at him. Zogrusz tentatively responded with the same gesture, and the man turned back to his charges with none of the screaming or panic that had marked Zogrusz's last interaction with the People.

His disguise was apparently good enough, at least from a

distance. Still, his pulse quickened as he approached the stone walls of the small town. Even if he passed as a man, how could he be sure that as a stranger he wouldn't be greeted with more of those sharp weapons? Not that such things could hurt him, of course . . . but Zogrusz found he was quite excited about finally conversing with something else. These creatures on this world circling their unremarkable star did not know how rare intelligence truly was in the cosmos.

And indeed, the tall man in his coat of beast skin standing beside the town's open wooden doors did lower his spear threateningly when Zogrusz attempted to walk past him.

"Hold," the man growled, the spearpoint of chipped obsidian glittering in the sun. "State your name and purpose in Xochintl."

Zogrusz repeated the wave he'd exchanged with the old man, nearly stabbing himself on the spear. The guard blinked, clearly surprised. Aha, so this greeting was only done from afar. Good to know.

"Hello!" Zogrusz said loudly. "I am Zogrusz!"

The corners of the man's mouth twitched, as if he was fighting to hold back a smile. "Are you now?" he asked, the spearpoint dipping.

The man thought he was jesting. Zogrusz quickly scoured the store of knowledge he'd gleaned so far and learned that humor was a way to forge bonds of friendship. This seemed like a promising tactic at the moment.

"Ha-ha!" Zogrusz bellowed, stretching his mouth so wide that he felt his skin might split. "I am joking, of course! I am not Zogrusz! I am . . ." Zogrusz summoned up the memories he'd recently pilfered from the man watching his animals. "I am Napuatl!"

The guard relaxed further. "Are you any relation to the Napuatl of this town? He is a shepherd – indeed, he is out in the fields you just passed."

"Oh?" Zogrusz exclaimed, feigning surprise . . . and masterfully, he had to admit. Communicating with these animals was even more interesting than he had hoped. "No! I have never met this man."

The guard scratched at his cheek. "Truly? I thought I saw you wave to him."

Zogrusz inwardly berated himself. These creatures had better eyesight than he'd thought. "Ha-ha! That man is also named Napuatl? What a remarkable coincidence!"

The man shrugged. "It doesn't matter. I take it from how you first introduced yourself that you're here to visit the shrine?"

Shrine? Zogrusz reached into his store of knowledge but found nothing about a shrine. He should have drunk deeper of the shepherd Napuatl and not just skimmed the surface of his mind. Zogrusz had been enjoying the spontaneity of this conversation and was loath to enter this man, but he supposed he should learn more about this town. Perhaps he could find the answer without delving too far.

As luck would have it, the image of an impressive stone building decorated with skulls and tufts of black feathers was at the forefront of the guard's thoughts. This must be the shrine. Why would he want to go there? But if this man thought that was an acceptable reason for him to enter the town, so be it.

"Yes! I have long wanted to go to the shrine. I hear the bones and feathers are very pleasing to look upon!"

From the crinkling of the man's forehead, he must have said something wrong. Still, the guard stepped aside, motioning with his spear for him to pass through the doors.

"Enter, then, friend Napuatl, and may the dark blessing of Zogrusz be upon you."

At the sound of his name, Zogrusz barely kept his grip on the man-cloak he wore. If it had fallen away, he would have reverted to his true form, and wouldn't *that* have been an extremely unfortunate turn of events, but with an act of will he tamped down his frisson of surprise and reasserted his control over his disguise. Instead, he smiled as he walked unsteadily past the guard and through the great wooden doors, his mind whirling.

How had that man known his name?

Lost in his thoughts, Zogrusz nearly collided with a woman carrying a basket overflowing with vegetables. She danced around him, snarling some imprecation that in his troubled state he couldn't quite catch, and then she continued along the single muddy road bisecting the small town. Stone buildings loomed on either side of this avenue, and behind these he glimpsed more rudimentary structures of wattle and daub. There were many men and women, squatting in the shade outside the entrances to buildings and clustered around where fruit was laid out on colorful blankets. Shrieking children chased each other around the legs of the adults, and a few small, graceful creatures lounged in the shadows – cats, Zogrusz learned after consulting the knowledge he had already absorbed. He noticed that the townspeople were dressed in dyed cloth shifts and dresses, very different from the animal skin jerkin he'd summoned out of his memories. But perhaps his garb was not so unusual, as no one had even spared him a second glance as he wandered down the street.

The commotion was overwhelming, an intoxicating mélange. Stray thoughts bombarded him, along with sounds and smells unlike anything he could have imagined. If he'd known how to render himself invisible, he would have stopped in the middle of the road and let these sensations wash over him; since he did not – nor did he want to draw any undue attention to himself – he continued walking, while also trying his best to keep the illusion he had created absolutely flawless. To help himself focus, Zogrusz concentrated on the delicious nectar that had drawn him here. It hovered in the street, pulling him along as if plucking at some primal need. He couldn't help but taste the air with his man-tongue, and even though the flavor was diluted, it still thrilled him. He was much closer to the source of what had sustained him while he slept.

He found he was not surprised when the trail ended in front of the structure the guard at the gate had called the shrine. It was the most impressive building in this town – taller than Zogrusz even in his true form – and was the only one decorated with bones and feathers and other small talismans. Clearly, this was a place of great importance to these People.

Zogrusz pushed through the hide flap covering the entrance and found himself in a single large room. The day trickled through in places where the irregularly fitted stones of the walls were not perfectly joined, and that was the only light in the chamber. Something strange-smelling had also been burned here recently, making the interior even murkier. Reed mats were scattered about, surrounding a great flat chunk of stone in the middle of the room, and Zogrusz could tell that the object placed on this rock was of some importance.

It was a statue. Not large – perhaps only as tall as his forearm was long – but it was intricately carved, though also evidently ancient, as some details had been effaced by time.

Still, there was no doubt about what it was supposed to represent.

Him.

Zogrusz traced the lines, marveling at the skill that had summoned his likeness from the stone. Huge bulbous eyes above a nest of writhing mouth-tendrils, a thick muscled body with the nubs of wings poking out over sloping shoulders.

How marvelous. How beautiful.

"You there!"

Zogrusz turned. A cadaverous old man in flowing robes stood framed in the entrance to the shrine. From his expression and the tone of his voice, Zogrusz suspected he was angry.

"Hello!" Zogrusz cried cheerfully. He nearly waved but then stopped himself. The man was almost certainly too close for such a greeting.

"You dare touch our god Zogrusz?" the man snarled, letting the hide flap fall as he strode into the chamber, his hands clenched.

Zogrusz snatched his fingers back from the statue. "Apologies!" he cried. "I was overcome by the workmanship."

The man scowled, but Zogrusz sensed a slight softening in his mood. "I understand, stranger. I remember my first time in this room, when I felt His presence looming over me. But you cannot so blithely stroke the visage of our dread lord! Such disrespect might summon His wrath, and all of Xochintl would suffer."

"What delightful nonsense!" Zogrusz exclaimed, clapping his hands together. "Did you make it up yourself?"

Even in the gloom, Zogrusz could see the man's face darken. Oh no, he'd miss-stepped again.

"Nonsense?" the man hissed. "It is the wisdom of our ancestors! It was *they* who Zogrusz appeared before and whispered his dread words. And so long as we honor him in this place, he will not return and punish us for our failings!"

Zogrusz thought back to that night in the clearing. He remembered introducing himself several times – apparently, at least one of these animals had been listening.

"How do you know he is so vindictive?" Zogrusz ventured. "Perhaps he is a friendly god."

The old man barked a mirthless laugh. "Ha! Friendly? He is the Lord of the Abyss, the Night-bringer, the Devourer of Souls. And yet He has bestowed great wealth and power on our tribe in return for our fearful devotion. It is our glorious mission to spread His dark shadow over all these lands."

Zogrusz couldn't help but smile at the man's words. "So you will go out and bring others to worship Zogrusz? To fear him?"

"Of course!" the man replied. "Our warriors have defeated a dozen tribes, and all of them have cast down their pathetic spirits in favor of Zogrusz!" The man's expression turned shrewd. "Perhaps you are here from one of these peoples to steal His holy statue? Is that it?"

Zogrusz held up his hands placatingly. "No, no! I promise your fears are mistaken! I was merely curious."

"Curious," the old man murmured, his eyes narrowing. "But you are a stranger. Why should I not call for our warriors to come and bleed you out as a sacrifice to our dark lord?"

Zogrusz had the sudden giddy desire to let his man-mask slip for a moment. He would take great pleasure in seeing the look on this man's face if one of his mouth-tendrils squirmed loose. But he hesitated, unsure what kind of chaos would result if he revealed himself.

He needed to leave this place and consider his next course. Whatever the animals of this town were doing in this shrine in front of that statue had kept him fed during his long sleep, and before he upset the situation here he should think very carefully about what he was doing.

The old man was still watching him for a response to the threat he had just made. Well, he'd try his best to satisfy him.

"Oh, no!" Zogrusz cried, covering his mouth with his hand. "Please, no bleeding! I prefer my blood inside me!"

The man frowned, his eyebrows rising. Apparently, this was not the reaction he had been expecting.

"Then away with you," he snapped, jerking his head in the entrance's direction.

"Yes, of course!" Zogrusz said, hurriedly crossing the chamber and flinging aside the flap. He waved jauntily at a few nearby women who had stopped their conversation to stare at him in surprise, and then he began striding purposefully down the street in the direction of the town gate, his stolen man-body thrumming with exhilaration from this fascinating exchange.

HALFWAY TO HIS MOUNTAIN, Zogrusz climbed a small hill and gazed back at the town. There had been no alarm raised behind him, no spear-carrying warriors rushing in pursuit, so it seemed that the old man – the priest, he'd realized, after having more time to sift through the knowledge he'd absorbed – had let him go. Despite being the servant of what he believed to be a fearsome god, the fellow didn't truly seem all that terrible. That pleased Zogrusz.

"They are interesting, aren't they?"

Zogrusz blinked in surprise, glancing down. Sitting on its haunches in the grass beside him was a cat, its little face turned up to regard him. It had golden eyes and pale fur the color of the moon. The animal must have followed him from the town.

"I didn't know your kind could speak," Zogrusz said, squatting down beside the animal.

"Not all of us can, Zog," said the cat in a voice that seemed far too deep for such a little creature. Then it stretched languidly and yawned, its claws kneading the ground.

Bemused, Zogrusz ran his hand down its fur. The sensation was pleasant.

"The question arises," the cat continued, arching itself into his touch, "why you didn't shed your disguise in the town, particularly after that awful old man threatened you. Stomp about and send the poor little humans fleeing."

"Humans," Zogrusz repeated, rolling the word around in his mouth as he straightened. "That's what you call them?"

"That's what they are," stated the cat, rising and coming to rub itself against his leg. "They don't really think of themselves as a distinct species, so it's probably why you haven't drawn the term from their minds."

"I see." Zogrusz frowned, suddenly realizing he felt no wash of emotions and memories flowing from this animal. "Why can't I look into your thoughts, cat?"

"Call me Rhas," it replied. "And it's because I don't want you to. It's a bit rude, honestly."

"I'm sorry."

"It's all right, as you clearly don't know any better." The

cat batted at a bug flying past its head. "But let's not get too far away from my question. Why didn't you terrify those humans down there?"

Zogrusz shrugged. "They all seemed to be having a nice day. It would have been a shame to upset them."

The cat was quiet for a long moment, and when Zogrusz glanced down, he found it was peering up at him with an almost unsettling intensity.

"Is something the matter?"

"You are not what I expected at all in an Eldritch Horror."

"Is that what I am?" Zogrusz asked, his interest rising. "An Eldritch Horror?"

"I thought so," the cat replied slowly. "But now I'm less sure. To be honest, I assumed you would be a lot more . . . horrible."

"Huh," Zogrusz said, his gaze drifting to the faint outline of the moon in the darkening sky. "Rhas, please tell me more about Eldritch Horrors."

"My knowledge is limited," the cat admitted. "Your kind are rare, and usually exist very far from here. But occasionally you venture forth, especially when young . . . and growing."

"I've seen them," Zogrusz murmured, remembering the sleeping Old Ones. "I don't think they hunger as I do. What could satisfy such vast creatures?"

"If one of them wakes, the universe trembles in fear," the cat said matter-of-factly. "At least those pockets of the universe that can feel fear. For that is what Eldritch Horrors feed upon, as I'm sure you've realized. Terror. Dread. Panic." It cocked its head to the side as it regarded him. "Have you noticed the different flavors of each of these?"

Zogrusz nodded slowly. "That first night, in the clearing,

when the People fled before me . . . the taste was so sweet it made me dizzy."

"Something similar happens to humans when they eat sugar cane or overly sweet fruits," the cat explained. "It is a great rush, but the effects recede quickly. If you instill panic it will be delicious, but not nearly as filling as other forms of fear." The cat sat back on its haunches and pointed its face in the direction of the stone town. "The humans down there still fear you, but it is more of an existential dread. You are a vague presence used to threaten them with punishment."

Zogrusz concentrated on the river of fear flowing from the town. "You're right, it is different than before. Now it is not so sweet, but I feel more . . . sated."

The cat swished its tail, and Zogrusz sensed it was satisfied with what he'd said. "Good. So if you turn into a giant monster and go stomping around, you will get that flood of delicious fear, but you'll soon find yourself hungry again. And then it becomes a vicious cycle where you need to create even more panic, but the effects will dissipate faster and faster. Eventually, you'll spend all your time chasing humans around to stay alive. What you have right now down in that village is far more . . . sustainable. Not as tasty, but much better in the long run. And that's why I first asked you why you hadn't transformed into your true form in the town and started a mad panic. I thought you must know about your nature, but apparently you do not."

"It just didn't seem like the proper thing to do," Zogrusz said, peering with interest at the talkative little cat. "Who told you all this?"

Rhas raised a paw and began licking it in a way that Zogrusz could only describe as arrogant. "I'm a cat," it said airily. "We are very perceptive. And intelligent. Also, as the true masters of those humans down there, I would prefer if you didn't send them all rushing around in a blind terror. Far more likely then that they'll forget to feed us."

"Oh? What do you eat?"

"Plenty of things," the cat replied. 'Mice. Fish. Birds. And bits of souls. We draw a little away from humans by rubbing our heads against them, which creates a disturbance in the psychic realm through vibrations that fracture the foundation of their souls."

"How ingenious."

"Yes, well, you can see how we don't want the status quo disrupted too much. Humans make fantastic livestock, but it's best if they don't suspect they're being fed upon."

"I see," Zogrusz said, looking at the moon-colored cat with newfound respect.

"Wonderful," the cat said brightly. "It seems we understand each other. I'll be off then, Zog. There's a sunny spot calling to me and a nice old lady who usually stops by in the afternoon with fish heads."

"Goodbye," Zogrusz said. "It was a pleasure talking to you, Rhas. I hope I can meet you again."

"Very likely," the cat replied, and then with a twitch of its tail that might have been a farewell, it scampered down the hill, quickly vanishing into the long grass.

"What a nice fellow," Zogrusz murmured as he turned back to his mountain.

HE WAS NOT EXPECTING the emotions that flooded him when he again stood at the entrance to his cavern. Staring out at the boulder-strewn stillness, listening to the silence (save for the scurrying insects), smelling the musty air, he suddenly felt profoundly alone. Even if their souls were slowly being eaten by their cats, Zogrusz couldn't help but feel jealous of the humans, always around others of their kind. The memory of his conversations with the old priest and the guard made him feel slightly better . . . and he supposed there was nothing stopping him from going out and mingling with the People again. Perhaps after another sleep he would venture forth once more.

Zogrusz wandered around his cavern, claws clasped behind his back. Would he feel happier if he could make this space more . . . homely? He thought back to the shrine in the town and the statue inside it. The beauty of that carving had filled another emptiness that he hadn't even known had existed. Zogrusz crouched and picked up a rock the size of his hand. He pressed his claw into its surface and was pleased to see a furrow appear. Sticking his tongue from his mouth and concentrating hard he began to etch the same design he'd seen on the shrine's statue. Time ceased to have meaning as he worked – it might have taken him just the night, or perhaps several days passed, but finally he was done and held up what he had made. His own face stared back at him from the rock, large pupilless eyes set above a nest of mouth tendrils, and he'd even added some details that he remembered the statue as lacking, such as the creases in his broad forehead and the subtle intimations of scales. A warmth filled him, and it took Zogrusz a few moments to put a name to this feeling.

Satisfaction.

He set down the carving on the floor of the cavern. No, he thought with a frown, that didn't seem right, and so he piled together a few loose rocks and perched it atop this little cairn. That was better, but still he felt like his creation deserved a better resting spot. Zogrusz remembered the flat piece of stone the statue had stood upon in the shrine.

Surely he could make something similar. He searched the cavern until he found a good-sized boulder. He turned it over, tapping until he felt a spot that seemed weaker than the rest, then struck this imperfection a sharp blow with his fist. The rock broke apart into two pieces, one of which was about the size he had envisioned for what he wanted to make. He saw it in his mind's eye clearly: a block of stone, with a small plinth on top where his carving would sit, and its sides decorated with designs of the moons and stars and planets he had visited in his journeys.

Zogrusz settled down beside the chunk of rock, his excitement rising. This first attempt would be crude, he knew, as he learned how to shape the stone with his claws and whatever else he could find to use as tools, but he felt confident that with enough effort he could make something wonderful. He laughed, surprising himself, the sound rebounding off the walls. Zogrusz sank one of his claws into the rock and worked it back and forth until he felt a crack open up inside, then struck it hard enough that the piece slid away cleanly, revealing what would become the first side of the block. He paused before he continued, once more looking about his cavern. What else could he create?

Zogrusz lost himself in his labors. After completing the altar upon which his first crude attempt at a carving would rest, he fashioned a great, rough-hewn chair from one of the chunks of stone scattered about the cavern, large enough that he could recline in it even in his true form. And since he thought he might also want to relax while wearing his man-disguise, he made another throne, but this time human-sized. His thoughts wandered as he carved this second chair, revisiting everything that had transpired since he had woken in his cavern, and Zogrusz decided he should also have somewhere for the cat Rhas to rest if he ever visited. So despite the difficulty of carving such a tiny piece with such massive hands, he carefully formed a low, flat divan that looked like something the cats he had seen sprawled in the sun in the town might enjoy. He hoped so, anyway . . . and he also hoped that one day Rhas would indeed lie here, and know that Zogrusz had been thinking of him. Zogrusz suddenly realized that he'd come to think of the cat as male, perhaps because of the deepness of Rhas's voice. He supposed he'd continue with that assumption until informed otherwise.

When he'd finished these first few furnishings for his cavern, Zogrusz collapsed into his mighty chair and wiped his dusty hand across his scaled brow. Gazing at what he'd done, he felt another upwelling of satisfaction. He'd worked for quite some time – several days, at least – but he knew the vision in his head that had slowly been forming would take much longer to realize. He would fashion a tiered ziggurat in the center of the cavern, upon which he would place his throne, and beside this he'd smooth and level a space where he could sleep. Also, he'd set benches beside the pool of water so he might sit and watch the phosphorescent fish in its depths. And the walls . . . he imagined them covered with many carvings, records of his voyage between the stars and his time here on this fascinating world. Such an effort would take many years, but this did not trouble him. He would work until he tired and then sleep and work some more.

After all, he had all the time in the universe.

3

Something was wrong.

Sunk deep in his dreams, Zogrusz at first tried to ignore this vague sense of unease. But it was insistent, a nagging itch that demanded to be scratched, and with a tremendous effort he finally hoisted himself from the black womb in which he floated and clawed his way towards consciousness. As the dreamscape receded behind him and his awareness returned, that irritation became a throbbing ache . . . and then, when he fully breached into the woken world, he was consumed with blinding agony.

Zogrusz groaned, rolling onto his side as he clutched at his stomach. It felt like his insides were being devoured by his own hunger. The vast reservoir that had been filled by the fearful dread of the People when he had gone to sleep had been almost completely drained – now just a tiny trickle still flowed from outside, and Zogrusz suspected that was all that was keeping him alive.

What had happened?

With some effort, he pushed himself into a sitting position. The cavern whirled, and it took a great effort of will to make the spinning stop. How long had he been asleep this time? Had the humans forgotten him?

Zogrusz climbed unsteadily to his feet. The tiered pyramid he had constructed in the center of the cavern tilted alarmingly, but then righted itself as he found his balance. Zogrusz gazed up longingly at the throne he'd set at the ziggurat's apex, but then dismissed the idea of dragging himself up there. If he let himself rest, he might never rise again.

Zogrusz gritted his fangs, his claws pressing into the palms of his clenched fists. He took a stumbling step towards the mouth of the tunnel that led outside, but then paused in surprise. He had changed again, like the last time he had woken from his sleep – he had grown larger and stronger, and he sensed a new ability. Zogrusz concentrated on the darkness choking the entrance to the tunnel, and it writhed like a thing alive. Momentarily forgetting the gnawing pain inside himself, Zogrusz coaxed forth a shadowy serpent, twining it around his arm before letting it dissipate. It had felt solid, as if he'd somehow given substance to the black.

A pang like a metal spike piercing his stomach made him wince. The exploration of this new power would have to wait; his immediate concerns were far more pressing.

The twisting tunnel passed in a blur, and then he burst out of the mountain and stood swaying in the harsh sunlight. Far below him, the rows of crops and herds of animals were gone, much of the land reclaimed by forest. Blinking, he tried to focus on where the stone town had stood, but now there was just a wild tangle of trees. He saw no humans or even wisps of smoke to suggest they still dwelled somewhere nearby.

Yet that small rivulet of worshipful dread persisted.

Were there humans squatting in the jungle who remembered him? Zogrusz bounded down the mountain, his huge strides devouring the distance. Why should he bother with a man-disguise at this moment? The memory of how delicious the taste of blind panic had been on that long-ago day in the forest made his insides twist. He wouldn't mind at all if someone saw him right now.

Zogrusz quickly reached where the village had been. Surprisingly, the trickle of fear remained attenuated, as if it was still coming to him from very far away. His true form was now taller than the trees, and he waded into the jungle, using his great claws to pull aside the branches so he could see what the canopy had hidden. A flock of colorful birds burst from below as he did this, startling him.

Ruins. Tumbled walls veined by creepers, roots buckling the remnants of foundations. The forest had reclaimed Xochintl and was devouring its corpse.

The People were gone. They had been the first conscious beings he had encountered, and their dread had sustained him for the turning of an age. But something had happened, and they had vanished.

Or had they? Zogrusz raised his gaze from the ruins and stared out over the undulating green expanse of trees. Somewhere out there someone feared him. Perhaps the People had abandoned this place but still held fast to their old beliefs, and if he followed this trail he could find them again.

With a newfound resolve, Zogrusz walked into the jungle, his perception fixed on that distant, thready, life-giving pulse.

∽

THE DAY DEEPENED as he traveled farther and farther from his mountain home. Eventually, the forests thinned, then vanished entirely, replaced by grasslands pockmarked by lakes and copses of stunted trees. Great herds of animals bounded away from him as he approached, their curved horns glittering in the sun, but from the lack of shepherds he could tell that these were wild beasts. There was evidence that humans were about, however, as a road of fitted stones wended through the plains like an impossibly long snake, vanishing into the hazy distance. And after following it for a while, he encountered a lone wagon pulled by shaggy, plodding creatures.

He realized there were humans on it before he saw them, as Zogrusz suddenly tasted a rush of sweet panic. It was delicious but hardly made a dent in the emptiness inside him – as he had swelled in size, so too had his appetites. When his vast steps brought him closer, he glimpsed a tiny figure seated behind the hairy animals, lashing them on frantically. Zogrusz felt a stab of guilt about causing such terror in the poor fellow, but he also appreciated the sustenance. Still, he tried not to appear overly threatening as he passed the wagon and its driver, and he hoped that after he had disappeared over the horizon, the man would come to dismiss this as just some strange vision.

It would be much harder for the next humans Zogrusz encountered to believe he had been nothing more than a figment of their imagination.

The town hemmed the road, maybe two dozen small buildings in total. A few people were scurrying about like insects after their rock had been overturned, but most were huddled inside, staring in awed dread at the monstrous giant striding across the plains. Zogrusz saw himself in their thoughts in all his scaled glory, and he had to admit he did look rather impressive. He turned towards the little village and waved, enjoying the thrill of confusion that rippled through the watcher's minds.

He drank deep of their fear, and for a moment he almost felt sated. But he was like a bucket with a hole at the bottom – their terror briefly filled his aching emptiness, but then just as quickly it drained away, leaving him as hungry as before. The cat Rhas had been right – the panic conjured up by his presence was not nearly as filling as the worshipful dread that had previously sustained him.

He really needed to recover the previous state of affairs.

Night settled over the plains, and the thin trickle of terror he followed strengthened slightly as he neared its source. Evidence of habitation grew more common, the pinpricks of light scattered about suggesting towns, and the faint clamor of many minds infringed upon his thoughts. No great upwellings of fear, though – it was a moonless, cloudy night, and to the few that were outside, he was but a massive shadow as he passed. Zogrusz also experimented with his new power, weaving himself a shroud of darkness that would drink the faint starlight and hide him even if the clouds parted.

He was so lost in testing his capabilities that at first he didn't realize he'd arrived at his destination. The city rose from the edge of the plains like a clenched fist, many buildings and a forest of thin towers girdled by a mighty wall. Beyond it spread a darker plain than the grasslands, and it took Zogrusz a moment to realize he was staring at the sea.

This city was a hundred times larger than the village outside his mountain. A thousand. The abilities of architects and stonemasons had improved dramatically while he slept, and he felt a strong urge to wander among these great buildings. What inspiration could he find inside? The thought made his pulse quicken.

But he did not want to send those living here fleeing in panic . . . at least until he understood who still feared him within these walls. The avalanche of fear that would result if he arrived at the city in his true form would be intoxicating – and it made his mouth tendrils twitch in anticipation just thinking about it – but as the cat had warned him, he would have to continuously create larger and more terrifying spectacles if that was the path he went down. So after he'd approached as close to the mighty walls as he could while remaining unseen, Zogrusz folded the great majesty of his form into the man-cloak he had worn before. Then when he stood upon the road leading to the city, he also allowed the darkness with which he had cloaked himself to dissipate into wisps of shadows.

He'd chosen a spot that was empty of travelers, but soon after beginning the trek towards the looming walls, he heard the clopping of hooves. A wagon was coming up behind him, a hunchbacked old man huddled behind a pair of agitated horses.

Zogrusz could guess why.

"Ho, stranger!" the driver called out, pulling his horses to a snorting halt when he reached where Zogrusz stood in the middle of the road. He looked around, clearly expecting to find something else here.

"Hello," Zogrusz said with a wave.

The old man squinted down at him blearily. "Did ya see anything strange here, laddie? Me horses are dancing like they caught a whiff of a whole pack o' garanth."

Zogrusz made a show of peering into the long grass fringing the road. "No, I didn't see any garanth." From the old man's thoughts he pulled the image of huge ink-black lizards with manes of curving spines.

The driver grunted. "Ya wouldn't, they're clever bastards. Never come this close to Amotla before, though." He flicked a length of braided reeds across the backs of his horses, but this did little to settle the stamping beasts.

"Still," the old man continued, "something's got them upset. Might be you should get in the back until we reach the city." He jerked his head at the wagon behind him, which Zogrusz saw was full of fruit. "Jus' don't go eating the melons, is all I ask."

"Thank you," Zogrusz said, climbing up into the back of the rickety cart and finding a spot where he could sit among the mounded green fruit.

"Welcome," the old man said, turning back to the road after he saw that Zogrusz had settled himself. "The Burning Scrolls teach us ta care for strangers. Never know when someone could be Anecoya herself in disguise." With a crack of his whip he sent the wagon lurching forwards again, and when he spoke next, he had to raise his voice to be heard over the plodding horses. "Not that ye look much like a god, I must say."

"Oh, that's wonderful."

"What?"

"I said that's wonderful . . . because I don't look like a god."

The old man lapsed into silence at this, and Zogrusz worried that he had made a serious mistake. But after a moment the driver only shook his head. "Yer certainly a strange one."

"Truly, you have no idea."

∾

ZOGRUSZ SLIPPED inside the old man's mind as they trundled towards the great city, but he found no answers to satisfy his questions. The fellow's mental landscape was overwhelmingly dominated by thoughts of a clear liquid called pulque, a bottle of which was waiting for him at his home. From what little Zogrusz could extract, they were approaching Amotla, the greatest city of these lands and ruled by the priest-king Cozotl. His rummaging unearthed nothing about a dread god named Zogrusz, but there was plenty concerning the goddess Anecoya.

It seemed he had some competition.

Mosaics adorned the walls of the city, images of a red bird in flight illuminated by flames flanking the great gates. There were other people passing into Amotla at this late hour, and the bored-looking guards waved them along without even bothering to inspect the wagon or Zogrusz, sitting among the fruits as he stared up in awe at the soaring fortifications.

Truly, these humans had built something incredible here. And beautiful – the vibrant pictures set into the walls were comprised of countless small colorful stones perfectly arranged. Could he do the same in his mountain sanctuary? Zogrusz imagined graven images flowing into such mosaics and filling the cavern's walls, and he shivered in excitement at the thought. What clever little creatures these humans had become!

The wagon passed through the gate and entered a great market square that must have been bustling earlier in the day. Now only a few merchants remained, and they were selling confections of spun sugar and meat threaded on long sticks to laughing men and women wearing feathered masks. Houses of white stone rose around the square, their doors and windows gracefully arched, many also boasting balconies with wrought-iron balustrades. One building recessed in the city loomed over all the rest, its domed roof ringed by slender minarets.

Zogrusz was so overcome by the majesty of what the humans had created that he didn't realize the wagon had come to a halt until the old man spoke.

"Well, friend, here's where we part. I have ta deliver these melons, and I canna imagine you want ta come visit a fruit warehouse, what with all the city to explore."

Zogrusz nodded absentmindedly as he climbed down from the back of the wagon, still looking about wide-eyed.

The old man chuckled, shaking his head. "I can see this is yer first time in the Queen of Cities. Enjoy yourself, lad, but make sure ta keep a hand on yer money-pouch and yer wits about ye." Then with another flick of the reins, he sent the wagon lurching forward again.

Zogrusz didn't even think to say farewell or thank the old man, as he was too distracted by the incredibly rich stew of thoughts and emotions filling the square. Briefly he entertained the idea of shedding his disguise and sending the humans here scurrying in blind panic. He could almost taste the delicious flood of fear that would result, and the hollowness that had been slowly growing inside him ached in yearning.

But not yet. He would resort to such crudity only if he felt his survival was truly at stake. Until then, he'd try to discover where that trickle of dreadful worship was coming from.

It was much stronger here in the city proper, and he knew he was close to the source. But there were so many ambient psychic distractions that he was finding it difficult to know where exactly he should search. Zogrusz slowly turned, his gaze sweeping the pavilions and stalls of the market square. His curiosity was drawn to where a crowd had gathered in front of a covered stage. Elaborate wooden carvings decorated its frame, and Zogrusz realized that one of these images depicted him in his true form, though his head was ridiculously large and some of his writhing mouth-tendrils were grasping drooping flowers. His portrayal was just one of several, and the others included a grinning dog and a solemn human child holding an hour-glass. Looming over all these carvings was a great red bird with wings outspread, its feathers resembling tongues of flame. Bemused, Zogrusz wandered towards the stage, and as he drew closer he noticed movement atop its roof – several humans were crouched up there, almost invisible to those watching from below.

Excited murmurs rippled through the crowd as some-thing descended towards the stage. It was a cleverly constructed wooden doll with fabric mouth-tendrils and stunted little wings, suspended by threads that allowed for each limb to move independently. Zogrusz found he was grinning watching this representation of himself alight on the stage and begin to amble back and forth. How marvelous! So these humans remembered him! But the dread that had kept him alive as he slumbered had not orig-inated from this puppet show, for he could sense that the watching humans did not fear him.

In fact . . .

Zogrusz frowned as the puppet suddenly changed its gait. Now it strutted across the stage, radiating arrogance through the skillful manipulation of those above, and a few scattered guffaws rose up from the watchers. He sensed tension, like those around him were waiting for something with bated breath. This wasn't really fair, Zogrusz grumbled internally – he had never comported himself like this puppet, even though he *was* a far more advanced and powerful being. In fact, he had tried to avoid upsetting humans whenever he encountered them . . .

Zogrusz gasped when some white liquid poured from above to splatter on the puppet's oversized head. Laughter erupted from the crowd as the wooden Zogrusz began running around in a panic, mouth-tendrils flapping comically. Another puppet swooped down from where it had been hidden, a red bird that chased the Zogrusz off the stage to applause and cheers. It flapped in a circle, then settled on the platform and spread its wings wide. Zogrusz noticed that flames were painted onto the bird puppet, as if it had been set on fire.

He frowned as several other puppets were lowered to join the bird on the stage. The humans clearly remembered him, but now derision had replaced veneration. It was no wonder that he had awoken on the brink of starvation. They did not fear him anymore.

Or most of them, anyway. Zogrusz sniffed, focusing once more on what had drawn him to the city. Someone here still held fast to the old ways, he was sure of it. He turned away from the stage and began pushing through the crowd of masked humans, following that faint trail. Behind him, the bird-puppet screeched, and to Zogrusz it sounded mocking.

~

AMOTLA WAS A LABYRINTH.

Narrow streets twisted between buildings that rose like canyon walls, eventually spilling into empty plazas drenched in darkness. Zogrusz felt eyes watching him hungrily from the shadows, but none dared confront him as he pushed deeper and deeper into the city. The number of lit torches dwindled, with some areas black as pitch, a heavy blanket of clouds obscuring the moon and stars.

He was drawing closer.

Finally, Zogrusz found himself before a crumbling archway sunk slightly below street level, at the base of an abandoned building that once had been impressive. The taste of fear was strongest here, flowing out of this entrance like a river, and he paused for a few long moments to greedily gulp down what was welling up from below. He could sense many consciousnesses nearby, minds clustered together in joined purpose, and Zogrusz passed through the arch slightly unsteadied as he started on the passage sloping down.

He heard them first, a low droning. The sound strengthened as he descended, and his pulse quickened, thrumming in his veins. This was the source. This was why he still existed, even though the town of Xochintl had long since vanished.

The corridor opened up into a larger space. Once it might have been a catacomb, as the vague outlines of bones were visible set in niches along the walls, but now it had been repurposed for something else. A dozen ragged humans knelt in the chamber, their foreheads pressed to the floor, all facing where a dark slab of stone had been pushed against the far wall. And set atop this roughhewn altar ...

Zogrusz almost cried out in joy. His own visage stared back at him from across the room, though it looked far older than when he had seen it last. The passage of time had not been kind – several of the mouth-tendrils ended in stumps, and some of his features had been lost to erosion, but Zogrusz knew that this was the same statue that had once been displayed by the People in a place of great honor.

A tug on his sleeve drew his attention, and he found an

older woman in dark robes had appeared beside him. One of her eyes was missing, and scarring that almost looked ritualistic covered the rest of her face. She studied him with pursed lips, then motioned for him to follow her back outside the chamber. With a last, lingering look at the stone carving, Zogrusz joined her in the corridor.

"Who are you?" the woman hissed as something sharp and cold pressed against his stomach. Zogrusz glanced down in surprise and found that the point of a curving dagger had parted his jerkin and was poised to disembowel him . . . if he actually had bowels that could be removed in such a way.

"I am Napuatl," Zogrusz said calmly. "I am one of the People."

A tremor of surprise passed across the woman's face, and the certainty behind the dagger wavered. Zogrusz sensed the confusion churning within her, and he took this moment to slip into her thoughts and learn what was happening here.

She was a priestess of the old ways, the last in a long line stretching back to when the remnants of the People had been brought in chains to serve in the houses of their conquerors. For five hundred years they had kept their ancient traditions alive despite their dread lord failing to protect them from the armies of the sea people (Zogrusz felt a pang of guilt about this), though their numbers had dwindled, and now just a few remained who still believed. Peering deeper into this woman's mind, Zogrusz saw cracks in the foundation of her faith, that even she doubted their dread god would someday return.

All this Zogrusz gleaned in those moments of uncertainty after he had introduced himself, but then her one eye narrowed suspiciously, the sharpness poking him returning.

"Impossible. I do not know you."

"My ancestors escaped the destruction of Xochintl. Long have I searched for others." This explanation he plucked directly from her mind, for Zogrusz could see it was what she fervently wanted to hear – that the People still survived somewhere else, and when they finally faded away in Amotla it would not mark their end.

The dagger slipped from his midsection. "Welcome my brother," she said, her expression softening. "As you can see, we still hold dread Zogrusz in our hearts. Though for how much longer I do not know, as our children have turned away from the Nightbringer to embrace the fire bird of the subjugators."

"Fire bird," Zogrusz murmured, his thoughts returning to the performance in the market square. "When I entered the city, I saw a puppet show and a bird defecated on me – uh, I mean on our dread lord."

The old woman's lips twisted. "Anecoya. It is she who has laid our People low, why we are forced to hide down here. If her priest-king Cozotl discovered this sacred statue, he would have it dashed to pieces!"

"Cozotl? Does this human king dwell in the greatest stone building of Amotla?"

She nodded, though she looked confused by his choice of words. He had to remember what the cat Rhas had told him about humans not actually referring to themselves as humans.

"Yes, he does . . . and his ten-thousand bright spears."

"Excellent. I believe I shall go pay him a visit."

AN UNFAMILIAR EMOTION took root in Zogrusz as he wended his way through the streets, his gaze fixed on the great dome swelling over the city like a second moon bubbling up from under the world's crust. He thought of his followers, the ones whose devotion had sustained him for so long, and how they were now forced to huddle in crumbling darkness for fear of retribution. He thought of the lines of suffering carved into the face of the old woman leading the ragged remnants of the People. He thought of the laughter and good cheer that had filled Xochintl when he had walked its streets before the armies of this city had come.

Anger. It burned in his breast, bright and hot. The People had saved him. They were *his* People, and they still – even after all this time – believed he would make right the wrongs done to them. He remembered the snickering of the crowd when the red bird had befouled his puppet. The citizens of Amotla had reveled in his humiliation, just as they no doubt enjoyed their dominance over everyone they had made slaves. Lives of ease made possible through the toil of the conquered.

Well, they had made a terrible mistake. He was awake now, and they would experience the vengeance of something born in the cold darkness beyond the stars. They thought they were the masters of everything on this world? He was a creature of the cosmos and had trod the dusty surface of a hundred dead planets. The shadows trembled, agitated by his wrath.

Lost in his dark mood, he hadn't realized that he'd gotten close to the great citadel until its mighty outer wall loomed over him. Zogrusz sneered as he stared up at the distant crenellations. The arrogance of these humans, to believe they deserved to rule all they saw. He could burst forth from within his man-cloak right now and grow to the limit of his true form, and the walls would barely reach past his knees. He imagined these fortifications toppling over, the rush of delicious fear that would erupt from the people of Amotla as they scurried before him like terrified ants.

Zogrusz's gaze returned to the tower-fringed dome of the priest-king. That was where this Cozotl ruled. In his mind, Zogrusz saw the palace exploding as he erupted from within, great chunks of stone raining down on the city as he bellowed into the night. Yes, that was how his revenge should begin – with the utter destruction of the palace-temple dedicated to their ridiculous bird-god. He would lay waste to the city's heart, and these people by the sea would learn the folly of daring to humiliate an Eldritch Horror.

Zogrusz followed the wall until he arrived at an open gate. Guards flanked this entrance, but he wrapped himself in shadows and passed them unseen. Beyond was a path cutting sword-straight through the garden to the palace proper. At night it was a shadowy tangle speckled with motes of light – some were insects, flickering as they drifted lazily, but pale blue radiance was also seeping from flowers clinging to trellises of wrought copper.

Zogrusz let his cloak of shadows dissipate as he strode the path, his feet ringing on the metal bricks sunk into the earth. He did not care who heard him – soon this entire edifice would come crashing down, torn apart by his rage. What could these puny humans do to him, a creature of the void? Perhaps he would make this priest-king kneel before him and beg for mercy.

"Pardon."

Zogrusz halted abruptly, surprised by this voice. He had been so lost in his thoughts that he had not felt the intrusion of another consciousness.

"Can you help me?"

Zogrusz turned. A small girl stood just off the path, staring up at him. She was dressed in robes so white they almost glowed in the darkness, and her fair, intricately-plaited hair fell nearly to her waist. Zogrusz was not very experienced in guessing the age of humans, but he thought she was not yet halfway to adulthood. He peered past her, looking for some older guardian, but saw no one else.

"Hello," he muttered, not sure what else he should say.

"Oh!" the girl-child exclaimed, dropping into a curtsy that nearly caused the circlet resting on her brow to slip from her head. "I'm so sorry I didn't greet you properly." She paused for a moment after she straightened, clearly gathering herself. "Hello," she said, her tone more formal than before. "Can you help me, good sir?"

Zogrusz's eyes flicked from her to the great dome and then back to her. What was he doing? He had a city to destroy.

"I'm sorry," he said. "I'm very busy."

The girl's face fell. "But . . . but . . . it's Lord Whiskers. He's . . . he's . . . ." She sniffled, then wiped at her cheek with the back of her hand. The sadness flowing from her had a purity unlike anything Zogrusz had ever experienced before. He'd never peered into the mind of a child, and the innocence was disconcerting.

"What is wrong?" Zogrusz asked, shaking his head to clear it.

The girl raised her arm, pointing deeper into the garden. "My kitten is lost. I think he's somewhere in there." An image formed in Zogrusz's mind of a tiny white cat with black paws. "I know I wasn't supposed to take him outside," she continued, her words coming so fast now they were tumbling over each other. "But he's been so bored in our chambers and he just stays at my window watching the birds and I thought maybe I could let him just run in the grass a bit and chase the chipmunks and he'd enjoy it so much but I think something scared him and –"

Zogrusz held up his hands in a gesture of surrender. He was growing exhausted just listening to her.

"I will find it," he promised, and the girl-child gave what might have been a squeak of thanks.

If he could. The cat Rhas had somehow closed its mind to him . . . but perhaps not all of those creatures had such abilities, as he felt a glimmer of consciousness recessed in the garden close to here. Fear was rolling off it in waves, and it did not seem nearly as advanced a mind as the moon-colored cat had boasted, but that might be because it was very young. Zogrusz concentrated, willing the darkness the kitten crouched in to harden. It gave a startled chirp, and the girl-child beside him made a similar sound, clapping her hands to her mouth.

"That's him!" she cried. "He's so scared!"

Zogrusz lifted the cocoon of shadows swaddling the kitten with a thought. It drifted from the garden and settled in his hand, then melted away to reveal a tiny, shivering shape. Before it could flee he made a cage with his fingers, and it yowled miserably.

"Oh, it can't be all that bad," Zogrusz muttered sternly, too quiet for the girl to hear. "I've seen into her soul – it must be absolutely delicious. You should be quite grateful to have this one as your pet."

The cat did not seem to agree, scratching at his palm with its little claws. He wondered if it understood him – apparently, the power of speech developed late in these creatures.

"How did you do that?" the girl whispered, and he

turned from the cat to find her staring at him wide-eyed. "I thought you were the gardener. Are you a wizard?"

"*Hm*?" Zogrusz said, holding out the squirming kitten for her to take. "Oh, no. I'm an Eldritch Horror from beyond the stars. I've come to destroy your city as punishment for the crimes of your people."

The girl blinked up at him for a long moment, as if trying to parse what he'd just said. "That's too bad," she finally murmured, gingerly accepting her cat. "I like the city. You can get roast sweet corn in the market on festival days. You should try it."

"I'm sorry, but I'm very angry."

"Why's that?" the girl asked. She'd calmed the kitten and was running her fingers down its back, eliciting a pleased-sounding vibration. Fracturing her soul for later feeding, Zogrusz knew. Such clever creatures. He wondered if this entire escapade had been planned for this very purpose.

"Because your people took away something I cared about," he told her.

"Maybe we could just give it back?"

"No, no, I'm afraid that's impossible. This happened a long time ago. Many hundreds of years, I think."

The girl's face crumpled in confusion. "Oh. Then I suppose the people in this city aren't really to blame."

Zogrusz opened his mouth to dispute this and then closed it with a click. Surprisingly, she did have a point.

He grimaced, rubbing at the back of his neck. Things were more complicated than he'd first thought.

"You should go talk to my father," the girl suggested. "He's the king and very wise."

This roused Zogrusz from his ruminations. "Your father is Cozotl?"

The girl nodded enthusiastically. "Yes! He's probably in

his study right now working. Just please don't tell him I went into the garden."

"I won't," Zogrusz promised, returning his attention to the dome.

ZOGRUSZ WALKED unseen through the halls of the palace, pausing occasionally to marvel at the beautiful mosaics adorning the walls and the intricate stonework embellishing the lintels of the doorways. The craftsmanship was remarkable, far more detailed than what he had created in his mountain home. But rather than making him feel inadequate, the sight of such artistry quickened his imagination. He felt inspired, excited to discover if he could also fashion such wonders. He ran his fingers over one graven flower, tracing the delicate petals and thorned stem. He doubted his claws could etch so finely – no, he would need new tools if he wished to work stone in such a way.

Zogrusz shook his head, disappointed with himself that he had come so close to destroying this palace. He should be careful not to let his temper sweep him along in the future, lest he do something he ended up regretting.

But he needed to protect what remained of the People . . . so he would have to meet with this Cozotl and impress upon him the gravity of the situation. And he had an idea about how he was going to do that.

From the minds of the servants roaming these passageways, Zogrusz learned where the priest-king spent his evenings, and soon he found himself on the threshold of a larger and more impressive chamber than any he had yet encountered. The palace's great dome soared overhead, and a colorful scene of a familiar red bird hatching from a golden egg wreathed with flames had been painted on its underside. Shelves ringed the circular space, some filled with piled scrolls and books and others with stacked clay tablets, and in the center of the room was a table of black wood covered with paper. A man in white robes trimmed with gold was leaning over this mess, examining an unrolled scroll with a look of intense concentration. He was young, but there were traces of silver in his hair that matched the color of the circlet on his brow.

Zogrusz entered his mind briefly to confirm that this was indeed Cozotl, priest-king of Amotla and the father of the girl he had met in the garden. He didn't delve too far, but he could sense that the man loved his daughter and the city he ruled deeply. An arrogant man, but not cruel or selfish. Zogrusz was feeling better and better about not laying indiscriminate waste to the palace – this was a fellow who deserved the chance to redeem the sins of his ancestors.

Zogrusz shrugged off his cloak of shadows as he approached the table. Cozotl straightened in surprise when he realized he was no longer alone.

"Who are you?" he asked, his fingers closing around the amulet at his breast. "How dare you intrude?"

Zogrusz attempted his most reassuring smile, but this seemed to upset the king even further. Was he using too much teeth? Next time he'd keep his lips pressed together.

"I come on behalf of the People of Xochintl."

"An emissary?" the king said, his face creasing in confusion. "What are you doing wandering the palace at night? And where is this Xochintl? I do not know it."

"It was conquered long ago," Zogrusz said, coming to stand on the other side of the table. "And its descendants forced to serve in this city. I have come to demand that they be allowed to return to their ancient lands . . . and also that their god be treated with more respect within these walls."

The king sneered. "There is only one god exalted in Amotla, and that is Anecoya. You must be one of those ridiculous cultists who grovel in the dark before their demon – I have clearly been too lenient on you fools."

Then Cozotl sucked in a deep breath, and from his thoughts, Zogrusz knew the king was about to bellow for his guards.

"Apologies, I wish to talk to you alone," Zogrusz said, using his new powers to fill the king's mouth with clotting shadows. Cozotl's eyes bulged, his fingers scrabbling at his throat like he could dislodge the darkness Zogrusz had just conjured.

"I will let you breathe again if you promise not to cry out," Zogrusz said, wandering closer to the table and hefting a remarkably detailed little statue of a bird that had been helping to keep a scroll unfurled. The craftsmanship truly was exquisite. "So what do you say? Will you be quiet?" He traced the delicate beak, wondering what sort of tool had been used here . . . and how he could get ahold of one.

Cozotl nodded vigorously as his face purpled, and with a thought Zogrusz dispelled the choking shadows. The priest-king slumped gasping over his desk, the terror emanating from him in pulsing waves making Zogrusz almost dizzy.

"What . . . what are you?" he managed, massaging his neck.

"I am Zogrusz."

From his blank stare, this was clearly a name he had never heard before. Very well, then. It was apparently time to introduce himself again.

Zogrusz abandoned his man-disguise, though he did not swell to his full size, as that would have brought this palace crashing down. Instead, he chose to manifest himself as twice the height of the king, who gaped up at Zogrusz in shock.

Well, if this was the path he was going to go down, he supposed he would have to play the part.

"Kneel!" he cried, his mouth-tendrils writhing as he spread his arms wide. "I am Zogrusz, Eldritch Horror from the farthest void! Look upon me and despair, mortal!"

Sensing the man's rapidly elevating pulse, Zogrusz feared for a moment that he had gone too far and that Cozotl would faint or maybe even expire from this wave of fear crashing down on him. But the king stayed conscious, instead sinking to his knees as he stared up in wordless terror at Zogrusz. Perhaps he should tamp down the theatrics before he reduced the poor fellow to nothing more than a gibbering idiot.

"No longer will you worship that bird! Henceforth, I shall be the only god in Amotla, and all will fear me or . . . or . . ." Zogrusz hesitated, trying to summon forth a suitable threat. Eat their souls? A bit macabre. Kick over the city walls? Perhaps not macabre enough. "Endless night!" Zogrusz shouted triumphantly as inspiration struck. "I will wrap the world in endless night!"

"No," moaned Cozotl, clasping his hands together in an imploring gesture. "Please, mighty Zogrusz, spare us . . ."

"Then cast aside that ridiculous and annoying bird!" Zogrusz wanted to sweep the statue of Anecoya off the table to punctuate this command, but inwardly winced at the thought of such a beautiful work dashed to pieces.

"We shall!" cried the king, and in his mind, Zogrusz saw that he was being absolutely sincere. "Oh, glorious Zogrusz! You will be the new lord of Amotla, and we shall spread your dark gospel across the lands!"

"Dark gospel?" Zogrusz murmured, intrigued by the king's fervent proclamation.

Cozotl blinked, apparently surprised by the sudden change in Zogrusz's tone. "Y-yes. Your commandments! Your revelations! Please instruct us how to honor you!" The king snatched up the yellowing papers strewn across the table, crumpling and tossing them aside. "These are the Burning Scrolls, the teachings of Anecoya. All rubbish! We shall throw them into the flames, make them burn in truth! Only your words we will hold in our hearts!"

Oh, what an interesting idea. A sacred text to codify his worship and transform his cult into a true religion. "An excellent suggestion," Zogrusz agreed, stroking his mouth-tendrils thoughtfully. "And you, Cozotl, you shall help me write this . . . gospel." He glanced about at the scrolls filling the shelves. "You can write, can't you? If not, I suppose we can summon a scribe . . ."

"I can write!" Cozotl cried, as if afraid that Zogrusz would find his usefulness at an end if he could not. "Beautifully!" He scrabbled among the mess in front of him for a blank piece of parchment and a quill, then with a shaking hand dipped this feather into the inkstone on the table.

"Wonderful!" Zogrusz said as he paced back and forth. "Then let us begin. We shall call it . . ." He paused, considering what might be a suitable name for his new scripture.

The Dreadnomicon?

The Black Testament?

"We shall call it . . . the Book of Zog."

4

Zogrusz returned to his mountain almost a year later.

The creation of the Book of Zog had only taken a few days, with Cozotl furiously transcribing his words as he dictated its contents. The bulk of the book he wove whole cloth from his imagination (of which he was quite proud), but he did sprinkle the text with references to what he had actually experienced beyond this world, such as the unknowable horror of the Great Old Ones and the vast devouring darkness between the stars. Cozotl had seemed disturbed by the idea that existence was meaningless except to provide sustenance for eldritch cosmic beings, so Zogrusz had leavened these stark truths with some comforting pablum about redemption and an afterlife and karmic justice, most of which he had pulled directly from the king's mind.

The rest of his year away had been spent in a small village outside Amotla, near where much of the stone used in the city was quarried. It was there amidst the dust and the sound of tapping chisels that Zogrusz had watched sculptors summon forth all manner of wondrous things from within the formless rock. He'd kept himself invisible during the days, wrapped in his cloak of shadows, but at night he'd entered the workshops and attempted to recreate what he had witnessed. He learned of the tools used by these masters, the hammers and axes and picks, and when he finally departed this village, he carried enough implements with him to reshape a mountain.

Which was what he planned to do.

If humans with their ephemeral mayfly lives could manifest art that persisted down through the ages, what was an immortal like him capable of creating?

Zogrusz couldn't help but smile when he again stood at the threshold of his cavern and beheld his first crude fumblings. He kept the thrones he had made and the carving that now looked so ridiculously childish to remind himself of how far he had come, and then he set to work realizing his vision. He painstakingly smoothed the walls, scooping away the curving rock to create sheer sides that soared up to the cavern's roof. He snapped away the dangling stalactites, chiseling the ceiling until he had crafted something similar to the great dome of Amotla. He searched the deeper tunnels and caves of the mountain, amassing a hoard of different colored stones that he then broke into smaller chunks, and after mixing a cement like he had witnessed the stonemasons making – ash, lime, water, and volcanic rock – he affixed these stones to the ceiling. He had thought long and hard about what the overarching mosaic should depict, and had finally settled on an image of himself not long after arriving on this world, standing among the trees and animals with his head limned by the setting sun.

The walls were next, and using the tools he had appropriated from the stoneworkers, he memorialized the record of his long journey. He carved the Great Old Ones – or what he could remember of them – those confusing tangles of tentacles and many-jointed limbs and the vast profusions of eyes staring blindly out into the void. Then he etched the other wonders he had seen – the all-devouring maws of black holes, the moons ringed by glittering clouds of ice, the vast nebulas billowing across space like ink spilled in water, even the stark beauty of the dead worlds. He carved the shard-studded ice worm that had been the only conscious being he'd encountered until arriving here, as well as his view of this planet during his first approach.

Zogrusz passed into an almost dream-like state as he worked, and when he finally stepped back to admire what he had wrought he sensed a long time had passed, though this was difficult to measure under the mountain. Something had certainly changed in the world outside. That thin, life-giving trickle of worshipful dread that had sustained him was gone, replaced by a steadily strengthening stream. Cozotl must have made good on his promise and helped his faith spread among the people of Amotla . . . and perhaps even farther afield, for to Zogrusz it seemed like it was not only swelling but also drawing closer. Was it possible that the People had returned to Xochintl? The thought warmed his heart. If he stepped outside, would he again see ribbons of smoke curling from the rebuilt town?

Curious, Zogrusz set down the worn nubs of his tools (he would have to procure fresh hammers and chisels soon) and made his way through the winding tunnels until he stood once more on the mountain's flank.

And to his great surprise, he found he was not alone.

A collection of tents and other ramshackle structures had been erected farther down the slope, and from this makeshift little village delicious pulses of fearful prayer were flowing up to him. Zogrusz squinted into the distance, but saw no sign that Xochintl has been resurrected – no, his nearby worshippers were most definitely these pilgrims. For a moment he was confused about what they were doing here, but then he remembered that in his ramblings to Cozotl he had mentioned that he dwelled under a mountain near a town called Xochintl. Apparently, someone had delved into the histories and found where it had once been located.

He supposed it was lucky that none of them had dared venture into the cave that led to his lair. How surprising would that have been if he had set down his stone pick and turned to find a few of these humans standing slack-jawed at the entrance to his cavern! He'd probably have had to shift into his true form and stomp about to dissuade them from ever bothering him again. And watching the pilgrims milling down below, Zogrusz knew that eventually they *would* risk his wrath by entering the mountain – it was the nature of humans to be curious. If they were not, they never would have left the primordial jungle and advanced so far as a species.

But perhaps there was some benefit to having this tasty morsel right on his doorstep. Could he encourage these pilgrims to come to his mountain . . . while also keeping them outside? Zogrusz pulled on the dark curls of his man-form as he considered what he should do. Maybe he could turn the cave behind him into an imposing entrance, so all would know he did indeed dwell within. He imagined huge cyclopean pillars and statues of Eldritch Horrors, a temple façade worthy of his new faith. And he could use his power over the shadows to make the darkness within impenetrable to all but himself. He would have to do the bulk of the work in his man-form so as not to send the pilgrims fleeing in terror, but he had found the small, dexterous fingers of humans perfect for manipulating stone.

Excited to begin, Zogrusz reentered the cave to fetch his tools with a bounce in his step.

THE FRAME of the entrance he erected at night during a thunderstorm while the mountain was drenched in darkness, dragging the massive boulders that would become the great blocky pillars flanking the cave mouth. As lightning rent the sky and thunder crashed, he broke apart these rocks until they were a size manageable for a man to chisel into their last form, if said man had an inhuman patience and all the time in the world. He could sense the fear and confusion from the pilgrims down below huddled in their beds, for many of them could tell that the terrific cracks shivering the night were not just from the raging storm. But as he suspected, none worked up the courage to investigate what was happening high on the mountain of their dread god.

Zogrusz worked for a month undisturbed before someone dared approach. He was carefully shaping the mouth-tendril of a statue when he was startled by an unexpected voice behind him.

"Greetings!"

Zogrusz fumbled his hammer, nearly dropping it. He had been so lost in his labors that he hadn't felt another mind ascending the slope.

"I'm sorry!" the man said as Zogrusz turned, pressing his hands together and dipping his head in what Zogrusz guessed was a gesture of apology. "I didn't mean to scare you." This stranger was in the middle of his life-span, with a dusting of gray in his black hair, and despite the worry lines etched deep in his face, he was grinning broadly.

"It's fine," Zogrusz said, returning the smile as he set aside his tools and ran his fingers through his sweaty curls. "I was surprised, not scared."

The man nodded at this. "It must be difficult to frighten someone who would build a temple to our lord here on His sacred mountain."

Zogrusz shrugged. "I suppose so." He couldn't help but feel pleased about how naturally this conversation was flowing – the long sessions with Cozotl and then his spying on the craftsmen of the stoneworker's village had done much to improve his ability to interact with humans.

"My name is Izel," the man said, extending his hand. Zogrusz stared at it for a moment before realizing this was a greeting he hadn't seen before. He mirrored the gesture, and the man clasped his forearm warmly. "And what is your name, friend?"

"Ah . . . Napuatl," Zogrusz replied, hoping his slight hesitation went unnoticed. It apparently did, for the man's friendly expression did not falter. Izel took back his hand and used it to shield his eyes as he surveyed the work Zogrusz had done so far.

"It is remarkable," he said. "We've been watching your progress from down below, and now that I've seen it up close, it looks even more impressive. These details . . ." He stepped closer to the statue Zogrusz had been carving and ran his fingers along the gentle slope of its skull. *His* skull. "Do you think this is what our lord truly looks like? There is certainly some resemblance to what the Prophet Cozotl described, but this depiction of yours is almost . . . noble? I see little of the horror Cozotl claims he experienced when our god appeared to him."

Noble? Zogrusz decided he liked this human. He had been trying to capture the beauty and majesty of his true form in the stone, and it seemed he had been at least somewhat successful.

"Thank you," Zogrusz said, pride swelling inside him. He found the enjoyment he felt looking upon his creations was heightened even further when there was an appreciative audience.

"May I ask, Napuatl, *why* you are building this temple? You are the topic of much discussion among the others. And now that I come here and see you are so young – yet also so skilled – I am even more taken with this mystery."

"I . . . had a vision," Zogrusz said slowly. "I wanted to make something worthy of our . . . our god."

Izel nodded again at this, even more enthusiastically. "Of course. You have been divinely inspired. Most of us believe you must be a holy man who has experienced the dark touch of our lord on your soul."

"I suppose you could say that," Zogrusz murmured. He felt his own curiosity rising as he stared at this man who had climbed the mountain to meet him. Briefly he delved into Izel's mind and was immersed in a flood of memories and thoughts. Zogrusz saw a woman, young and laughing, and a small child with dimpled cheeks. His wife and his son. Both gone, dead, their memories heavy with sorrow . . . but there was something else as well, something that blunted this pain, an emotion he could not quite understand.

"And what has brought you here, Izel? Why have you made this long journey to pray at the foot of this mountain?" He hesitated, then gave voice to the most important question. "Why have you chosen to devote your life to Zogrusz?"

The man's smile returned, but there was an edge of sadness this time. "He saved me," he said. "I owe Him my life."

Now this was indeed intriguing. Zogrusz adopted the expression that he thought best conveyed how interested he was in the man's story. "But Zogrusz is a terrifying god. An avatar of the void. Why would such a being bother with the life of a mere human?"

The man spread his arms wide. "You have answered your own question, friend Napuatl! The revelations in the Book of Zog are what kept me from throwing myself under the waves after . . . after what happened." His expression turned more somber, and Zogrusz sensed he was reliving old and painful memories. "It was the Whispering Death. My wife . . . my child . . . I could not protect them when it came to the isles. They died in my arms. I was a fisherman on the Pearl Sea, and like the rest of my people, I followed the Reborn Goddess, Anecoya. As the Burning Scrolls taught, the goddess would protect us if we were worthy. She cared for us. Loved us. And so, as I clutched my son's body to my chest, I thought *I* must have failed the goddess. That She had turned away from us, and it was *my* fault for being an imperfect man. I went down to the docks and stared down at the jade water and began working up the courage to join my Ome and Mictlan. But then . . ." Izel swallowed, and Zogrusz realized the human was blinking back tears. "I heard the word of Zogrusz. A man had come to our village, and he was standing in the fishmonger's square behind me reading from the Book of Zog. Somehow I heard him over the waves and the wind and the shrieking of gulls. 'The cosmos does not care about you.' Those words . . . they pierced my breast and lodged deep in my heart. And I stepped back from the edge of the docks and went to listen to what the disciple of the dread lord was preaching."

"You felt saved . . . because the gods did not care?"

"Yes!" Izel cried, and the fervor in his voice sent a thrill through Zogrusz. "If the gods truly loved and cared for us, then it was *my* fault that my wife and son had died. Because *I* was not worthy, they had suffered terribly! This was punishment for my failure! But if the universe was uncaring . . . then I was not to blame. The words of Zogrusz untied the blindfold from my eyes. I saw that there is nothing greater that will descend to save us . . . if we wish to live in a better world, we must strive to create it ourselves! Zogrusz is my god because He is the only one who presents the truth of the universe honestly. All the others lie for our devotion . . . but not Him!"

A numbness had spread through Zogrusz during the man's passionate speech. He had wanted their worship, their fear . . . but this was something else entirely. He swept out his arm to indicate the distant tents.

"Are there others who believe as you do?"

Izel nodded enthusiastically. "Many. The ones who have come to this mountain . . . they were lost like me, consumed by guilt for things they could not control. Zogrusz taught us that these tragedies were not because of the action or inaction of the divine. They just . . . happened. And this revelation liberated our souls from grief."

Zogrusz stared at the man, shocked into silence. He realized suddenly that there was no terror flowing from him. Izel did not fear him . . . in his own strange way he *loved* his new god. Zogrusz had always wondered if he could derive some sustenance from worship when it was twined with other emotions . . . but apparently not. So while he was pleased that this man had risen above his personal tragedies through his interpretation of the Book of Zog, if everyone in the world thought similarly then Zogrusz would quickly find himself starving again. Luckily, from the delicious river flowing into him at this very moment – even from some of the devout pilgrims just down the mountain – not many shared Izel's perspective. And perhaps that was why this man had been the one to finally climb up here. Still, it was an intriguing – if slightly unsettling – development. He would have to reinforce the dread horror of his faith, lest his followers grow too comfortable and he find himself starved by their loving devotion.

Izel must have interpreted his silence to mean that Zogrusz wished to return to his labors because he took a quick step back.

"Goodbye, friend Napuatl," he said, again pressing his hands together, and in his mind Zogrusz saw that this could be as much a gesture of respect as well as an apology. "I will leave you to your sacred task. Thank you for listening to my ramblings, it was . . . good to unburden myself. Especially to such a holy man."

"Wait," Zogrusz said hurriedly as the man turned away. Izel hesitated, glancing back at him in curiosity. "Perhaps . . . perhaps you can return . . . friend Izel. It is nice to have some company."

The lines on the man's face deepened as he smiled. "I would like that. See you on the morrow, then."

Izel's visits became a regular occurrence, and Zogrusz found that he looked forward to their chats so much that he was disappointed on the days when the man did not ascend the mountain. The once-fisherman had a wry sense of humor and a folksy wisdom that Zogrusz appreciated – never had he spoken so long and so deeply with a human, and he learned much about the workings of their minds and how they understood their existence. His own ability to converse improved dramatically during these days, as he further learned how to interpret the subtle hints and mannerisms that underpinned every interaction between these fascinating animals. He still made mistakes, he knew, but Izel seemed to simply accept that a hermit who had devoted his life to single-handedly building a shrine to a dark god would have more than his fair share of eccentricities.

So his heart lightened one morning when he emerged from the cave's entrance to find that Izel was already waiting for him. His back was to Zogrusz as he leaned against the plinth of a half-carved statue of an Eldritch Horror, gazing out at a bloody dawn welling up from beneath the horizon. It was a rare treat that Izel would come up here so early, and Zogrusz found that he was affecting the very human quirk of smiling as he hurried over to greet the man.

But then he stopped, a coldness washing through him.

Something was wrong. Very, very wrong. Izel's consciousness should have been seeping out to stain their surroundings, but Zogrusz could feel nothing. And even if Izel were asleep on his feet, Zogrusz should have been able to see stuttering images from whatever dream he was experiencing. It was like . . . it was like he was dead.

Yet he clearly was not.

An unfamiliar emotion coalesced within Zogrusz, and he did not like at all what it made him feel.

Concern. He was afraid for his new friend.

"Izel," he said, coming to stand beside the man. "Are you alright?"

The man turned to face him, the movement oddly slow and deliberate.

Zogrusz hissed in dismay. Izel's eyes were gone . . . replaced by something else. Blackness filled the gaping sockets, but Zogrusz knew they were not truly empty. The dark had a substance; it was both unfathomably deep and as shallow as a rain puddle. It was familiar – he had stared into such a pit before, at the very edge of reality, far beyond the stars.

He was looking into the void itself.

"What are you?" he asked, and for the first time since he had left the place of his birth, Zogrusz felt true fear.

The thing inhabiting Izel did not smile or nod a greeting. Its expression remained slack, clearly ignorant of how humans acted, but Zogrusz could sense an intelligence watching him from the cold depths.

"*The nectar flows, Sower. Squeezed from the flesh of ripening fruits, it dances on the tongue and quickens the essence. Such a delicious vintage. We are pleased.*"

It was Izel's voice but distant, as if echoing up from the depths of a deep chasm.

"What did you call me? I am Zogrusz, not this . . . Sower."

"*A true name shared so freely. Foolish. This one left the creche too early, learned nothing.*"

"And who are you?" Zogrusz asked, more harshly than he intended. He wanted to grab the shoulders of this creature and shake it, but he did not know what it could do to hurt Izel.

The void-thing continued staring at him blankly, unperturbed by his agitation. "*We are a Reaper, almost finished with our fifth cycle. This one traded his name freely, so we will do the same. Ycthitlig we are, but on our worlds we were known as the Crawling Dread. A long time since that was uttered."*

"Ycthitlig," Zogrusz repeated, grimacing at the barbed strangeness of the name. "You are an Eldritch Horror."

Its expression still did not waver, but Zogrusz felt something had changed in how the creature was regarding him. *"Both Horrors, but not the same. This one Sows while we Reap. Once we also Sowed, but we finished our cycles and sank within our chrysalis. Larva to pupa we became, a step closer on the way to ascendance . . . but still so far away."* It studied Zogrusz intently, the force of its attention making his skin prickle. *"This one is second cycle. Only two times has this one's abyss been filled, two times has he slept and woken. Unexpected, to find a world made so ripe by such a young Sower."*

"What do you mean, ripe?" Zogrusz asked, his apprehension rising.

"This world is ready for the Harvest." The thing that had called itself Ycthitlig turned away from Zogrusz, staring once more out at the red dawn. *"We are coming."*

Izel suddenly shuddered so violently that it was nearly a spasm. He swooned and might have fallen if Zogrusz's hand had not flashed out to grab his shoulder. The man glanced at him with wide, terrified eyes . . . eyes that once more were the jade of the Pearl Sea.

"Napuatl," he croaked. "My friend. What . . . what has happened? How did I get to this place?"

Zogrusz forced a smile he did not feel. "Izel. I think you must have walked in your sleep. I found you standing here when I arrived. How do you feel?"

Izel swallowed hard, kneading his temple with shaking fingers. "I . . . I have a headache. But I think if I lie down for a while I will feel better."

"Go back to your bed," Zogrusz urged. "Rest. Our dark lord does not need you today. If you feel well on the morrow come visit."

Izel nodded. "Yes . . . yes. Sleep is what I need." He attempted a wavering smile. "And hopefully when I wake I won't find myself freezing up here again."

"Take care," Zogrusz said as Izel began to make his stumbling way down the scree-strewn slope.

The man waved a farewell without turning around, and so he did not see the concern creasing the face of the disguised Eldritch Horror.

ZOGRUSZ ATTEMPTED to work for a while on one of the steles scattered near the entrance, but he found he couldn't concentrate on his carving and so eventually he wandered once more into the mountain and returned to his cavern. His thoughts whirled as he dragged himself up the tiered steps of his ziggurat and flung himself down on his throne. He had shed his man-cloak, but he did not swell to his full size, as his true form no longer fit within the confines of his home. And so Zogrusz perched on the edge of his seat with his chin on his knuckles (mouth-tendrils twined around his forearm) and considered what had just happened.

Another Eldritch Horror had come to his world. Or had it? Ycthitlig had spoken to him through Izel, but Zogrusz suspected his friend had merely been a conduit and that the physical form of the creature was still very far away.

We are coming.

The words chilled him. Ycthitlig – the true Ycthitlig – might right now be swimming through the dark, following whatever thin trickle had first turned its attention to this world.

A trickle that Zogrusz was likely responsible for. Ycthitlig had called him a Sower. What else could it mean other than his actions here had manifested the dread that Eldritch Horrors fed upon? He had sowed the seeds that were now bearing fruit, the number of his worshippers growing across these lands. And Ycthitlig had claimed it was a Reaper. The term unsettled Zogrusz. One who reaped waded among crops, cutting down what had grown. They plucked fruit from vines and crushed them into juice. They ripped up what was spreading beneath the ground.

Zogrusz did not like those comparisons.

Ycthitlig had claimed that it had once sowed and had spoken of experiencing many 'cycles'. Zogrusz suspected that this referred to the long sleeps he found he could not resist after the hollowness inside him was finally filled. Each time he rested he awoke changed, larger and possessing new powers, but if Ycthitlig had spoken true, then eventually he would transform into something else entirely. Larva to pupa. Sower to Reaper. Reaper to . . . Great Old One? Or were there more steps along the way?

Zogrusz shook his head, banishing this speculation for another time. What was important right now was when Ycthitlig would arrive. He doubted that the Horror would have bothered with this . . . sending if its appearance was imminent. Hopefully, it was years away . . . decades . . . In truth, Zogrusz did not know how long he had wandered the cosmos. Perhaps he had spent centuries searching for a suitable world on which to feed.

What would happen when Ycthitlig came here and began its reaping? Would any shred of consciousness remain? Or would this planet become as dull and lifeless as the countless other worlds Zogrusz had visited?

The thought appalled him. He remembered Amotla, with its soaring dome and mosaic-encrusted walls. All those diligent craftsmen working for years to shape a block of stone into something beautiful. Everything that had been created would be rendered meaningless. And the people . . . Zogrusz thought of the innocent little princess in the garden. The kind fruitmonger. Wise Izel, who had lost and then found his will to live. Could he abandon everyone here to be reaped and simply set out into the cosmos again, questing for another world among the stars with the spark of intelligence? How many times had Ycthitlig 'ripened' a world before it finally transformed from a Sower into a Reaper? Had it once been like Zogrusz, worried about what would happen to the world it inhabited?

And there was something else . . .

Recently Zogrusz had again begun to feel full past the point of satiation, bloated with the flood of worshipful dread the spread of his new religion had unleashed. What had Ycthitlig said? Something about an 'abyss' being filled, which led to the end of a 'cycle' and the growth of his size and powers. But should he sleep with this threat traveling to his world? *Could* he choose not to sleep? In the past, the compulsion had been overwhelming. And what could he do when the other, far stronger, more evolved Eldritch Horror finally arrived? Fight? Beg? Appeal to its sense of mercy?

Zogrusz's head sank deeper into his hands. What was he going to do?

THE MOUNTAIN SHOOK.

Zogrusz came awake, his awareness returning sluggishly. He lifted his head from the floor of the cavern and looked around in confusion – he had no memory of falling asleep, just a rising exhaustion that had made it harder and harder to focus on his work. Yet now here he was . . . How much time had passed? And had he truly felt the shiver of stone beneath him, or had that only been in his dreams? Surely if there had been an earthquake –

Another trembling, and in the distance he heard the grinding and clattering of rocks as they shifted. Zogrusz climbed to his feet, glancing up at the ceiling in apprehension. Could he survive having a mountain fall on him? Maybe. He was more concerned about the mosaic he had painstakingly arranged. What he had created here was supposed to be immune to the ravages of time, but perhaps that had always been a foolish conceit.

He frowned as something finally worked its way through his sleep-fogged mind. There had been something strange about that last vibration. Earthquakes welled up from deeper underground, but he could have sworn that this one had emanated from *outside* the mountain, and the faint sound of falling rocks had almost certainly come from the tunnel leading to the surface.

He had to go see what had happened.

Zogrusz hurried up the passage, staggering as the strongest tremor yet struck and dust sifted down from above. He could sense that he had again changed after waking, but at this moment he could not take the time to explore the new power coiling inside him. That would have to wait until after he understood what was going on.

If there was an after. A cold fear gripped Zogrusz as he imagined an enormous Eldritch Horror straddling his mountain, mouth-tendrils dangling from the clouds wreathing its great head. His true form had grown ten times by the end of his second cycle as a Sower . . . how much larger would a fifth-cycle Reaper be? Large enough to stride these lands like a colossus and tread kingdoms beneath its clawed feet?

As he suspected, the elaborate entrance he had made at the cave mouth had collapsed, light trickling through the gaps between the tumbled blocks and bits of shattered masonry. He certainly could clear the way in his true form, but that would take some time, and Zogrusz desperately wanted to know what was happening outside. So instead he donned his man-cloak and wriggled his way through the rubble.

Zogrusz emerged into the brightness of the day, expecting to see Ycthitlig the Crawling Dread's shadow covering these lands, but there was nothing. He turned slowly, wondering what could have happened – the magnificent statues of Eldritch Horrors had been pulverized into dust, the mighty pillars he had set beside the entrance knocked down like saplings in a storm. The rest of the mountain seemed intact, as if it had just been his hard work that had been the target of this destruction . . .

Zogrusz blinked in surprise. One of the pilgrims had ascended the mountain and was picking her way across the rocky slope. She was young, barely a woman, and the hood of her golden robes was thrown back to reveal a shock of bright red hair.

Oddly enough, she didn't look pleased. She was scowling and her hands were bunched into fists as she stomped towards him.

"Excuse me," Zogrusz said when she drew closer. "Did you see what happened –"

A blur of movement, and he was suddenly flying backwards with the breath driven from his chest. Zogrusz slammed with tremendous force into the side of the mountain, the rock crumpling beneath him. He lay there for a moment, dazed, then a hand closed around his ankle, and he was dragged out of the crater he had just made.

"What –" he slurred, trying to focus on the girl who was hauling him across the stone.

"How *dare* you!" she cried, cutting him off, then spun around in a circle while still holding onto his leg. His fingers scrabbled helplessly as he was lifted from the slope, and when she released her grip, he went spinning into the ruin of the collapsed entrance. Zogrusz bounced off a plinth where once a statue had stood, his head striking its edge hard enough that he knew his skull would have broken like an egg if he truly had been only a man, and then he landed awkwardly in a heap amidst the devastation. He sprawled there, staring up at the lip of the cave mouth curving above him, unable to form a thought coherent enough to understand what was going on.

As he did this, a familiar face thrust itself into his field of vision, blocking his view of the cave's ceiling.

"Rhas," he croaked, wondering if the sharp little feline features staring down at him in what looked like mild disappointment was a hallucination produced by the tremendous blows his head had just sustained.

"Zog," the moon-colored cat said. "You look terrible."

I feel terrible he wanted to respond, but before he could do that, his leg was yanked hard again, and he was thrown violently against the rock wall.

He considered shifting into his true form, but that would probably collapse the cave mouth, and then even less of his work could be salvaged. Instead, he staggered to his feet, and drawing upon his power he crystallized the shadows to form a wall of gleaming blackness between himself and the rampaging girl.

Who was clearly not just a girl.

"You think *this* will save you?" she scoffed, now reduced to a vague blur on the other side of the barrier. "From *me*?"

"Who are you?" Zogrusz yelled, momentarily distracted by the feeling of warmth running down his scalp. He reached up and was shocked to see that his fingers were stained red. She had made him bleed!

"As if you don't know!" the girl snarled, and then the wall started shuddering as she struck it again and again, cracks spidering across its surface.

Zogrusz gaped, shocked at what he was seeing. "Are you . . . Ycthitlig?"

The battering ceased. "Yickthlig?" the girl said incredulously. "What in the hells is that? It sounds like a dog retching!"

Light erupted on the other side of the barrier, as if something had suddenly burst aflame. Then the hazy shape of the girl reared back, and Zogrusz frantically tried to reinforce his shadow-weaving for what he expected was coming.

It did not matter. A wave of force pummeled the wall, and it was shattered into slivers of darkness. The girl stepped through these dissipating fragments, her long red hair writhing like it was alive, a sword of flame roiling in her hand.

Zogrusz sighed in resignation, preparing to adopt his true form. Clearly, he was not winning this fight in his man-disguise.

The girl stalked forward, brandishing her burning blade, but then halted abruptly as Rhas suddenly materialized in front of her.

"Out of the way, cat," she snarled, glittering embers tracing the passage of her sword as she slashed the air.

Rhas watched these motes wink out of existence with no apparent concern. Then his tail flicked about in what Zogrusz interpreted as mild annoyance.

"Oh, calm down, Anecoya," he said. "You're embarrassing yourself."

Anecoya?

"You're that bird?" Zogrusz blurted.

"I am a goddess!" the girl fairly screeched.

"Right now a petulant goddess," muttered the cat.

"He *stole* my people," she said angrily, gesturing with her flaming sword at Zogrusz. "And he must be punished for such audacity!"

Anecoya attempted to move past Rhas but paused when a threatening rumble emanated from the cat. "You always said I had to protect my flock!" she fairly whined, now addressing Rhas directly. "Well, how can I protect them if I allow them to be stolen by another shepherd! This is *my* world!" Anecoya stamped her feet, and Zogrusz felt the mountain tremble.

"Behave yourself!" Rhas said. "So far, Zog has shown impressive restraint, but he will fight if you continue this behavior. And what happens when beings such as yourselves brawl? Floods! Earthquakes! *Cataclysms*! No one can worship either of you if they are *dead*." The moon-colored cat rose from his haunches and began pacing back and forth in front of the fuming goddess. "I taught you better than this, Annie," the cat muttered, his voice softening. Zogrusz thought Rhas sounded almost disappointed.

Anecoya flushed at Rhas's admonishment, but anger still blazed in her eyes. "Then what," she said with cold sharpness, "am I supposed to do? Meekly relinquish the people I raised up from fledglings?"

Rhas twisted around to face Zogrusz, who had watched this exchange in mute astonishment. The cat looked tired, as if this situation was absolutely exhausting.

"Do you have a more comfortable place for us to talk, Zog?"

For a moment the unexpected question made his mind go blank. Then he swallowed, running a hand through his bloody, dust-coated curls.

"Uh, yes. Yes, I do."

"WHAT IS THIS PLACE?"

Zogrusz turned back to where the red-haired goddess was standing at the threshold of his cavern. Her gaze slowly traveled along the elaborate carvings incised into the walls, lingering on the throne atop its ziggurat and the crude idol that had been his first fumbling attempt to work stone.

"This is my home," Zogrusz said simply, not in the mood at the moment to elaborate further. He'd compelled the cut on his brow to stop bleeding, but the wound still pulsed painfully.

"It can't be," Anecoya muttered. "It's too . . ." Her words trailed away, as if she didn't want to finish that thought.

"Too what?" Zogrusz asked, but her answer was a scowl as she followed him into the cavern.

"It's quite remarkable, Zog," Rhas said, filling the silence after hopping up onto one of the ziggurat's lowest tiers. "I did not know Eldritch Horrors held such appreciation for the art of humans."

"Art isn't only for humans," Zogrusz murmured, still fingering the gash on his head.

Rhas looked at him curiously, cocking his little head to one side. "Apparently not," he finally agreed, then began grooming himself.

Zogrusz returned his attention to Anecoya, who had stopped a few steps into the cavern and was staring upwards, her face slack with surprise.

"The ceiling," she said softly, "It looks like . . ."

"The dome of Amotla," Zogrusz finished for her, with some satisfaction. "It was my inspiration. I chose a mosaic for the underside rather than a painting, but the dimensions of the arch are virtually identical, I believe."

Anecoya pointed at the image looming over them. "That's you, isn't it? In the jungle."

"The first day I arrived on this world."

"And you gave yourself a halo," Anecoya said. "Do you think yourself holy, demon?"

"Halo?" Zogrusz replied in confusion. "No, that's the sun setting. I thought it looked dramatic."

The red-haired girl snorted at this, rolling her eyes.

Zogrusz thought back to what was painted on the underside of Amotla's great dome. "In the palace of the priest-king, the image was similar. A golden egg hatching – that must have been your first moment in this world."

"My first moment?" Anecoya sneered. "Demon, I *created* this world. I dreamed it into existence while I lay nestled in my egg."

Rhas made a sound that was something like a cough, and they both turned to where the cat lay sprawled on the step. "That's . . . not entirely true, Annie."

"And how would you know that?" the red-haired goddess demanded, hands on her hips.

"Because, my girl, I am not just a cat."

"Of course," Anecoya replied with an exasperated sigh. "You're the god of cats. I figured *that* out long ago."

Rhas stretched deeply, his entire body quivering at the effort involved. "I'm a little bit more than that, Annie. You see, you didn't make the world . . . because *I* am the world."

"What?" the goddess and the Horror exclaimed.

Rhas did something with his shoulders that almost seemed like a shrug. "I suppose I just like cats, and that's why I choose this form. They are as close to perfection as any creature that has arisen on my surface."

Anecoya was staring at Rhas in incredulous disbelief. "I don't believe it," she said. "If that was true, why not tell me this a thousand years ago?"

Rhas sighed, looking over to Zogrusz. "You know, I don't like you all looming over me. Is there someplace we can relax?"

"Uh, of course," Zogrusz muttered, gesturing at the benches beside the pool with the phosphorescent fish. He hurried over to the little divan he'd fashioned long ago after his first meeting with Rhas and hefted it. "I made this for you," he told the cat – or whatever it was – as he carried the divan across the cavern and set it down beside the larger benches. Then he gestured grandly for both his guests to sit.

"Much appreciated," Rhas said, hopping down from the ziggurat and sauntering over to the divan. The cat watched the glowing fish in the water for a moment, then jumped onto the stone where Zogrusz had carved a smooth cat-sized indentation and promptly curled up. "It's very comfortable," Rhas assured him, punctuating this statement with a loud purr.

"Trying to fracture our souls?" Zogrusz asked as he also plopped down on one of the benches.

The cat paused his pleased vibrations and chuckled. "Ha. Sorry about that – my imagination does get carried away sometimes."

"Like telling me I didn't make this world?" Anecoya said as she came to stand next to the pool with her arms tightly crossed.

Rhas sighed. "Well, that was true, Annie. And to be honest, I'm surprised you never questioned this. You hatched only a thousand years ago, but you must have noticed that the world was far older than that."

"I thought when I'd dreamed it into being I'd made it old," she sniffed.

"Well, you didn't. This world has been around for several billion years, though I've only been here for the last two hundred thousand. I suppose I might have existed before that, but my . . . emergence coincided with the very event that drew both of you to this world."

"When the animals here began to think," Zogrusz guessed.

"Many animals think, Zog," Rhas corrected him. "But there is a higher plane of thought that is quite rare and takes many eons to manifest, if it ever does. Consciousness. Life that is aware it is alive, that can question its place in the universe and consider what the future may bring. When that spark ignited in the minds of those long-ago humans, I was suddenly born as well. Now, I try to represent and care for all life on this world, but my . . . advanced state is, I believe, because of all those complex human minds constantly churning. I am their total knit together and given form."

Anecoya's eyes narrowed suspiciously; she hadn't yet followed Rhas's advice and sat on the empty bench, stubbornly remaining standing. "Then why tell me a completely different story after I emerged from my egg?"

"Because it was what I thought you needed to hear," Rhas replied with another long-suffering sigh. "I wanted you to care for this world and its inhabitants. I thought that if you believed it had all been your creation, you would treat them better. And to be honest, I didn't have the answers you wanted. I do not know where you came from or what you are. One day a golden egg fell from the sky, and when it finally hatched a hundred years later, you tumbled out groggy and disoriented. Perhaps I was wrong to lie to you . . . but you *have* been a good goddess to these humans."

"Did you hear that, demon?" Anecoya said, turning to Zogrusz. "I am a good goddess. I taught them love and compassion, not to grovel in fear before a terrifying monster."

"I am not a demon or a monster," Zogrusz replied sharply, the anger that had been smoldering since her completely unwarranted ambush suddenly flaring hotter. "I am an Eldritch Horror. And until a few moments ago, I didn't even know you existed!"

"How could you not know about me?" Anecoya retorted. "You *stole* my worshippers!"

"And your worshippers *stole* my worshippers! I woke up to find the town that venerated me in ruins, and my people had been dragged off to *your* city! And *you* are angry? I have the right to be furious! Your Amotlans could have just left my People alone!" Zogrusz was surprised to realize he had risen from his bench – he was dangerously close to losing control of his temper.

Anecoya blinked, her lip curling in revulsion. She was staring at something on his face, and when he reached up, he felt rubbery flesh dangling from his chin. He was so upset that he'd let his man-disguise slip, and a few mouth-tendrils had squirmed loose. The look on her face at seeing this sliver of his true form made him even more indignant.

Very well, if she wanted to keep escalating this situation . . .

Zogrusz shrugged out of his man-cloak, reveling in the surprise and fear that shivered her face as he swelled to twice her height. He stretched out his scaled arms, unsheathing his curving claws, and spread wide the stunted wings on his back. Ribbons of darkness twined around his true form like glistening black serpents, and he felt the new power that had manifested in him upon waking stir, pleading to be unleashed.

Anecoya had taken an instinctive step back as he came to loom over her, but then her expression hardened, and the flaming sword materialized again in her hand.

"*Enough!*" Rhas's booming voice echoed in the great cavern.

They both looked at the cat; his hackles were raised, and he was glaring like he wanted to dismember both of them.

"Stop it! The only two cosmic beings on this planet and you're acting like children!"

Anecoya's sword guttered and went out, and Zogrusz supposed that if he was still in his man-form, he'd have shared her flush of embarrassment.

"The others were right," the cat continued, "you outsiders are trouble."

With a thought, Zogrusz shrank himself down to a more human proportion, though he did not don his man-cloak again.

"Others?" Anecoya ventured, then hesitated for a few moments before moving over to a bench and sinking down stiffly. Zogrusz did the same, letting the ribbons of darkness he'd summoned dissolve and the new power bubbling inside him subside.

"That's what I call them," Rhas said, aggressively scratching behind his ear. He still sounded annoyed, but not as much as a moment ago. "Though I do actually know the names of a few circling the nearest stars. They are like me – the aggregate of all the lives on their worlds given form and will and then finally awareness with the emergence of consciousness. Communicating with them is like yelling from one mountain top to another, but over time we've pooled what knowledge we each have gained from our respective experiences." Rhas pointed his little nose at Zogrusz and then Anecoya. "And *that* is how I know your kind are trouble."

"*Our* kind?" the red-haired goddess repeated, glancing at Zogrusz warily.

"Cosmic beings," Rhas said hastily. "I didn't mean to imply you were in any way related. You are both from different species – Zogrusz is a very young Eldritch Horror, and Annie, my dear . . . well, I don't know what you are. The other world-consciousnesses I'm in contact with have never encountered your species before. But just like Zog, you feed off the emotions of the intelligent minds on this planet . . . in a way, you're both really feeding off of *me*." His tail lashed back and forth, as if trying to dismiss this last statement as not so important. "That makes you both sound like parasites, which would not be accurate. What we have is more of a . . . symbiosis. The love and fear and devotion the humans direct towards you feeds you, yes, but they also receive something important in return. Faith in something greater nourishes the soul. It helps give purpose and structure and binds together communities. So as troublesome as you cosmic beings can be, until now I have been glad you both found your way to my world."

Zogrusz swallowed, suddenly remembering what he had been expecting to find earlier when he'd rushed outside. A Reaper, drawn to this world by what he had sown.

"Rhas . . ." he began, then faltered as they both turned to him. His mouth-tendrils writhed nervously as he tried to think of the best way to tell them of the threat he knew was coming . . . and his part in bringing it to this world. "Perhaps you shouldn't be glad I'm here."

"A REAPER?" the red-haired goddess scoffed after Zogrusz had finished telling of Ycthitlig's visitation. "And what is it going to reap? Eldritch Horror cultists? Fine by me."

"I would be surprised if such a being would traverse the cosmos just to snack on a few minds," Zogrusz muttered, annoyed that she would be so cavalier about the lives of his followers.

"Then we fight," Anecoya said confidently. "You're an Eldritch Horror. It's an Eldritch Horror. With me at your side, we can banish it back to whatever abyss it crawled from."

Zogrusz shook his head emphatically. "No, no, no. You haven't seen them out there, in the void. The Great Old Ones. They are . . . beyond comprehension. Incredibly vast and ancient."

"But this isn't a Great Old One," she countered. "You said it was a Reaper, some lower tier of Eldritch Horror."

"Still far beyond what I am," Zogrusz said. "Just how much stronger I don't know. But given how much my power has increased each time I wake and that Ycthitlig claimed to be an entirely different class of Horror . . . I believe it likely we could not stand against it even if there were a dozen others just like us."

"I'm not frightened," Anecoya said, almost sneeringly. "You haven't seen my full power yet either."

"Zog is right," Rhas suddenly interjected. The moon-colored cat had been quiet during Zogrusz's story and the argument that followed, eyes closed and motionless except for the occasional twitching of his ears. "Whatever is coming is almost certainly well beyond our ability to repel. There are . . . legends among the web of world-minds I am in contact with about the arrival of Eldritch Horrors, and how in their wake planets simply . . . go dark. Scoured clean of consciousness. I've never been sure how much weight to put in these stories – we world-minds love to gossip and pass along rumors that extend in whisper-chains across the universe – but the common understanding is that an Eldritch Horror puts a world in great danger. Which was why I was so confused, Zog, when I witnessed how you interacted with the People of Xochintl and then your behavior in our first conversation. I could not imagine that *you* were going to end life on my surface. But if you are just here to prepare the way for something far greater and more terrible . . ."

"Then what do we do?" Anecoya exclaimed, throwing up her arms. "I will not abandon this world *or* my devout." She frowned, glancing at Zogrusz. "And what happens to you after this . . . reaping? You also won't have any followers left."

"I believe," Zogrusz said slowly, trying to convey his uncertainty, "that I am supposed to leave this world to its fate. And then travel elsewhere in search of other planets suitable to feed an Eldritch Horror. Establish another faith that assuages my hunger and helps me grow stronger . . .

and in time whatever beacon this creates will draw another Reaper. Eventually, after enough worlds are sown, perhaps I will change into this higher stage of Horror."

"So is that what you will do?" snapped Anecoya. "Fly off and leave this world to die? Continue on your journey to become some sort of all-powerful evil god?"

Zogrusz's mouth-tendrils fluttered in agitation. The idea of deserting this world was difficult to even consider. Humans had proven themselves to be remarkably complex creatures capable of creating all sorts of wonders. And he simply *liked* them. Nearly every interaction he'd had with humans had been interesting and exhilarating, from that first exchange with the guard outside Xochintl all those years ago to his conversations with the fisherman Izel at the end of his last cycle. And then there was Rhas. The cat would cease to exist if the minds on this world were extinguished.

"No," Zogrusz said softly. "I will do what I can to help stop Ycthitlig."

Suddenly Anecoya snapped her fingers. "What if we halt this flow of dread that is drawing the other Eldritch Horror here?"

"And how would we do that?" Zogrusz asked, suspecting he knew where she was going with this.

The red-haired goddess shrugged, her expression carefully innocent. "We get rid of your cult."

Zogrusz folded his arms across his scaled chest. How convenient – exactly what she wanted anyway. "And how do you propose to do that?"

"Oh, I don't know . . . a crusade?"

Zogrusz snorted. "Some goddess of love and compassion you are."

Anecoya narrowed her eyes, anger clouding her face

again. "I'm a pragmatist. As the humans know, infections cannot be allowed to spread. It must be cut away, or the rest of the body will sicken and die."

"I'll die as well," Zogrusz retorted.

"That's a sacrifice I'm willing to accept," she said, her smile sickly sweet.

"You're speaking of mass murder," Rhas scolded her. "Purging hundreds of thousands, perhaps millions of the minds that are part of me." The cat shook his head sadly. "I'm disappointed, Annie. I thought I raised you better than that."

Anecoya scowled, hunching her shoulders as she crossed her arms. "It was just an idea," she muttered sulkily.

"She's right, though," Zogrusz admitted, which brought a confused glance from the goddess. "If we can't fight Ycthitlig, we have to dissuade it from coming here. And the only way we know how to do that is to uproot what I have accidentally sown." He saw Rhas stir and continued hastily before the cat could object. "But it will be difficult, because I learned how resilient belief can be. The remnants of my people survived centuries of persecution from those who followed her"—one of his mouth tendrils extended towards the goddess—"religion of kindness. It would not only be monstrous but also very difficult to ensure that no traces of my religion remained, and we don't know how little dread devotion Ycthitlig requires to find this world."

An uncomfortable silence descended after Zogrusz finished speaking. Anecoya looked impatient, like they were wasting their time sitting around in a cavern hoping for a flash of inspiration, while Rhas had adopted one of those inscrutable cat-postures with his head raised over his outstretched paws, a pose Zogrusz had seen commonly represented in stone at the entrances of many Amotlan buildings. It was impossible to know what Rhas was thinking: it might have been about mass murder or munching mice or defeating rampaging elder gods.

After a good long while of listening to the many-legged insects scurrying along the walls, Anecoya gave an annoyed grunt and abruptly stood. "This is pointless. Come find me if a plan materializes. Until then, I'll be preparing a welcome for this Yickthleg. If he wants the world, he'll have to take it from me!" The goddess's blazing gaze fell on Rhas, as if he might challenge this statement, but the cat continued staring straight ahead with serene indifference. Anecoya's mouth twisted at the lack of reaction, then she turned sharply on her heel and strode back towards the tunnel leading outside. After her footsteps had faded, Zogrusz also looked at the cat, but Rhas spoke before he could open his mouth.

"I am in communion with the closest world-minds, Zog," the cat murmured, his tail flicking back and forth. "Let us hope they have a better solution to our problem. For if they do not, I fear we must prepare for the worst."

Zogrusz wandered his cavern in a daze while Rhas remained on the little bench lost in whatever passed for conversation between world-minds. He lingered in front of the first carvings he had made on the walls, those abstract depictions of the Great Old Ones pulled from the dimmest recesses of his memory. Mad profusions of eyes nestled amongst writhing tentacles, fanged mouths endlessly gnawing at the darkness. Did they dream of the worlds they had sown and reaped? In some dark crevice of their beings did they feel guilt for the minds they had consumed on their journey to becoming . . . whatever they had become? Were they gods now? Demons? What had Rhas said, before quickly correcting himself? That Zogrusz was a parasite feeding off this world? Were all the Great Old Ones nothing more than vast parasites burrowed into the skin of the universe?

When he finally turned away from the carvings, his thoughts still troubled, Zogrusz found Rhas had vanished without saying farewell. That annoyed him slightly, but he supposed the cat or world-mind or whatever he truly was must be very distracted by the apocalypse Zogrusz had just revealed to be looming.

After making sure the tantrum that had shaken his cavern had broken nothing, he made his way outside and surveyed the ruin of the temple entrance. There was perhaps slightly more that could be salvaged than he had feared, but it would still be many months of hard work to repair the damage Anecoya had caused. And spending what time he had before Ycthitlig arrived doing *that* seemed rather pointless.

What would be a better use of the time? Perhaps understanding what new power had manifested while he slept. Not that he harbored any delusion that he could defeat or drive away the Reaper . . . but if Anecoya and Rhas were going to stand against the Eldritch Horror, then he would also be beside them, and any slight advantage would be welcome. So taking a deep breath, Zogrusz reached down inside himself and tried to explore his new ability. It felt different from his shape-changing or shadow-weaving, like it was something that could be pushed outwards, rather than a power molded into existence. He gazed out from where he stood on the mountain slope, concentrating on a curving line of birds etched against the brilliant blue of the sky. With a flicker of will, he summoned the new ability and let it slip its leash, trying to direct it towards that distant flock.

The air in front of him rippled as an invisible wave rushed forth. He lost sight of it quickly, and for a moment Zogrusz thought it had simply dissipated – which would have been rather disappointing – but then, in the far distance, the birds dropped like stones from the sky.

Interesting. The sensation of sending out this attack had been similar to when he'd delved into the minds of nearby sentient beings, but this was far more concentrated and violent. It was some sort of telepathic attack – a psionic blast, he supposed he could call it. Whether it would work against another Eldritch Horror, he did not know – he suspected it would not – but it was at least another weapon in his arsenal. Now he wished he'd unleashed it on Anecoya when she'd first assaulted him – the expression on the arrogant goddess's face if he'd pummeled her with psychic energy would have been quite satisfying to see.

Or maybe it would have slid away like water from a duck's back. He had no way to know if this power would faze other cosmic beings in the slightest. Perhaps he could test it on her when next they met – he owed her at least one good sucker punch.

Zogrusz sighed deeply, suddenly realizing he had forgotten to put on his man-disguise before he'd left the cave. He peered down the mountain at the pilgrim encampment, expecting to see it in panicked turmoil, but the ramshackle collection of tents and huts looked to have been abandoned. Perhaps his followers had fled when the temple façade had collapsed, or they'd seen Anecoya tossing him around and decided wisely that they should all be somewhere else at that moment. And truly, what did it matter if a few of the pilgrims were hunkered somewhere and could see him right now in his true form? They knew he dwelled in the mountain, after all. There really was no point in remaining hidden, not with the end of the world rushing towards them all.

A pang of sadness accompanied that thought. If these were the waning moments of human civilization, he wanted to experience its glory one last time. He yearned to feel the bustle around him again, hear their babbling conversations and smell the food they fried on the streets. Witness once more the colorful churn of humans in their dyed clothes, metal flashing at their wrists and neck, iridescent feathers woven into their hair. For a moment he stared at the horizon, where he knew somewhere by the sea the white-stone domes and minarets of Amotla blazed in the bright sun, and then with a final glance back at the ruined entrance, he began to pick his way down the mountainside.

ZOGRUSZ TRAVELED MOST of the way at night wrapped in his cloak of shadows, consuming the distance with his trueform's massive strides. He saw little benefit to sowing panic, and he didn't want to cause a riot in the city when he eventually arrived, so when he glimpsed the white-spear towers of Amotla shining in the moonlight, he donned his mancloak – as he had those many years ago when he had first come to the city – and made the final approach on foot. This time no kind old man offered the back of his wagon to Zogrusz, so by the time he reached the mosaic-adorned walls, dawn had broken, its rosy blush staining the spires.

He joined a procession of farmers bringing carts laden with vegetables into the city. The market square just beyond the gate was far livelier than he remembered, as it seemed most of Amotla's households were in competition at that moment to buy the freshest produce and meat. Zogrusz strolled through the clamor, drinking deep of the sights and sounds and smells, sincerely hoping that this was not the last time he would enjoy the delightful chaos of a human city.

He spent the day exploring the winding streets and any buildings he found architecturally compelling. A foray down a random alleyway deposited him at a familiar archway, but the passage that had once led to the little chamber where the tattered remnants of the People had prayed to his idol and kept their faith in him alive – kept him alive, truth be told – had long ago been bricked up. However, the Church of Zog was very much alive in the city – he must have passed a dozen temples in his wanderings, all built from black stone with graven Eldritch Horrors guarding the entrances. His was not the only faith in Amotla, as there seemed to be just as many houses of worship devoted to a certain red-haired goddess, great wooden birds perched atop circular roofs with outspread wings, flames blazing in the braziers that filled the temple courtyards. It pleased him that Cozotl had allowed the two faiths to co-exist peacefully, despite the command he'd given long in a fit of pique. Clearly, there were plenty of humans to go around . . . so her ambush had been very much an overreaction.

As he turned away from the blocked-up passage, Zogrusz noticed something that gave him pause. Overlaying the bricks was a web of truly epic proportions, with several large spiders adding to it with admirable industriousness. But this, by itself, was not what had drawn his attention. No, it was that his name was written in a curling, elegant script across the top of the web. He blinked, for a moment wondering if he was experiencing some sort of hallu-cination.

'*Zog*,' the glistening threads spelled out, '*Tallest hill. Twilight.*'

He briefly entertained the notion that this might be Ycthitlig, but quickly discarded the idea. Communicating through spiders seemed a bit understated for an Eldritch Horror . . . and there was only one being out there who called him Zog.

Zogrusz checked the sky and saw that it was already

starting to purple. Well, if Rhas truly wanted him to be punctual, he wouldn't have used arachnids to deliver this message. Shaking his head, Zogrusz began retracing his steps back to the city gates.

TRUE NIGHT WAS STILL a way off by the time Zogrusz reached the top of the tallest hill outside Amotla – though truly it was little more than a knoll rising above the otherwise perfectly flat grasslands. No trees or shrubs infringed on his view, so he found a comfortable spot to sprawl in a patch of purple clover and watched the darkness steal over the city. Motes of flickering light drifted around his head – tiny bugs that veered away abruptly after drawing close, as if sensing there was something very wrong about him.

"Zog."

He glanced over and saw that Rhas had appeared in the grass beside him. The insects swarmed the world-spirit, dancing about as if attracted by the moon-glow of his fur.

"Rhas," Zogrusz said, nodding a greeting. "You have news, then? A plan?"

The cat gave his head a little shake, dislodging a bug that had settled on his nose. "Damn things," he muttered before turning to look up at Zogrusz. "I wish I could have chosen what life developed on this world. Even I don't like insects, and they make up more of the total organic mass of me than any other animal."

"Despite being so small?"

"There are a lot of them, Zog," the cat murmured, swiping at a bug that had gotten too close. "So, so many. Which is partly why I do like spiders – they eat a huge amount of these little monsters."

"I assume you didn't bring me up here to complain."

Rhas's ear twitched. "No. I wanted to discuss a . . . a possibility. Truly, I don't know if it will help us solve our problem, but it's the only avenue I can see that gives us even the slightest hope."

The world-mind's cryptic comments stirred Zogrusz's curiosity . . . and ignited another small spark inside him, something he hadn't been expecting. Hope. Had Rhas discovered a way to save this world?

The sound of someone trudging through the grass drew their attention, and a moment later Anecoya's red hair – now a bloody crimson in the fading light – emerged from below as she ascended the hill. Zogrusz briefly entertained the thought of trying out his new psionic blast and sending her tumbling back down the slope, but he decided he wanted to hear what Rhas was going to propose. He was also fairly sure utter chaos would result if he knocked her over now.

He'd do it later.

When the goddess reached the summit, she put her hands on her hips and scowled at them both.

"Well? I hope you have a good reason for dragging me all the way here."

Rhas stretched deeply while Zogrusz climbed to his feet.

"I can't say I have a solution," the cat admitted, "but perhaps – and this is a very unlikely perhaps, I must admit – I have found a *path* to a solution."

Rhas paused – somewhat dramatically – and Anecoya made an impatient gesture for him to get on with it. "The universe is full of cosmic beings," the cat finally stated, his gaze lingering on Zogrusz before shifting to Anecoya. "Entities of great age and power. We world-minds know little about most of them – they exist on the periphery of our understanding, occasionally deigning to interact with one of the life-forms we harbor . . . or even sometimes wreaking devastation on us. Eldritch Horrors are some of the most well-known of all cosmic beings because their appearances have resulted in the destruction of so many worlds. But when I asked the others about how to survive a visitation by a Horror . . . a Reaper . . . silence. The other minds had never heard of a world persisting after attracting such an entity's attention."

"Then you are doomed," Zogrusz said glumly, the spark of hope inside him guttering. "*We* are doomed."

"As I said, perhaps," the cat continued. "You see, while we world-spirits might not know how to stop an Eldritch Horror, that does not mean no one in the universe does."

"Another cosmic being," Anecoya guessed.

Rhas bobbed his head in a cat-approximation of a nod.

"But you said these entities are mysterious and unknowable," Zogrusz said.

"They do not respect *my* kind very much," Rhas admitted, flicking its tail to disperse a swarm of the glowing bugs. "But perhaps they will treat with their own."

"You know where one is," Anecoya said slowly, her eyes widening.

"I do," Rhas replied. "Or at least I think I do – the world-mind that told me of this being's presence is . . . less than reliable."

"Why's that?"

Rhas's golden gaze flicked to Zogrusz. "First you must understand something about world-spirits. We are only as advanced as the creatures that comprise us. Humans are quite intelligent, at least compared to organisms on other worlds, which is why I am so clever and perceptive."

Anecoya snorted, but Rhas continued undeterred.

"However, one of the closest world-minds to me is quite . . . rudimentary. This is because consciousness only recently emerged on its surface . . . and it is very different than what arose here. It's a kind of communal intelligence, the aggregate of the organic substance that covers the world."

"Isn't that what you are?" Zogrusz asked.

"Yes . . . but here each human is a distinct individual. On this other planet, it's not the same. Rather, it's all one organism. One big . . . fungus."

Anecoya blinked, clearly startled. "You mean a mushroom?"

"Something like that," Rhas said. "Which makes it very difficult to communicate with, because it's both so foreign and so simple. But it was quite insistent in its own . . . unique way that a cosmic being is currently nearby. That this being actually visited its surface and is still lingering in its system, with no apparent plans to leave."

"Does it know what kind of being?" Zogrusz asked. "After all, it would be quite the disaster if it turned out to be another Reaper."

"After much parsing of its rather disjointed ramblings, the name that I drew forth was 'the Wanderer.' And it's a name with which I'm familiar." Rhas scratched behind his ear, then continued. "Now, as cosmic beings go, the Wanderer is one of the most well-known and reasonable. Sometimes it is even helpful, if the stories are true. The general understanding is that it drifts through the universe collecting knowledge. Why, we do not know. But there is no record of it being aggressive or dangerous . . . which suggests it would be safe to approach."

"And do what, exactly?"

Rhas gave Zogrusz a look like the answer should be obvious. "We ask what we can do. Surely this Wanderer knows much about Eldritch Horrors and whether any world has ever defeated one or dissuaded it from going through with its . . . Reaping."

"So we travel to where it is and ask its help," Zogrusz said. "But what if it says no or has no answers?"

"Then we have lost nothing but time," Rhas said.

"And we don't know how much of that we have," Zogrusz murmured, glancing up at the darkening sky like he expected the stars to wink out and Ycthitlig to suddenly appear.

"We will have to fly there as quickly as possible. Zog, I've seen you in your true form . . . I can't imagine you travel very fast with those stunted little wings."

"They brought me across the universe," Zogrusz replied, slightly offended.

"But not quickly, I'd wager," Rhas continued, turning his golden eyes to the red-haired goddess. "Which is why we need your help, Annie. It's time for you to spread *your* wings."

"I've never left this world," Anecoya said, and to Zogrusz she sounded a little nervous. "What if I can't fly between the stars?"

"You are a cosmic being," the cat assured her. "You were born to soar on solar winds."

The goddess grimaced, but the world-mind's words had clearly heartened her somewhat. Then she shifted her attention to Zogrusz, pointing at him accusingly. "Are we sure we can trust him? He's one of *them*."

"I told you Ycthitlig is coming," Zogrusz reminded her through gritted teeth.

"And perhaps you want us off this world when it arrives," she continued, folding her arms tightly across her chest. "To make the reaping easier."

"This is my idea, Annie," Rhas told her with a sigh. "Not his. And I trust Zog. I've watched him for centuries."

Anecoya blew out her cheeks. "Fine. The demon and I will go to see this Wanderer."

"I'm coming as well," the cat said. "I can't imagine what catastrophes would result if you two were left alone to do this."

"You can leave?" Zogrusz asked in surprise. "I would have thought you were confined to this world."

"For a short while," Rhas informed him haughtily. "And it will only be a sliver of my full consciousness that accompanies you . . . though it will still be *significantly* smarter than both of you."

Anecoya rolled her eyes at this but didn't bother arguing. "And so when do we leave?"

"As soon as possible," the cat answered. "Now, if you both agree. There is no telling how much time we actually have."

Anecoya nodded. "Very well, cat. I've always trusted you, so I suppose I shouldn't stop doing that now. If you think this is the best course . . . I'm with you."

"As am I," Zogrusz added, then looked at the goddess. "But can you truly transport both of us?"

She smirked and took a large step backwards. "Oh, yes," she said, raising her arms above her head with the palms turned outwards. A shimmering began at her hands, then quickly spread until the edges of her limbs and body blurred, contorting and swelling. Zogrusz shielded his eyes as a blazing light erupted in the center of her form and raced outwards, consuming Anecoya. When it subsided, she was gone, and in her place was an enormous bird large enough to pick up an elephant in its claws, its feathers crackling like flames. Its head swiveled, sword-sharp raptor gaze skewering Zogrusz, and he found he was having trouble looking away from a curving beak that looked easily capable of rending his man-form in half.

"You might have to change your shape or at least get out of those clothes," Rhas said, scrambling up onto one of the scythe-like talons furrowing the grass. "It gets rather hot on her."

6

Zogrusz's previous experience of traveling through the dark between the stars had been very different. It was clear to him now that his journey to Rhas's world had been like a seed drifting on the breeze, a leisurely exploration into the unknown, and far more time than he'd realized must have elapsed during his wanderings. Clinging to Anecoya's back now, he marveled at the speed of the goddess as she surged through space, the distant light of the stars blurring and elongating around them. Zogrusz also remembered the cold kiss of this vast emptiness, but that had been banished by the intense heat welling up from beneath the feathers in which he crouched. He was certain a human would have instantly exploded into crackling flame if they had clambered up onto the goddess.

Rhas however seemed to be enjoying this feeling. He had found a comfortable spot to curl up in the pocket formed where the crest of feathers below her mantle flowed into her wings, and he looked as content as a cat sleeping in the afternoon sun. After a while, he seemed to sense

Zogrusz's attention, his golden eyes sliding open to settle on the Eldritch Horror.

<Zog>

His name blossomed in his mind, uttered in Rhas's distinctive voice. Zogrusz stared at the cat in surprise, wondering if this had been his imagination.

<It's not. I've made a bridge between our thoughts because sound cannot travel out here>

Zogrusz concentrated, trying to form a response. *<How? >* he asked, the word reverberating in his skull.

Rhas winced. *<No need to think so loudly. And to answer your question . . . I **am** consciousness. A vast, interconnected web of minds. Speaking like this is far more natural for me than using my mouth>*

Zogrusz glanced at the back of Anecoya's blazing head as she plunged through the darkness. *<Can she hear us?>*

<She could if I wanted her to> Rhas responded. *<And in a moment I'll bring us all together so we can discuss important matters. But first . . . I wanted to talk to you privately. About Annie>*

Zogrusz couldn't restrain his surge of dislike at the mention of the bird-goddess.

Rhas's mental sigh slipped through his head. *<Your feelings are understandable. She has been less than pleasant towards you>*

<I'd go so far as to say antagonistic>

<Yes, and for that I'm sorry. It is at least partly my failing – I was the first being she encountered after emerging from her egg, and I've done my best to guide her into becoming a good goddess for my world. But I did not prepare her for the truths that she was neither unique nor responsible for all creation. When she awoke from her sleep this time to discover that another cosmic being now inhabited 'her' world and had

leached away some of the devotion that sustained her . . . I admit, she reacted badly. I should have prepared her better, but I thought she would sleep for another few centuries. Perhaps you can try to look at it from her perspective? Her reality was upended, and for the first time in a thousand years she felt threatened. Her continued belligerence is because she doesn't know how to act towards you. Are you a rival? An enemy? A . . . colleague?>

<Right now we are allies> Zogrusz grumbled. *<And we should be united in common purpose . . . unless she wants to lose everything she has ever known>*

<Quite right> Rhas quickly agreed. *<I just beg you not to judge her too harshly. I've known her since she was a fledgling, and she is not terrible. Impetuous, yes, perhaps a bit arrogant . . . though I believe those flaws are a rather immature attempt to deal with her insecurities. She is very young, you know. By the standards of cosmic beings, she's still a child>*

Zogrusz attempted the telepathic equivalent of a shrug. *<I will . . . try to be understanding>*

<That is all I am asking> said Rhas, and Zogrusz could sense he'd pleased the world-mind. *<I've hoped for a long time that you two would eventually be able to . . . coexist>*

Zogrusz snorted, causing his mouth-tendrils to flutter, but the sound was swallowed by the airless emptiness.

<Let me bring her into this conversation> Rhas said, and a moment later Zogrusz felt the touch of another mind – broiling hot when compared to the world-spirit's cool equanimity.

<Annie, how are you doing?>

<Rhas!> Anecoya exclaimed, her exuberant voice filling Zogrusz's head. *<I feel incredible. I never knew how constrained I was on our world . . . I can finally push myself to the very limit!>*

<Good, good> Rhas replied. <*Your true home is the space between the stars. I'm glad you finally can experience it*>

<*We are almost there, I think*> Anecoya continued, her excitement so infectious Zogrusz felt his own pulse quickening. <*I can sense the star you pointed me towards growing closer*>

<*And that means we should discuss what will happen when we arrive. Annie, Zog is here sharing this mind-link*>

<*I can feel him*> she replied tersely, her thoughts flavored with distaste.

<*Yes, well, we should make sure we are all in agreement about our strategy. First, while you two are why I hope the Wanderer will grant us an audience, I strongly believe it is best if I do the talking*> Rhas paused, as if expecting an objection, but after none were raised, he continued. <*I must stress that we should strive to avoid conflict at all costs. The Wanderer is an old and powerful cosmic being who has survived threats we cannot imagine over countless eons. Almost certainly it wields powers we cannot comprehend. You must keep your temper in check, even if the Wanderer is rude or dismissive*> Rhas did not specify to whom he was directing this statement, but Zogrusz had a strong suspicion it wasn't him.

<*Very well*> Anecoya muttered.

<*Excellent*> Rhas said. <*And that certainly also means no . . .*>

Zogrusz glanced in surprise at the world-mind as its thoughts trailed away. Something was wrong. Rhas had risen and was now perched on Anecoya's shoulder, staring off in the direction they were flying.

<*Oh. We're there*>

One of the brightest points of gleaming light in the star-spattered distance suddenly swelled. Zogrusz hadn't realized just how fast Anecoya was moving, and he found the speed at which this point was expanding more than a little disconcerting. Then with a violent flaring of her wings that sent Zogrusz tumbling forward clutching at burning feathers the bird-goddess arrested her approach. Zogrusz looked to Rhas, expecting the cat to have been thrown from Anecoya's back, but the little creature seemed somehow to be firmly rooted despite being so small and light.

It was a binary stellar system, with a large yellow star and a much smaller bluish-white companion dancing in attendance. Zogrusz couldn't see much in the way of planets except for a few vast gas giants girdled by rings and surrounded by moons, although some rocks drifting in the system's large asteroid belt might have been approaching planetary size.

<I . . . sense something> Anecoya murmured. <A presence>

<Go to it, Annie> Rhas instructed her, and the great bird began to move again, though this time much more sedately. She glided towards the swarm of floating rock-and-ice chunks, and after a moment Zogrusz also felt something strange. It was a tickling in his head, like spiders scuttling across the surface of his brain . . . but behind that silken touch loomed something vast and ancient and watchful.

Zogrusz's gaze was drawn by a flash of bronze recessed among the tumbling debris. Anecoya must have seen it as well, as she angled herself in that direction, swooping around a large ball of dirty ice and passing through the glittering cloud trailing in its wake.

<Is that what I think it is?> Rhas's voice reverberated in Zogrusz's head, edged with panic.

He was too numb to answer. Anecoya murmured something in an awed whisper he could not understand.

It was a fish the size of a moon, drifting between the asteroids like it was a leviathan haunting the ocean's depths.

The light from the twin stars made the scales around its massive blunt head glow a deep copper, though its coloration shifted to gold and then a muted bronze farther down its great length. Its fins were motionless, its vast milky eyes staring blankly ahead, and if not for the very slow sweep of its tail back and forth, Zogrusz would have thought the creature was dead.

With some effort, Zogrusz finally managed a coherent thought. <*The Wanderer is a fish?*>

<*A WORLD I VISITED IN MY YOUTH HAD AN OLD SAYING: 'TEACH A MAN TO FISH, AND YOU'LL FEED HIM FOR A LIFETIME. GIVE A MAN A FISH, AND HE'LL SWIM BETWEEN THE STARS'*>

Stunned silence descended, and Zogrusz imagined the others were also listening in their heads to the fading echoes of this pronouncement. Something from outside had pushed its way into the mental bridges Rhas had fashioned to link their minds, a hoary presence that reminded Zogrusz of what it had been like to drift between the sleeping Old Ones and experience the intoxicating power of their dreams.

<*A PHOENIX, AN ELDRITCH HORROR, AND A CAT THAT IS NOT A CAT. HOW UNUSUAL. COME, YOU MUST ENTER AND TELL ME WHAT BRINGS YOU HERE*>

The fish's great jaws slowly unhinged, opening wide. A strange opalescent light painted the inside of its mouth, making jagged teeth the size of glaciers gleam. Zogrusz couldn't see exactly where this radiance was coming from, but he thought it was welling up from deeper within the fish.

<*Rhas . . .*> Anecoya whispered in their minds, as if the other being would not hear her if she was quiet enough. <*What should I do?*>

<I suppose we have to go inside> Rhas said in what sounded like resignation.

<I was afraid you were going to say that> muttered Anecoya, but still she banked on invisible currents, adjusting their approach so they were headed on a path directly for that gaping fanged maw.

<Are we sure this is wise?> Zogrusz asked, eyeing the great glistening teeth with unease.

<You know, there is a fish at the bottom of the ocean that uses light to attract its prey> Rhas murmured, <luring it into a mouth that does not look that dissimilar to this one . . .>

<If you want me to turn away and fly as fast as I can in the other direction, tell me now> Anecoya said sharply, her thoughts flavored by what might have been fear.

<There's something strange inside> Zogrusz said, peering between the fangs. <It's not . . . I don't think this thing is truly a fish, at least like we understand them>

Anecoya muttered something unintelligible and angry, but she stayed her course, passing between two enormous teeth that reared around them like canyon walls. Zogrusz imagined the mouth snapping shut, the fangs looming above plunging down to impale Anecoya, and he let out a little sigh of relief when this did not happen.

<Oh> Anecoya murmured as they emerged from the forest of teeth and beheld clearly for the first time what lay beyond.

There was no throat leading into darkness, no flesh fringing the inside of the mouth. The fish had been gutted, its insides scooped out and replaced with . . . something else. Filaments infused with nacreous light webbed the interior of the creature, forming softly glowing pathways that occasionally intersected to create broader platforms. These pearlescent threads vanished into the hazy distance, but

Zogrusz thought they were anchored on the gray walls curving up around them. He wondered if the fish was truly still alive, despite its languid swimming – there were no bones or organs or blood, just this strange lattice filling the entirety of the vast hollow space.

"I think we can safely assume that the Wanderer is not the fish."

When he heard Rhas's voice, Zogrusz glanced at the cat in surprise.

"There's air," Rhas said, then as if to prove this point yawned deeply. "Somehow."

<*I'm going to land*> Anecoya told them over their mental bridge – perhaps she hadn't realized that sound traveled in here, or maybe she simply preferred to communicate telepathically when in her bird-form. After all, Zogrusz hadn't heard her speak since she'd transformed, so human-style speech very well might be impossible with her avian physiology.

Anecoya settled onto the closest of the suspended platforms, a wide disc connected to a half-dozen of the threads like it was a spoke in a wheel. A few of these paths were so narrow human children would have had to walk single-file, while others were wide enough that Zogrusz thought he could have navigated them in his true form. The grade of these filaments varied as well – some ascended to link up with higher platforms, while others descended into what would have been the bowels of the fish, and the rest branched out at roughly the same elevation they now stood. Zogrusz tried to tell what else might be hidden in the far recesses of the fish, but the skein of threads was far too thick to see clearly. He understood why Anecoya had alighted here – she never would have made it through that dense tangle.

<Everyone off> Anecoya commanded, and after an apprehensive glance at the opaque substance below, Zogrusz slid carefully from her back, though he was not willing to let go of the tuft of feathers he was gripping tightly until he was sure the platform wouldn't shatter beneath him. He decided he would stay in this smaller version of his true-form until he was absolutely sure it could support a greater weight.

Rhas had already leaped down and was pawing at the thread as if this could help him discern what it was made of. Zogrusz had thought it would feel cool and hard, perhaps like polished stone, but instead it was warm and slightly sticky, which suggested to him it might be organic. Perhaps hardened saliva or some other bodily secretion.

A rush of hot air stirred his mouth-tendrils, and Zogrusz turned to see that Anecoya had assumed her human form. The flush in her cheeks was nearly the color of her hair; she looked exultant, the grin on her face revealing a pair of deep dimples. He'd never seen her smile, Zogrusz realized, and he had to admit it was far more pleasant than the scowl she usually sported.

"So where is this Wanderer?" she asked, brushing a stray lock of hair out of her eyes.

"I don't know," Rhas replied, "but it looks like he's sent a welcoming committee."

Zogrusz realized what the cat was talking about a moment later when movement on one of the higher threads drew his gaze. An insectile creature with many-jointed legs was scuttling along its underside. A pendulous barbed stinger hung from the end of its thorax, and transparent wings of veined membrane were folded upon its back. More of these creatures were now coming into view farther back on the same thread, and all were moving with the same frantic purpose. Towards them.

"Let's not rush to judgment here," Rhas said. "I'm sure they are servants of the Wanderer."

"They don't look friendly," Zogrusz muttered, reaching inside himself to ready his psionic blast.

"Now Zog," Rhas admonished him sternly, "I'm disappointed. You of all beings should understand that outward appearance has no bearing on one's inner character."

The closest of the creatures had halted its mad scramble and was now staring down at them from one of the threads crisscrossing above the platform.

"Greetings, good sir!" Rhas called up to it loudly. "Thank you for your hospitable welcome! We have traveled from very far indeed to meet your master and ask –"

The cat broke off his speech, yowling in surprise as the creature spat a glob of viscous goo. Rhas just managed to jump away before the substance splattered on the platform, where it hissed and smoked, eating away at the opalescent material beneath their feet. Zogrusz stepped hurriedly away from the deepening hole, wondering if this stuff could dissolve even his true-form's flesh. The creature perched above them spread its serrated mandibles wide and made a chittering sound that might have been laughter.

Not friendly, then. Zogrusz blasted it with his psionic attack, sending it tumbling from the thread. He must have stunned it, because the insect did not even try to spread its wings as it plummeted out of sight. An enraged keening rose from its brethren, the onrushing horde uncasing their wings as they leaped from the filament they had been clinging to.

Zogrusz raised his claws, but before the insects could reach them, a flame suddenly erupted, and the swarm veered away as Anecoya swung her blazing sword.

"Back to back!" she shouted over the harsh droning, and immediately Zogrusz realized the wisdom of this idea. He set himself as she'd suggested just as the throng of creatures began to circle them. For a moment the swarm hesitated, as if unsure about the best strategy to attack, and then one of the insects proved itself the bravest – or perhaps the most foolish – as it suddenly darted from the rest of its kind and hurled itself at Zogrusz. He reacted purely on instinct, swiping with his claws and catching it in its distended abdomen. The creature exploded in an eruption of green ichor, splattering Zogrusz, though thankfully the creature's blood turned out not to be as corrosive as its spit.

A crackling pop sounded from behind Zogrusz, and then Anecoya shouted in triumph. "Ha! Got one!"

The demise of their kin incensed the creatures further, and they surged forward in a flurry of clacking mandibles and thrusting stingers. Zogrusz felt something sharp scratch a fiery line across his belly, but he didn't have time to check the severity of this wound. He was too busy plucking the insects from the air, crushing their carapaces and making their swollen bodies burst like overripe fruit. Several of the creatures swooped at his head, but he scattered them with another wave of psychic energy. His mental attack was much weaker this time, and he doubted he had the reserves in him for a third attempt. Still, he'd been successful in disorienting the creatures, and as they bumbled about in a daze, he lunged closer and began smashing them into oblivion.

A cry of pain from Anecoya made him whirl around. His pursuit of the stunned creatures had carried him away from her, and after leaving where he'd been positioned the insects had descended to surround her from all sides. He waded back into the blizzard of beating wings and shifting chitin, taking hold of the goddess by her arm and dragging her stumbling out of the swarm. Her golden robes were in tatters, and blood flowed freely from a long cut on her shoulder close to where his claws were grasping, and he quickly released her for fear that he might make the injury worse. This was ill-timed, because just as he did this, one of the larger creatures latched onto her back and wrenched her from her feet, pulling her once more into the insect whirlwind. For a frozen moment she met his gaze with shocked eyes, and then she was gone.

"No!" Zogrusz cried, lunging after her, but before he could reach the swarm something erupted from its center and he was thrown backwards. He landed in a heap not far from the edge of the platform, momentarily stunned, and after blinking away the dark spots in his vision, he saw Anecoya had once more assumed her bird form. The creatures seemed panicked by this development, the coherency of their swarm dissipating as they fled in every direction to escape her snapping beak. But Anecoya would not be denied her revenge, plucking the creatures from the air and swallowing them. In moments they were all gone, either disappeared into her gullet or reduced to specks in the distance.

"Well, that was interesting."

Zogrusz looked down to find Rhas sitting between his feet. "Where did you go?" he asked. A ripple passed through the great bird as Anecoya reverted to her human form – her robes were intact again, and the wounds he could still see seemed to have stopped bleeding. Her face was pale, though, her hair in wild disarray.

"I thought it best if I stayed out from underfoot," the cat replied, arching his back as he stretched. "Annie, are you all right?"

Anecoya ran a shaking hand through her disheveled curls. "I'm fine," she said, watching the creatures warily as they dwindled.

<BRAVO!> They all jumped as the word reverberated in their heads. *<TRULY AN EXEMPLARY PERFORMANCE. I VERY MUCH WANT TO MEET YOU ALL>*

The light infusing one of the pathways extending from their platform suddenly strengthened into a rich golden hue, picking out the thread clearly against the tangled knots of ganglia.

<PLEASE, FOLLOW THE YELLOW SPIT ROAD>

THE FISH WAS NOT AS empty as Zogrusz had believed. Traveling the glowing golden filament, he glimpsed strange things sequestered down branching paths or perched on floating platforms. There was what looked like a house made of coral balancing on crustacean-like legs, its door a great shell; the gleaming black statue of some four-legged animal, upon which blood-red flowers were blooming; and a jade head with eyes that followed them as they passed, its lips set in a disapproving frown.

"It's a collection," Rhas murmured.

"Wander the universe for an eon or two and you probably pick up a few things," Anecoya replied, rubbing at the fading wound on her shoulder as she stared at a massive corvid crouched on the limb of a silver tree. The bird cocked its head, regarding them as they passed with eyes of glittering obsidian. Zogrusz wondered if it felt any kinship with the bird-goddess.

"I think we have arrived," Zogrusz said when he noticed that the filament they were following terminated at a far-larger platform than any he had yet seen. Most of this great space was empty, though something large and jagged was thrusting up from the platform's center. It almost resembled the stalagmites that had formed in his cavern after many ages of water dripping down from above, but as they neared, Zogrusz realized that the haphazard pile was actually a great chair. Ensconced in this throne was a tiny, wizened being that looked like a human male who had lived several centuries too long, dressed in faded red robes patterned with silvery geometric designs, a sphere of shimmering gold hovering beside him.

"Aha!" the man cried, clapping his desiccated hands together sharply. "My unexpected but not unwelcome guests! I am known in many places as the Wanderer, but I invite you to use the name first given to me – Ixiathyco-lapsus k'Veringian. Or Ixia, if that's easier to remember."

Rhas settled on his haunches a hundred paces from the Wanderer, Anecoya and Zogrusz taking up positions flanking the world-mind.

"Greetings, Ixiathycolapsas k'Verin -"

"Ixiathycolapsus," interrupted the ancient creature.

Rhas's tail swished in annoyance. "Excuse me?"

"Ixiathycolaps*us* not Ixiathycolaps*as*. On my home world – which is now a cinder orbiting a dead star, bless its memory – using the wrong vowel there could be construed as a declaration of war. Or a desire to mate . . . which, come to think of it, might be why my species went extinct."

Rhas blinked his golden eyes slowly, as if struggling to process these bizarre ramblings. "Ixia, then."

"Very acceptable," the Wanderer said with a grin that nearly cracked his face.

"Greetings, Ixia," the moon-colored cat tried again after a moment spent collecting himself. "I am Rhas, the avatar of a planetary world-mind. And my companions are Zogrusz and Anecoya."

The old man shifted, leaning forward in interest at the

introductions. Zogrusz noticed with a trickle of unease that his flesh seemed to be connected to the throne on which he sat, several ropes of the pearlescent material passing into his body.

"Yes, the Phoenix and the Eldritch Horror. It has been quite a long time since either of your races have entered my home. Welcome, welcome." He frowned, squinting at them. "And both of you are orphans, it seems. More and more interesting."

"Orphans?" Zogrusz repeated, sharing a confused look with Anecoya. "What do you mean by that?"

The old man sank back, spidery fingers curling around the armrests of his throne. "Ah, you already wish to trade information? Right into negotiations, then. But I doubt this knowledge is truly why you have come. Well . . . perhaps I can give you this small insight as a gesture of good faith, especially after you helped me with my little pest infestation."

"The insects?" Rhas blurted.

Ixia sighed deeply. "Yes. I don't know where I picked up the damn things. Killing the queen first was smart, I have to say. They lost quite a bit of coordination when the Horror here – Zogrusz, is it? – when he blasted it with his mind." Ixia chuckled as if amused by the memory, shaking his head. "What was I saying? Oh yes, orphans. Quite rare to encounter cosmic orphans, and two at the same time is unprecedented, even for me."

"What are you talking about?" Anecoya fairly growled in annoyance, but if the Wanderer noticed her tone it did not bother him.

"I suppose as orphans you simply wouldn't know," he continued as the golden orb came to drift above his age-spotted head. "Very well, let me start at the foundations.

You see, my dear, there are two ways that a cosmic entity emerges. The first is that an otherwise mortal being makes themselves . . . more than what they once were. It may surprise you to hear this, but I was born merely a man on a backwater world at the fringes of creation. My journey from the floor of that swamp-hut to the belly of dear Galuga here is a fascinating tale, let me assure you, but we shall save that for another time. The other sort of cosmic beings, of course, are simply born or . . . how should I say it . . . spring into existence. You both belong to such species. And most entities like this do not waste their time raising their own progeny. No, since most cosmic beings have significant telepathic powers, they are simply imprinted with the knowledge they need to understand what they truly are when still very young. But occasionally, before such a process occurs, a juvenile cosmic being wanders away from their nursery, or perhaps their parents fall victim to something out there that feeds on celestial creatures. I call these unfortunates orphans. The imprinting does eventually take place . . . but now it happens when this orphan encounters its first sentient creature, and their still-gestating personality is shaped by this experience. Both of you, I can confidently say, were imprinted by a mortal. A human, to be precise, on one of the many worlds where that species has arisen."

Zogrusz thought back to the first time he had entered another mind. The woman had been nursing her babe beside the campfire as he watched from the darkened jungle . . . had his nature been irrevocably altered at that moment? Was this why he had always felt such an affinity for humans and the reason why when he had finally met another Eldritch Horror the creature had seemed so . . . alien? He felt light-headed, overwhelmed by what this

ancient traveler had just claimed. One of the abiding
mysteries of his existence may have finally been solved.

"You called me a Phoenix," Anecoya said, apparently not
as dizzied by these revelations as Zogrusz. "What is that?"

Ixia raised a knobby finger, wagging it at her. "If you
desire more answers we shall have to negotiate a trade. I
didn't acquire all that I have by simply giving away secrets
that are coveted by others." He blinked watery eyes. "Or is
that why you have traveled so far? To learn about your
kind?"

"No, no," Rhas said hurriedly to forestall Anecoya, as she
appeared ready to demand just such answers. "We have a far
more pressing problem."

The old man raised a bristly white eyebrow and steepled
his fingers. "I am listening."

"The world we reside on – my world – is in danger. We
have learned that an Eldritch Horror Reaper is coming to
harvest its life."

"Of course," the Wanderer mused, gesturing at Zogrusz.
"No doubt this Sower here has seeded it with just the sort of
dread that Horrors crave."

"I didn't realize what would happen," Zogrusz muttered
defensively.

Ixia nodded. "I suppose you would not, being an orphan.
And now, having been shaped by the humans you first
imprinted with, you do not wish to witness the destruction of
this world. Or at least not be the one responsible for it." A series
of high-pitched chimes sounded from the golden sphere
hovering over the Wanderer. He glanced up and then chuckled.
"Yes, yes. This does remind me of the Helias Conundrum. But
say no more, as I would rather not scare our dear guests away."

Zogrusz shared a glance with his companions. Rhas gave

a confused cat-shrug, while Anecoya looked ready to stomp over to the throne and start shaking the old man until his few remaining teeth rattled out of his head.

"I will provide what assistance I can in this matter," the Wanderer continued, leaning forward again, his smile now almost predatory. "But in return, I will need you to perform a task for me. You see, my ward has gone missing, and I want her back."

THE MOON WAS a small gray circle picked out against the roiling orange and red chaos of the gas giant, one of the dozens that accompanied the massive planet. There was nothing from afar that indicated it was special, but the Wanderer had insisted that this was the celestial body in the system where life had arisen, and Rhas had later confirmed that he could sense the buzzing crackle of consciousness as they made their approach.

<Anything yet?> Zogrusz asked the world-spirit, who had curled up in the space between Anecoya's vast wings again not long after they had flown away from the fish. Their earlier telepathic conversations had improved Zogrusz's ability to project his thoughts, and now he was able to communicate without Rhas first constructing the bridge between their minds.

<It's . . . garbled> Rhas replied, this statement flavored by his frustration. <Communicating is very difficult with such a rudimentary intelligence. It . . . says something descended from the stars claiming association with the Wanderer. What happened after the world-mind — or, I suppose in this instance, the moon-mind — isn't very clear. The phrase it keeps repeating is

that this emissary from the Wanderer 'went below' and is now gone. I do not know what that means>

Zogrusz traced the shallow cut on his belly with a claw; the wound had mostly healed, but it itched. He wondered what else they might encounter that could hurt them – after all, *something* had happened to Ixia's ward to keep her from returning, and Zogrusz could only assume that whatever sort of creature the Wanderer kept as a companion was a cosmic being as well. The old man had been evasive about the exact nature of his ward, but he had assured them that there would be no doubt once they'd found her.

<Where should I set down?> Anecoya asked, interrupting Zogrusz's musings.

<Were you not paying attention, Annie? The Wanderer said his ward was investigating an anomaly in the largest crater on the moon>

<I remember> Anecoya grumbled in reply *<I just wasn't sure if we wanted to go to the exact same spot where she disappeared. You know, just in case the reason she disappeared was still there>*

<Let us risk it. We should try and finish this task as quickly as possible, because we don't know how much time we have left>

Zogrusz felt a telepathic surge of affirmation from the Phoenix as Anecoya spiraled down. The moon was uniformly gray, and from a distance Zogrusz had thought this meant the surface was covered in the regolith that he'd encountered on other dead worlds during his wanderings. But as they drew closer, he realized that something was different here. The texture was wrong, not the fine-grained dust he remembered, and it flowed together into an endless carpet that completely draped the hills and mountains and valleys.

Anecoya also seemed disturbed by the strange substance

covering the ground, and she did a few extra gyres in the sky before descending to land.

<It won't hurt us> Rhas assured her. <That must be the fungus that has become sentient. I wonder what sustains it — I don't see anything else on the moon it might feed on>

<Hopefully it doesn't rely on eating foolish travelers coming to visit> Anecoya murmured, but still she swooped down and gently settled on the surface, raising a cloud of glittering silver spores.

Zogrusz leaped off her back into this dissipating mist, his clawed feet sinking deep in the spongy ground. More of those spores rose up, and his mouth-tendrils twitched at the smell. It reminded him of sulfur, harsh and acrid.

"I can't say I'm enjoying this," Rhas muttered after joining Zogrusz on the surface. The cat was light enough that he could stay on top of the fungus, but still Rhas kept raising his paws and giving them a shake after each step, as if he found the feeling of walking here uncomfortable.

Light flared as Anecoya reverted to her human form. "*Ew*," she said, wrinkling her nose in disgust at the aroma.

A crackling sound made Zogrusz turn, and he took a surprised step back when he suddenly found himself face to face with . . . himself. An Eldritch Horror molded from gray fungus had appeared, nearly identical to him in size and shape. Some details were missing, like his individual scales and the creases in his broad forehead, but there was no doubt what this thing was supposed to represent.

"Rhas . . ." Zogrusz said, raising his hands so he could react quicker if this simulacrum made any sudden movements, and it mimicked this action.

"It's all right, Zog," the cat said. "This is the mind of the moon."

"It still can't be too smart," muttered Anecoya, coming

closer to inspect the fake-Zogrusz. "Since it's really just a big mushroom. Also, it chose to take *his* form."

Rhas winced. "Please be polite, Annie. We are guests, and I don't know exactly how much this mind understands. It's not stupid . . . We just are radically different. In some ways, I'm more like you than this world-mind is to me. At least all our consciousnesses arose from within the folds of a brain – or brains, in my case – and not by whatever process brought about awareness in this organic mass we now see all around us."

Zogrusz had a strong desire to reach out and break away one of the dangling gray mouth-tendrils. "So what do we –"

"Wait," Rhas said, his voice slightly strained. "It's communicating with me. It . . . welcomes us. It has a name, but it's not something we can easily understand, since it's not a collection of sounds . . . more like a smell." Rhas sniffed, his whiskers shivering. "That smell. The smell of the fungus."

"What should we call him?" Anecoya asked. "Sir Stinky?"

Rhas flashed her an exasperated look.

"It smells like rotten eggs to me," Zogrusz said. "We could call it . . . Egg."

"I don't think it cares," Rhas said. "That sounds fine. Now be quiet, and let me concentrate – speaking with a sentient fungus is harder than you might imagine."

Anecoya and Zogrusz dutifully fell silent as the two world-minds engaged in whatever could pass as a conversation. The fungal-Zogrusz was absolutely still, but Rhas's tail kept lashing back and forth in fairly obvious frustration. Finally, the cat stopped staring at Egg, blinking his golden eyes as he turned to the two cosmic beings.

"Well. That was interesting . . . and exhausting. I hope

you never have to cobble together a coherent story from an entity that communicates mostly through electrical impulses. But from what I can gather, the One-From-The-Sky arrived on the moon and somehow opened a dialogue with Egg here. How, I don't know – I would have thought only other world-minds could parse out meaning from this fungus. But anyway, the One claimed to be a . . . servant, or companion, perhaps, of the Wanderer. Egg isn't being too clear here. The One told the moon-mind that she had come to, and I quote, 'go below by passing through the Door'."

Anecoya and Zogrusz glanced at each other in confusion and then out at the endless rolling seascape of fungal swells. "Door?" Zogrusz said, wondering if this was a problem of translating from mushroom-talk to flesh-and-blood-speak.

Rhas offered another of his cat-shrugs. "I do not know. But Egg says the Door that the One entered is nearby, just over that little hill."

Zogrusz's gaze followed where Rhas's face was indicating. It looked like everywhere else on the moon, a line of rumpled mounds coated with the omnipresent gray fungus.

Anecoya was already striding in that direction, shimmering spores erupting from the ground in her wake. Rhas bounded after her, and after a last lingering look at his fungal clone, Zogrusz followed as well. And it was because he was behind his companions that he saw Rhas stumble. At first, he thought the cat had just caught his paw on the spongy ground, but then Rhas staggered a few steps before coming to a swaying halt.

"Are you all right?" Zogrusz asked as he came to loom over Rhas.

The cat shook himself, dislodging more of the glittering spores. "I'm fine. Just a little dizzy."

"Do you want to ride on me?"

Rhas golden eyes blinked up at him, his expression unreadable. "That would be much appreciated."

Zogrusz bent and scooped up the cat, depositing him on his shoulder. Immediately Rhas found a comfortable spot and curled up, his dangling tail tickling Zogrusz's mouth-tendrils.

"Thank you, Zog," Rhas said, and as Zogrusz started walking again, he felt a pleasant vibration emanating from the cat.

"No eating my soul," Zogrusz warned him teasingly, to which Rhas responded with something like a cat-snort.

Anecoya had stopped at the top of the small hill and was staring down at whatever lay beyond. Zogrusz slogged up after her, wading through fungus that reached nearly to his knees. When she heard him approaching, she beckoned him on faster.

"I think we found our door," she said when he arrived beside her.

The slope was far more pronounced here, dropping almost vertically into a broad, circular depression. It looked like many of the other meteor-impact sites they'd already seen on the surface, but unlike the rest, this one was not completely covered with the fungus, the gray arms stretching only partway to the barren center of the crater. These fungal limbs became black and withered before they could reach where a massive stone hatch was set in the ground . . . and it was flung open, revealing an abyss so black that even his void-fashioned eyes struggled to pierce the darkness.

"I hate going underground," Anecoya muttered as she started to descend the slope, dislodging a large chunk of fungus with an annoyed kick. "It's no place for birds."

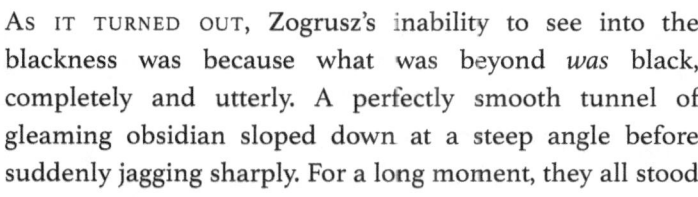

As it turned out, Zogrusz's inability to see into the blackness was because what was beyond *was* black, completely and utterly. A perfectly smooth tunnel of gleaming obsidian sloped down at a steep angle before suddenly jagging sharply. For a long moment, they all stood at the edge of this hole staring into the seamless dark.

"What is this place?" Anecoya shouted at the fake-Zogrusz, which had reformed on the closest patch of healthy gray fungus and was watching them silently.

"Egg does not know," Rhas told her from his perch on Zogrusz's shoulder. "The door has been here since consciousness first sparked on the moon, but it had been closed until The-One-From-The-Sky opened it. As you can see, something kills the fungus before it can get too close."

"Do you have any guesses?" Zogrusz asked, reaching out to grasp the darkness welling up from below. His powers seemed unaffected by the strangeness of this place, ribbons of shadow writhing at his command.

Rhas's claws kneaded his flesh as the cat spoke. "A treasure house, perhaps, placed here by an ancient being? Or a refuge to hide from some threat?" The world-mind paused. "Maybe a prison? I've heard of powerful entities that could not easily be destroyed being encased inside the metal cores of planets or shoved into the accretion discs of collapsing stars. Perhaps this is something similar."

"There must be a reason Ixia's ward did not return," Zogrusz said uneasily, trying to extend his perception to gain some insight about what lurked below.

"The Wanderer *was* rather annoying," Anecoya murmured. "Perhaps the tunnel goes all the way to the other side and his ward passed right through the moon and kept going in an attempt to escape the old man."

"Well, we still need to know what's down there," Zogrusz said, his claws clicking on the smooth black rock of the tunnel as he stepped from the moon's surface. Anecoya sighed deeply, and a moment later light flickered along the gleaming black walls and ceiling as she summoned her blazing sword.

Time lost all meaning in the passage as they descended deeper and deeper. The tunnel twisted and turned, but never branched or opened up into larger chambers. Its serpentine path was almost unsettling – there seemed no reason for its odd contortions, as if the way had been laid down by madmen. No writing covered the walls, nor were there any images carved into the glassy surface, and after a while Zogrusz began to doubt if this passage had actually been made by intelligent creatures. He knew from experience that the desire to decorate and memorialize was powerful.

The tunnel eventually leveled off, and though it was difficult to measure the passage of time here, Zogrusz believed they had been descending for longer than the sun took to rise and set on Rhas's world.

And then the tunnel abruptly ended.

"Oh my," Rhas whispered as Anecoya sucked in her breath sharply.

Zogrusz could only stand there blinking in the light, wondering if what was before them now could be real.

The passage emptied onto a large balcony of sorts, beyond which was a space so vast it was like they were no longer underground. There was no sun, but a golden radiance infused the distant ceiling and illuminated a city unlike anything Zogrusz had ever seen before. It sprawled gracefully to the very limits of his vision, full of layered stone buildings that reminded him of beehives piled on top of each other, their higher tiers connected by slender arching bridges. Elsewhere, silvery domes bubbled atop squat structures, while spires of nacreous light thrust up from the ground. Many of these structures dwarfed the largest buildings in Amotla, and Zogrusz couldn't help but wonder how many ages it had taken to carve this place from the moon's rock.

Against all reason – and in stark contrast to the barren surface above – the city was absolutely draped with vegetation. Golden vines studded with red blossoms like drops of blood wrapped the iridescent towers, while explosions of verdant greenery filled the balconies and sky-bridges. Down below, the streets wending between the buildings were almost completely obscured by a thick canopy, and copses of trees also sprouted atop the tiered buildings. And yet this growth did not seem unchecked; no, it looked to have been carefully sculpted and maintained and only through diligent efforts kept from completely running wild and consuming the city.

And that was the most shocking revelation: the city was still inhabited.

"How is this possible?" Rhas murmured.

Zogrusz also wanted to know. Everywhere he looked he saw movement – on the arching bridges and the rooftop gardens and what could be glimpsed of the streets through the crimson foliage. Even though the closest of the creatures were too far away to see clearly, Zogrusz thought the manner in which they moved seemed strange. They undulated, their bodies long and serpentine.

"Come on," Anecoya said, and Zogrusz turned to see that she was descending a broad spiraling ramp that led down to a great park filled with twisting paths and brilliantly colored blossoms artfully arranged into vast flower beds.

Zogrusz followed, the feeling of Rhas's sharp little claws digging into his shoulder telling him that the cat was just as unnerved as he was about this hidden world. There were even birds down here, flashing jewel-bright as they flitted between the trees, and a gentle river pocked with circular water-craft meandered through the city. Zogrusz donned his man-cloak as he descended the ramp, eliciting a surprised chirp from Rhas. Surely whatever creatures lived down here would be less intimidated by his human guise.

The park at the bottom of the ramp was even more lush than it had looked from above. Ornate trellises supported all manner of blooming plants and provided shade along paths of perfectly-fitted iridescent stones. The rich fragrances wafting from the elaborate flower arrangements were almost intoxicating, and insects with beautiful painted wings fluttered between the blossoms.

Zogrusz stiffened in surprise when he saw a pair of the city's denizens approaching. They did indeed look like snakes, with the front half of their long bodies lifted from the ground, dressed in embroidered windings of shimmering silk that wrapped them in such a way that their short, stunted arms still had the ability to move freely. They seemed deep in conversation, forked tongues flickering, and it wasn't until they had nearly reached where Zogrusz and Anecoya were standing dumbstruck that they stopped and shifted their attention to the strangers. Zogrusz was expecting a hissing panic, but the two snake-men merely stared incuriously at them, their nictating membranes slowly blinking a few times, then continued on their way.

Zogrusz extended a telepathic tendril, but his attempt to

delve into their minds slid off something hard and smooth. There was some sort of barrier, not dissimilar to how beings like Rhas and the Wanderer shielded their thoughts.

"What is this place?" Anecoya muttered, her fingers flexing like she wanted to summon her fiery sword.

"I do not know," Rhas answered. "There are many mysteries and oddities in the cosmos, but I've never heard of anything like this. A race of powerful telepaths living deep inside a moon in a thriving city, while the overmind on the surface does not know they are here? It's . . . unbelievable."

"They didn't seem concerned to see us," Zogrusz added, staring after the snake-men as they slithered away.

"Which either means that they are so powerful that nothing frightens them," Rhas mused, "or that creatures that look like you two in your human forms visit often."

"Ixia's ward," Anecoya said sharply. "That's all we're here for. We find her and get out. Someone else can solve this mystery."

"Agreed," Rhas said, then coughed hard enough that Zogrusz felt the cat convulse.

"What's wrong?" Anecoya asked, concern softening her tone.

"I've been away too long," Rhas replied hoarsely. "The thread that reaches back to my world is growing more and more frayed – we minds deteriorate after leaving the web of consciousness that we arose from."

"So you might die?" Zogrusz asked worriedly.

"I may," Rhas conceded. "Though I am but an avatar. If I do not return to my world, the larger part of me that remained behind will be fine."

"You should have told us!" Anecoya said, anger clouding her face.

"You both needed my help," Rhas replied calmly. "And if

I dissolve out here, this would not be the end of me . . . just *this* version."

"Well, we'll get you back in time," Anecoya promised. "We find this ward, return her to Ixia, and get what knowledge he has about thwarting Eldritch Horrors. So we have no time to waste – the next snake I see I'm tying in a knot if it doesn't tell us what we need to know."

They followed the winding paths of iridescent stones, passing beneath trellises and arches of braided flowers. The trees here differed from any Zogrusz had seen on Rhas's world, with thick, bulbous trunks and crimson leaves that swayed back and forth despite the lack of a breeze. There were circular stone basins set in the shade of these trees, and it took Zogrusz a little while to realize that these must be the serpent-versions of benches, though they encountered no snake-men coiled in them.

Rhas's claws tightened again as a new sound drifted from up ahead where an abstract stone statue loomed over the treetops. It was a song – or at least it had the cadence of a song, even if the lyrics were incomprehensible gibberish – and to Zogrusz's ears the singer might have been a very young human. But what would a human child be doing in this city of serpent people?

"Ixia's ward," Zogrusz and Rhas said simultaneously, and then after sharing a look of surprise they moved in the direction the singing was coming from.

The path they were on spilled into a large circular space fringed by trees, which was empty except for the huge statue they'd seen from afar. A little blonde girl perched on the edge of the statue's plinth, her legs swinging, and in her hands she held a chunk of faceted black crystal, staring into its depths as she sang her nonsense song.

"She must be who we're looking for," Zogrusz said, but

just as he started to stride across the open space towards the girl, Anecoya stopped him suddenly with a hand on his arm.

"Wait," she said as he turned to her questioningly. "Look at the statue."

Zogrusz frowned but did as she asked. And then he saw it as well. What he had thought was an abstract carving was nothing of the sort – those flowing lines were twisting limbs, the grooves were filled with gnashing fangs, and clustered at the center of the statue was a scattering of eyes drawn from different species, all staring upwards as if watching something descend from above.

There was no doubt in Zogrusz's mind what this thing was supposed to represent . . . He was staring at a valiant attempt to capture in stone the chaos of an Eldritch Horror's true form.

He was not the first of his kind to come here.

7

"That looks a lot like you," Anecoya said, nodding towards the looming statue.

"It's an Eldritch Horror," Zogrusz admitted. "We all seem to assemble ourselves differently, but the pieces are always similar."

"Different, yet somehow all equally terrible," Anecoya murmured, shaking her head.

"Do you know what this means?" Rhas asked before Zogrusz could respond to this jab. "These snake-people are in danger, just like the humans of my world. A Sower has clearly been here and prepared the way for a Reaper."

"The Sower might still be here," Zogrusz said, looking around as if he expected to see an Eldritch Horror in its true form peeking at them from behind the trees. "I don't think my kind leaves until a Reaper arrives."

"All the more reason to grab this kid and get out," Anecoya said. "The Wanderer said you're different, yes? Other Horrors have most likely been shaped into beings with far less . . . compassion. And they probably won't look too kindly on us meddling in this place, especially if it's in the process of serving these creatures up on a platter."

Anecoya walked towards the singing child, whose attention was still absorbed by the chunk of black crystal she held. Zogrusz followed, unnerved by the thought that another Eldritch Horror was possibly somewhere on this moon with them. Wouldn't he sense it?

"Where *is* this Sower?" Zogrusz muttered to himself.

"Forget the Sower, where is the overmind for these snake-men?" Rhas said. "I can still hear the ramblings of the fungus on the surface, but nothing down here. It's like it's hiding . . ."

The girl broke off her singing when she noticed Anecoya approaching, her eyes widening in excitement. "Hi! Oh wow, who are you? I'm Qala. You're so beautiful! And your hair is so red! Can I touch it? Is it hot?"

"Uh, hello," Anecoya said, momentarily unbalanced by the avalanche of questions. "I'm Anecoya. And this is Rhas. The ugly one is Zogrusz."

"He's not ugly!" Qala said, squinting at him. He felt a presence slipping through his mind like the wind, and the ease with which the girl rifled through his thoughts was disturbing. She had tremendous telepathic abilities, unlike anything he had encountered before. "Oh, wait, yes he is," she finally said. Her eyes lit up again as she shifted her attention to the cat on Zogrusz's shoulder, her legs swinging so hard she kicked the stone of the statue's plinth with her heels. "And a cat! Well, not really a cat. But I love cats! Can I pet you?"

"I . . . suppose," Rhas said slowly, then cleared his throat. "But later. Qala, I think you're the one we're looking for. Are you the Wanderer's ward?"

The child's face instantly collapsed. "Ixia sent you to come get me?"

"Indeed," Rhas replied gravely. "He worries for you."

Qala huffed and folded her arms across her chest. "He's not worried about me, he's worried about his 'great project.' And he said I could stay down here until I found the Heart." Her face suddenly brightened as she held up the chunk of black crystal proudly. "Which I did!"

"Oh," Rhas said. "Then . . . you can leave this place?"

Qala chewed on her lip, her expression turning evasive. "I could . . . I suppose, but I made a promise to S'skesspa . . ."

"Whoever that is, he's not important," Anecoya said curtly, stepping closer to loom over the child, her hands on her hips. "We don't have time for games – *gah!*" She reeled back, raising her hand like she meant to summon her fire sword. One of the snake-men had appeared beside her, silently materializing into existence. Surprised, Zogrusz came within a heartbeat of shifting into his true form, but stopped himself when he saw the creature was not making any threatening moves, simply watching them with eyes of glittering obsidian. He was taller than the snake-men they had seen previously, and unlike the others had a great hood flared around his head, very similar to some of the more dangerous serpents on Rhas's world. His robes were more elaborate as well, a deep crimson trimmed with black, which matched the black patterning on his red scales.

"S'skesspa, I presume," Rhas said.

The snake-man did not reply, continuing to study them impassively, his forked tongue flicking.

Qala clapped her hands together happily. "Oh! You look *much* better than before!"

Cold reptilian eyes swung from them to the grinning

child. "These ones are who, Soulfisher?" he asked, his voice soft and sibilant.

Qala blew out her cheeks and rolled her eyes. "They've come to fetch me, S'skesspa. I'm so sorry, I told you I couldn't stay forever."

The snake-man's expression did not change, but his tail began lashing back and forth in agitation. "So soon? On our scales, your light is a balm. Convince you to stay, how can we?"

Qala slid from the plinth, her expression sorrowful. "I'll come back and visit when I can, I promise!"

Rhas's voice bloomed in Zogrusz's mind. *<There is something strange here. This snake-man is no ordinary mortal. It is a world-mind, but it refuses to link with me. In fact, I believe it is completely cut off from the web of planets with intelligent life. I've never heard of anything like this before>*

<Perhaps it is hiding?> Zogrusz asked, his gaze returning to the statue of the Eldritch Horror. *<Its people seem to know something about my kind>*

<They're not hiding> a new, cheerful voice piped up, startling them both. *<But oh boy, I bet they wish they had! You see —>*

"This one," S'skesspa said suddenly, drawing their attention from the mind-bridge. He was peering at Zogrusz through slitted eyes, his hood spread even wider. The changed posture suggested aggression, and Zogrusz took an instinctive step back. "It smells . . . familiar." The snake-man's tongue slipped from his mouth again, but this time it remained extended, shivering as it tasted the air. Suddenly S'skesspa recoiled, hissing in alarm. "It does! The Betrayer's stench clings to it!"

The radiance from above suddenly dimmed, plunging the park into twilight. This darkness was fleeting, as a moment later the light swelled again, but harsher, making the pale trunks of the trees around them gleam like shards of bone. A tremor shook the ground, and Rhas had to tighten his claws to keep from losing his grip on Zogrusz's shoulder.

"Calm!" the cat cried as the snake-man overmind trembled violently. "We come in peace!"

"No peace!" S'skesspa hissed, baring long curving fangs. "Keep away, you could not? This carcass you have come to pick over?"

Zogrusz was certain the snake-man was screeching at him, and he drew himself up. "I have done nothing to you or your world," he said indignantly.

The snake-man ignored his protestations. "Betrayer!" he cried again, pointing a clawed red finger at him. "Show yourself!"

A wave of mental force washed over Zogrusz, making him stagger. He felt barbed psychic hooks slip beneath his man-cloak, and before he could steady himself the world-mind yanked hard, his disguise sliding away.

Rhas yelped in surprise as the soft flesh he crouched on was replaced by sharp scales and hard leathery skin. Behind him, he heard the *whoosh* of flames igniting as Anecoya summoned her fiery blade. Strangely, Qala's expression was now one of intense but distracted concentration, as if she was straining hard to keep her focus on something else entirely.

Reality flickered.

It was only a moment, but during that brief fracture in time, their surroundings changed. Gone were the trees and flowers, though Zogrusz thought he glimpsed a few fossilized stumps. The statue of the Eldritch Horror beseeching the heavens also vanished, though shattered pieces of its plinth remained, including one with a few clawed toes clutching at stone.

Then the park returned, just as alive and vibrant as before.

The hooded snake-man was nearly thrashing now, tossing his head back and forth, his stunted arms clawing at his face.

"Rhas . . ." Anecoya said nervously, raising her sword so that it formed a crackling barrier between them and the clearly deteriorating world-mind.

Their surroundings shifted again, this time for a heart-beat longer. The iridescent stones sunk into the pathways were still there, but dulled by time. Zogrusz raised his head to look at the great city looming over the park, and surprise washed through him. Most of the hive-like buildings had collapsed in on themselves, the graceful archways that had webbed the city now sundered. The silver domes had been cracked open like eggs, reduced to jagged fragments, and the tamed vegetation that had once draped the city was gone. Zogrusz saw no movement, nothing to suggest that anything still inhabited these ruins.

Then the dead city was replaced again by its still-living twin.

"S'skesspa!" cried Qala, lines of tension etching her young face. "You must stop! I'm losing the thread! I can't . . . hold . . . on . . ."

Abruptly the snake-man world-mind stopped his convulsions, focusing on them with a frightening intensity. Bloody tracks marred his face where he'd scratched his scales, and he thrust a red-smeared claw at Zogrusz.

"You we trusted! Finally, Betrayer, our revenge arrives!"

Qala cried out, collapsing to her knees. The chunk of black crystal tumbled to the ground, and as soon as it slipped from her fingers, the verdant park disappeared, the crumbled devastation rushing in to take its place. Zogrusz looked around wildly, but this time the ruin did not melt away – it seemed here to stay, and even S'skesspa had vanished, leaving them alone. The silence was unnerving, as the hum of insects and the trilling of birds that had a moment ago filled the park had suddenly ceased.

Qala was hunched on the ground, swaying and clutching at her head. Zogrusz went to kneel beside her, hooking a long claw gently under her arm to keep her from collapsing. She looked up at him, and to his surprise, she didn't flinch from his true-form's visage.

"What is happening?" Rhas asked, and Qala shifted her attention to the cat on Zogrusz's shoulder.

"I lost my grip," she said dully, her voice sounding drained. She glanced at the black crystal lying beside her. "But not all of him returned to the Heart. A part of him escaped. The worst part, the angry part . . ." Qala took a deep breath, steadying herself. Then she scooped up the crystal, running a finger along an ink-dark facet. "But it's all right, I don't think he can hurt us."

The world spasmed, and a ridge of rock burst through the ground, obliterating what remained of the statue's base. Anecoya cried out as fragments of stone pelted her. In the distant city, one of the few spires still upright buckled and collapsed. Chunks of stone fell about them like hail.

"Or maybe he can!" Qala cried, her eyes wide. "We gotta get out of here!"

"Over there!" Anecoya cried, and Zogrusz turned to see a half-dozen snake-men slithering towards them . . . or at least what once had been snake-men, as they had been reduced to nothing but bones and a few scraps of withered flesh.

Ancient jaws unhinged to display yellowed fangs, and the sound they made was more of a dry rattling than a hiss.

Zogrusz positioned himself between the dead snake-men and Qala, unsheathing his claws. Anecoya did not wait for them to arrive, rushing forward with her burning sword upraised, but the snake-men showed no fear of the flames and lunged to meet her charge. Her sword struck a skull, and it exploded into fragments of charred bone, but the other dead snake-men closed around her with mouths snapping. Anecoya cried out, sweeping her sword in a broad arc to drive the creatures back.

"I'll stay with the girl, you go help Annie!" Rhas yelled and then leaped gracefully down from Zogrusz's shoulder.

It was the cat that had been forcing him to hesitate, and now unburdened by the world-mind, he rushed forward. The snake-men were single-minded in their desire to tear Anecoya apart, and they didn't even turn around when he closed a taloned hand around a spine and hurled the snake-man through the air. He brought a fist down on a skull, crushing it, then ripped apart another of the dead creatures, scattering its pieces everywhere. Anecoya severed the last snake-man in half, then kicked away its upper body when its arms tried to pull the rest of it close enough to bite her leg. Her lip curled in revulsion as she surveyed the dismembered creatures . . . many of which were still moving feebly.

"More are coming!" Rhas cried, and Zogrusz looked around until he saw movement in the distance, a line of black squirming closer. With the park's trees gone, he could see quite a way, and though the dead snake-men were far, he knew they were rushing in this direction as fast as their bony bodies could slither.

"Back to the tunnel!" Zogrusz cried and then staggered as the ground heaved and shuddered.

Something massive emerged from below in an eruption of stone, sending them all tumbling. Zogrusz scrambled back to his feet, peering at the enormous shape looming within the haze. He heard coughing behind him and glanced back to see Anecoya helping Qala to her feet. Both of them were coated in dust, and a very miserable-looking Rhas hunkered at their feet, the yellow-white fur of the cat now moon-like in truth, gray as lunar regolith.

The shadow recessed in the cloud of dust swelled larger.

"Anecoya!" Zogrusz bellowed over the rumbling. "Get them to safety!"

"I want to fight!" she shouted back, but he ignored her and ran towards whatever was approaching. He heard her splutter angrily behind him, then felt a great rush of heat as she assumed her bird-form.

Good – they could fly back to the tunnel entrance in no time.

As for him . . . he wanted answers.

Zogrusz unclenched the fist of control he kept over his shape. Immediately his body swelled, and in moments he had grown to the natural limits of his true-form, the stony stumps of the trees that had once filled the park nothing except a faint prickle on the underside of his massive feet. He bared scythe-like claws and set himself as the great shape surged closer.

Then the haze dissipated, and he saw it clearly for the first time. A massive serpentine skull wended its way through the shattered park, faint red light recessed deep within its eye-sockets. If the skeletal snake lifted its front body from the ground, it would tower over Zogrusz, even in his true-form, but so long as its head remained on the ground it barely came up to his knees. Still, its length was unsettling.

"*BETRAYER!*"

The monster's mouth had not opened, but Zogrusz knew it had spoken. And he could sense a familiar presence behind that voice.

"S'skesspa!" he shouted as the snake slithered closer. "Let us talk! I know nothing of what happened here –"

His protestations did not slow the monster in the slightest. It lunged at him with jaws wide, revealing rows and rows of jagged teeth. Zogrusz caught the snake by its neck just before it could latch onto him, and the mouth snapped in frustration, straining to be free. Focused on keeping the skeletal giant from biting him, Zogrusz didn't notice what the rest of the monster's body was doing until he felt its bony coils wrap his legs. He swayed, barely able to keep himself upright, for he knew that if he fell, the snake would twine itself around the rest of his body and attempt to crush him. He needed his hands to pull the snake away, but they were busy keeping the monster from sinking its fangs into his flesh.

Apparently, the world-spirit did not wish to talk.

Zogrusz gritted his teeth as the sharp snake-vertebrae pressed against his legs and midsection. He stared into the depths of the monster's eyes at the faint red glimmering and could feel the waves of anger crashing against him. Madness as well. The mind of the creature he was locked in a struggle with was a rotting mess, barely bound together by its festering hatred for the one it had called the Betrayer. One who had looked very much like Zogrusz . . .

His arms trembled. The snake was only bones, but it certainly felt like it was still sheathed in muscle. He honestly wasn't sure how long he could keep its teeth at a distance or his legs from collapsing under the relentless pressure of its constricting coils. In desperation, Zogrusz unleashed his psychic blast, but unsurprisingly, it flowed over the undead monster with no apparent effect. White spots were pulsing in his vision, and as if it knew he was weakening, the skeletal serpent redoubled its efforts.

Heat washed over Zogrusz, and he gasped in relief as the snake loosened its strangling grip. Burning wings battered the monster, and Anecoya's flashing beak struck its skull again and again – it did not break under the onslaught, but chips of bone flew. Zogrusz used this reprieve to wrest himself free of the snake, and with a tremendous effort heave it away from him. S'skesspa landed on its back, raising another great plume of dust, and thrashed madly in an attempt to flip itself over.

<*On me!*> Anecoya cried, her voice echoing in his mind.

Zogrusz fought through his dizziness and the sharp pain where the snake's bones had dug into his flesh, lunging at the fire bird as he folded his true-form into a smaller shape. He landed on Anecoya's back, clinging desperately to her blazing feathers as she lifted into the air. A horrific shrieking from below made him turn his head just in time to see the great serpent leap after them, its bony jaws clacking shut frighteningly close to the Phoenix's talons.

Anecoya's wings beat the air furiously as they flew higher and higher. From this vantage Zogrusz could see the true devastation of the city – it looked like it had been nothing but a shattered ruin for a long, long time. He could only take the briefest of glimpses before glancing down again, as the skeletal snake was surging after them, carving a furrow through what remained of the park. Its speed was impressive, nearly keeping pace with Anecoya as she flew, and by the time they arrived at the tunnel entrance high up on the wall, they were barely ahead of the deranged world-mind. She alighted on the balcony in front of Rhas and

Qala, then shifted into her human form as soon as Zogrusz slipped from her back.

"Come on!" she cried, immediately dashing for the passage that led back to the surface. Zogrusz followed her, scooping up Qala and the cat just as another tremor shook the underground city. Cracks spider-webbed the gray stone of the balcony, but luckily it did not break apart before they threw themselves into the tunnel. A monstrous bellow washed over them, and Zogrusz turned to see the massive skull of the serpent rise from below, the crimson light sunk in its abyssal eye-sockets blazing like flames in the void. He put his head down and fled deeper into the passage until a terrified gasp from the child he held made him twist around. The snake was trying to wriggle its way in after them, but its skull was too large, and the attempt was causing the frame of the entrance to buckle. Another terrible shriek came from the monster, but it was drowned out by the sound of the ceiling collapsing. When the dust settled, the way back to the city was completely blocked.

They hurried deeper, far enough that Zogrusz thought this section of the tunnel was still stable, and then turned. The rock pile was shuddering as the maddened world-mind raged on the other side, its muffled screeching filtering through the barrier.

For a long moment, none of them could muster the energy to say anything, until finally Qala broke the silence.

"Wow, that was exciting!"

8

"You look like something the cat coughed up."

Rhas grumbled in annoyance from his perch on Zogrusz's shoulder, then commented quietly about how *that* was rich coming from someone who literally lived in the belly of a space fish. Zogrusz had to admit that the old man wasn't wrong, though – they were dust-smeared and hollow-eyed, laced with bloody evidence of their fight with the undead snakes.

The golden sphere hovering over Ixia's shoulder pulsed briefly, and the grinning old man chortled. "Indeed, indeed. Such a pity we couldn't witness what happened down there. It looks like it was *very* interesting." He shifted his attention to Qala, who was loitering next to Anecoya with her tiny hand wrapped around the goddess's finger. The old man spread his arms wide, the glistening threads plunging into his ancient body rustling with the sudden movement. "My girl, I'm so happy to see you." Ixia beckoned, as if trying to entice her to come over and embrace him.

Somewhat reluctantly – at least from Zogrusz's perspective – Qala released her grip on Anecoya's finger and went to Ixia, then clambered up into his lap.

"Quite the adventure you've had!" he said, tousling her golden hair. "But you found what you were looking for, I see." The Wanderer's gaze was fixed on the chunk of black crystal the girl had rescued from the underground city, and she drew it close to her chest like she feared he might try to take it from her. "Is it everything you hoped it would be?"

"Suppose so," the girl mumbled.

"You sent her down there for *that*?" Anecoya said in exasperation. "She's just a child!"

Ixia gave Qala's arm an affectionate squeeze. "To be honest, I tried to talk her out of going. But once I told her of Hearts, she just had to discover what had been left behind."

"You were right," the girl murmured, squirming on Ixia as she attempted to get more comfortable, "when you said the Heart is haunted."

"Haunted?" Zogrusz exclaimed. "What do you mean by that?"

"Exactly what I told her," Ixia replied, reaching out to stroke a gleaming facet. "This here is what remains of the world-mind that was once all the consciousnesses on that moon. When its people perished, it did as well, leaving this shard of concentrated essence behind."

"I wanted to see if anything was still inside," Qala explained. "And there was."

"S'skesspa," Rhas murmured.

The little girl nodded. "I brought him back to life, gave shape to the world he remembered. But he wasn't . . . right."

"Death rarely improves one's sanity," Ixia murmured. "I've learned that before."

"How could you do that? Bring him back?" Rhas

sounded shaken, like he couldn't imagine resurrecting a dead world.

"Qala is a telepath," Ixia answered. "And one unlike any other I have encountered in all my time in this universe. Her powers are unparalleled."

The girl's face reddened, as if she was embarrassed by the praise.

"I doubt very many other beings – if any – could reconstruct a world-mind from the ashes contained within this rock. But my darling ward did . . . which I have to admit opens up all sorts of interesting possibilities."

"You're just happy because it means I'm getting stronger," Qala said. "And that means your project might succeed."

"Let us not get too confident," Ixia admonished her. "You did lose control of the ghost."

"Only a part," Qala said, somewhat defensively. "The rest was still in here. If he hadn't realized Zogrusz was an Eldritch Horror, I think I could have made all of him return to the Heart."

"What happened down there?" Zogrusz asked, confused by the back and forth between the Wanderer and his ward. "You're saying the city and the snake-men weren't real?"

"They *were* real," Ixia said. "Thousands of years ago. What you experienced down there was a memory given form and substance."

"Whose memory?" Zogrusz said, unable to hide his exasperation at this exchange. "Speak clearly!"

"The dead world-mind," Ixia replied.

"S'skesspa," Rhas said, and Qala nodded enthusiastically.

"Yup. He wasn't so bad before you guys arrived. I mean, he wasn't sane, but returning to life after thousands of years has to be pretty difficult to deal with." She held up the black crystal, letting it drink the harsh light spilling from the fish's innards. "We could try to summon him again, but I'm not sure if that's possible anymore. We left a big part of him raging down there in the ruin of his world . . . though I'm pretty certain he'll dissipate quickly and return to the Heart. Until that happens, I think what remains in here won't be able to manifest."

Ixia took the dark rock from Qala, staring into its shadowy depths. "When a cataclysmic event utterly wipes out an intelligent species, its world-mind perishes as well, though their passing differs from the death of their constituent parts. What is left behind is a residue of the aggregate consciousnesses that once gave it form. And an echo of the world-mind remains within . . . a ghost, if you will. These Hearts are eternal records of a species, since the substance they are made from is among the most durable in the universe. It could survive a stellar implosion or a descent into the maw of a black hole. I believe whatever entity designed this universe wanted these Hearts to persist forever as eternal histories of every sentient life that has existed. I think you can imagine why they make such fascinating objects of study." His eyes widened, as if something had suddenly occurred to him. "Oh!" he exclaimed, turning his attention to Rhas. "After this Reaper wipes out the cat's world, I would be very interested in obtaining his Heart. Perhaps we could come to some sort of arrangement?"

Rhas's reply to this was a menacing rumble, but the Wanderer was not deterred. "I suppose I should talk to your companions, since they might actually survive what is coming."

"I think you should do as you promised," Anecoya said testily. "And tell us how we can stop this Eldritch Horror from doing to our world what happened to the moon below."

Ixia spread his arms wide. "Of course, of course. I always keep my bargains." He lifted Qala from his lap and set her gently down beside his throne. Then he stood, a brief flicker of effort evident in his face, and began to pace with his hands clasped behind his back. The glistening threads entering his flesh stayed connected to him, pulsing with iridescent light. "You have quite a dilemma," Ixia said. "My instinct is always to solve problems though negotiations, but the thought of turning aside a Reaper that has traversed the universe with nothing but reasoned discourse is, unfortunately, ridiculous. So you need another method of deterring this Eldritch Horror, such as enlisting the aid of an even more powerful being, finding a weapon capable of slaying the creature, or excising from your world that which it has come to consume." He stopping his pacing and glanced at them hopefully. "I suppose that's not an option? You must know that Eldritch Horrors feed on a very particular kind of religious fervor flavored by fear and dread."

"Are you proposing we eliminate all of his worshippers?" Anecoya asked, jerking a thumb toward Zogrusz. "That was my first thought."

Ixia smiled indulgently. "You are quite the unusual Phoenix. Your kind is not often so . . . bloodthirsty. But no, I wasn't suggesting a cleansing of this Sower's followers."

"And why's that?" Anecoya asked, her hands on her hips. "Are you also soft-hearted?"

The Wanderer chuckled. "Far from it. Believe me, I care nothing for the lives of mortals. But let's just imagine you are successful at eradicating his faith, or convincing his followers that he is nothing but a big, loveable space octopus-man. And then what will happen when this Reaper appears in the sky above your world? I think after the first city is flattened by a tentacle the size of a mountain, the fear will quickly return. You don't honestly think that a hungry Horror will simply turn around and head back to the void if it arrives and there are no more cultists on your world? No, when I spoke of removing what the Reaper needs for food, I was referring to consciousness itself. If there are no human minds, it will have nothing to eat."

"You're speaking of genocide!" Rhas spluttered. "And my death!"

Ixia held up his hands to calm the angry cat. "As you all saw on the moon below, intelligence waxes and wanes. Another life-form will eventually arise on your world, and by that time, Zogrusz here would have been forced to leave so that he can assuage his hunger elsewhere."

"That is unacceptable," Zogrusz said, his claws digging into his palms. "We are here because we want to save the humans . . . and Rhas." Anecoya nodded vigorously at this, her jaw set.

The Wanderer sighed. "Then a fight it has to be. Very well. I shall describe for you all the allies and weapons that might give a Reaper pause." He cleared his throat as if preparing for a long speech. "First let us consider the Spear of Koth-Aman, forged by the Celestial Artificer himself. It is said that –"

<Zogrusz>

He startled as a whisper slipped into his mind, spoken in the Wanderer's distinctive drawl. He glanced at Ixia, but the old man wasn't looking at him, continuing to describe some spear that could purportedly slay an Eldritch Horror.

<I have walled off our minds. The cat cannot listen to what is said here>

<What do you want?>

<To discuss matters of some import with you>

Ixia was now gesticulating and speaking passionately to his rapt companions, but the outside world had faded for Zogrusz.

<Isn't that what we're doing? Out there, I mean>

<Unfortunately, no> Ixia told him. *<I am fulfilling my part of the bargain by providing a list of everything that I am aware of that might slay a Reaper. The chances of you or your companions enlisting the aid of anything of which I am speaking about now are so small as to not truly exist>*

Indignation surged in Zogrusz. *<Then why bother with this charade?>*

<Because I made a promise> Ixia replied calmly. *<To share my knowledge. It is not my fault if said knowledge is useless>*

Zogrusz considered interrupting the Wanderer as he was speaking to his companions, but the old man must have sensed this, as more words hurriedly spilled into his mind.

<Wait. Listen to me first. The world-mind's situation might be hopeless, but yours is not. When the Reaper arrives, it will consume intelligent life on the planet, and then your hunger will drive you to find sustenance elsewhere>

<No, I will fight> Zogrusz said.

<You will not> Ixia told him confidently. *<You are a prodigal Horror, having left the void before you were imprinted by the minds of the Old Ones. As I said before, this gap was later filled by the first humans you encountered. You are flawed, incomplete . . . but you are not broken. When the Reaper comes, it will correct this mistake. You will no longer be an abomination, an Eldritch Horror tainted by the empathy common to lesser consciousnesses. No, the Reaper will fashion you into the cosmic being you were always meant to be. You will deliver the world to your elder without remorse and then depart to find more species to prepare for future harvests>*

<*I will not*> Zogrusz said forcefully, and if his companions had not been so invested in what Ixia was saying, they would have seen his mouth-tendrils writhing angrily.

<*You will*> the Wanderer insisted. <*Beneath your stolen humanity you are still a Horror, and this . . . unnatural stain will be brutally removed by the Reaper's will*> Zogrusz could sense the confidence seeping from the Wanderer, and he knew the old man absolutely believed what he was saying. This realization frightened him.

<*You should not be so despondent*> Ixia continued. <*You are not a monster but a cog in a very important machine. Perhaps the most important machine in the universe*>

This odd statement pulled Zogrusz from his self-loathing. <*What do you mean?*>

Ixia's reply was tinged with a rising excitement. <*It is a secret I stumbled upon long ago . . . Eldritch Horrors perform a very important function in the cosmos. You should not hate what you are — for in truth, we all owe your kind a great thanks*>

<*Why?*>

<*To answer that, you must understand one of the fundamental truths of the universe*> The voice in his head paused, as if for dramatic effect. <*And that is that life will always organize into a higher state of being*>

Zogrusz mentally shrugged. <*So?*>

A telepathic sigh gusted through his mind. <*I can already tell this shattering insight is going to be wasted on you. Ah, well. I'll try and explain in very simple terms. You see, all life is made up of living cells so tiny as to be invisible to the naked eye . . . yet when they come together, they can form organisms of incredible complexity. So complex that consciousness eventually emerges. And as consciousness spreads across a planet, a world-mind like your dear friend Rhas comes into being. But I believe this is not the end-stage for the development of life. No, my theory is that*>

once enough world-minds web the universe something new will manifest: a singular consciousness that binds together all reality>

Ixia must have been able to sense Zogrusz's difficulty in following this explanation, because he suddenly glanced over at him and frowned.

<I'm speaking of the birth of God>

Zogrusz blinked in surprise. *<You think that as life spreads throughout the universe, it is getting closer and closer to becoming . . . one?>*

<Indeed. And this outcome must be avoided at all costs>

<Because . . .?>

Ixia heaved another sigh. *<Because we will lose our autonomy! Would you rather be free or nothing more than a cell in a body? I, for one, have no interest in being merely a . . . a **piece** of something else! And what happens when this God finally is born? It will be alone, for eternity . . . such solitude can only lead to madness, and then perhaps the end of the universe by cosmic suicide!>*

<Why are you telling me this?>

<Because I want you to understand what you truly are> Ixia said fervently. *<Eldritch Horrors are not monsters. Their harvests are like . . . like controlled burnings so that a forest might survive. If the underbrush is allowed to grow too thick, the old and rotten trees not removed . . . then there is the risk of a far greater disaster, and the utter destruction of everything. I believe the Horrors were created for a purpose, a very noble purpose, and one you should not shirk from fulfilling. You may have been corrupted by humanity's weakness when you arrived on that world, but after the Reaper comes, he will force you to realize that this Harvest is right and natural and necessary>*

<Enough> Zogrusz said to the Wanderer, attempting to untangle himself from their telepathic bond. *<I've heard enough>*

Ixia allowed him to go, but before the link was completely severed the old man dispatched one final message. <*Do not despise your true nature*>

Zogrusz sucked in his breath as his awareness returned and the Wanderer's words once again filled his ears.

" . . . and the Weaver in Darkness lairs in the most forsaken pockets of the universe, spinning her webs around stars as she waits for her prey. I strongly doubt even Reapers could break the strands she weaves."

Anecoya interrupted the old man with a frustrated growl. "A forsaken pocket of the universe? Of all these cosmic beings and artifacts you have just described, are there *any* that are not lost or hidden or a thousand star systems away?"

"None," Ixia replied blandly.

"Then why are you telling us about them?" she snapped.

He shrugged. "You wanted to know what could stop a Reaper from consuming your world. I am telling you, as per our agreement."

Anecoya whirled around, throwing up her hands as she stalked away. "This is a waste of time," she snarled, and for a moment Zogrusz thought she was going to summon her fire sword and start slashing at the strands webbing the inside of the fish.

"Then it is hopeless," Rhas sighed bitterly.

"To my knowledge, when a world attracts the attention of a Reaper, this has always been a death sentence. I am sorry, cat."

"I suppose we were just hoping for a miracle," Rhas said. The world-mind looked more than just dejected, Zogrusz thought – its moon-colored fur has lost its luster, and its breathing was a ragged panting. If they did not return soon, he suspected the cat would not survive much longer. "I am glad I was able to see another star system, at least. Very few world-minds have ever done that."

Rhas turned his haggard little face to Zogrusz. "Come, Zog. It's time to go home – I would hate to miss my own reckoning." The cat nodded in the direction of the Wanderer and his ward. "Ixia, Qala – farewell."

The old man bowed his head . . . and then jerked it up in surprise as the little blonde girl stomped over to Rhas and planted herself in front of him, hands on her hips. "Don't say goodbye, I'm coming with you!"

"What?" Zogrusz blurted in perfect unison with Ixia, Rhas, and Anecoya.

The girl beamed at the cat. "I want to see your world! It sounds nice. And I'm bored with this fish."

"You . . . you can't *do* that," the Wanderer spluttered. "Weren't you paying attention? There's a giant monster coming to consume life on that world!"

Qala shrugged. "I'm not scared. And you always said I could leave whenever I wanted. Well, I want to."

Ixia's mouth worked soundlessly, and his ashen skin had somehow paled even further.

Qala ignored him, bending down to scoop up Rhas, and then hugged the cat to her chest so hard his eyes looked like they might pop out of his head. Or perhaps the world-mind was simply extremely shocked about this sudden turn of events.

"Come on!" Qala cried. "Let's go ride the bird again!"

9

The mood was somber on the flight back to their world. Rhas curled up again in the comfortable spot he had found between Anecoya's wings, and Zogrusz hoped that once they alighted on the planet again, the cat would regain his vitality – Rhas was his oldest friend, and now that he knew what a danger his kind posed to worlds, he couldn't help but appreciate the kindness shown to him during their first meeting. It would have been perfectly reasonable if the world-mind had spurned him or tried to banish him from the planet, but he had not. Rhas had thought he was different from other Eldritch Horrors. It must have been a terrible surprise when Rhas had realized that the real threat was not Zogrusz, but something else his presence would eventually attract.

This was what he brooded about as they soared through the black between the stars. Now that their flickering hope had been fully extinguished, a sharp-toothed guilt was gnawing at his insides. The Reaper was coming, and a feast awaited it.

Anecoya was silent as well, though Zogrusz could sense

the smoldering anger rolling off the goddess. She was incensed that the Wanderer had tricked them into rescuing his ward when he knew there was no chance they could use the knowledge he offered to avert the coming cataclysm. It had taken all of Rhas's considerable diplomatic skills to keep her from tearing apart the fish.

Although the three of them remained quiet on the journey home, each lost in their exhaustion, guilt, or anger, Qala more than filled the silence with her breathless chatter. It was literally breathless, since sound could not travel in the depths of the cosmos, but she also rarely paused for even a moment in her telepathic ramblings. Zogrusz attempted to wall off his thoughts from the girl so he could fully sink into his melancholic despair, but her words kept pouring into his mind with the same liquid ease as before.

<Can I have one of these feathers? Do they stay hot even after they come out? Why do you think those snakes on the moon built their city underground? Do you think it was weird they were wearing clothes? How does a snake even put on clothes?>

He did not offer any answers to this cascade of questions, and eventually her babbling faded into a hum in the back of his mind . . . though she never stopped talking. None of the others seemed inclined to engage with her either, but this did not deter the girl in the slightest. It was not until the cloud-banded majesty of Rhas's world appeared that she finally fell silent.

It did not last long. *<Can you hear them?>* Qala murmured, her excitement seeping across the link between their minds. *<So many thoughts! I've never . . . I've never . . .>* She trailed away, and Zogrusz glanced at her in mild concern where she was sitting cross-legged. She had a vacant look on her face, before shaking her head fiercely, as if to clear it. *<It's so rich! Ixia always said I shouldn't go to a*

world filled with intelligent life until I'd learned to control my powers, and now I can see why. And I thought the fungi were a bunch of chatterboxes!>

Anecoya entered a steep descent, forcing them to hold tight to her feathers, and when she broke through the clouds, Zogrusz saw a familiar fang of black rock. He felt a pang of homesickness as they turned in a wide gyre over his mountain, and he peered down at the rocky slopes to see if there was still an encampment of his followers. He didn't see any makeshift buildings or threads of smoke, which suggested they hadn't returned after Anecoya had terrified them. His faith was still strong elsewhere in the world, though, as the thin trickle that had stretched all the way to the other star was once more a raging flood. Despite how delicious this was, the knowledge that it was this sweet nectar drawing Ycthitlig ever-closer was sobering.

Rather than swooping down to the ruin of his temple's façade, Anecoya alighted on a foothill near the mountain – perhaps even the same one where Rhas had first approached him all those years ago. Back then, wildflowers had speckled the green field on its summit, but this was a bleaker season and what grass remained was sere and brittle.

The cat rose and moved stiffly over to the edge of the bird's great back. It clearly wanted to get off, so Zogrusz scooped Rhas up and deposited the cat among the dying grass. Immediately a shudder passed through Rhas, his tail quivering with pleasure.

"Oh, that is *so* much better," he said, and Zogrusz could see the years that had accreted during their journey melt away.

Qala stumbled past the cat, her eyes wide and lips slightly parted. "How do you all deal with this racket?" she breathed, then blinked furiously. "Millions of minds, every one its own small little universe . . ."

A wave of heated air buffeted Zogrusz and nearly sent Qala sprawling as Anecoya shifted into her human form. The long flight seemed to have done little to soften her mood – her jaw was clenched, and her gaze looked sharp enough to cut glass.

"So that was all just a huge waste of time," she snapped. Sparks drifted from her crackling hair, and around her feet the grass had blackened.

"No, it wasn't!" Qala cried, grinning as she spread her arms wide. "You brought me back with you!"

Anecoya snorted, turning away from the little girl. "And what are you going to do about the Reaper? Annoy it to death?"

"Annie . . ." Rhas began, but the Phoenix cut the cat off by throwing up her hands and stalking away.

"I was preparing to defend this world when you pulled me away to go on this fool's errand," she said, jabbing a finger at Zogrusz. "Don't bother me again until *his* friend gets here."

Her hair ignited into flame, crimson feathers emerging as her body rippled and twisted. In a heartbeat, she returned to her avian shape, and then with a shriek she beat her blazing wings and lifted into the sky.

Zogrusz watched the Phoenix until she was nothing but a fading ember in the unmarred blue. A sniffle from Qala brought his attention to the girl, and he saw that she was staring after Anecoya with a dejected expression.

"Don't worry about her, my dear," Rhas said, and Zogrusz was relieved to hear some of the old energy in the cat's voice. "She's just not very good at dealing with frustration. I promise she will apologize later for what she said. In the meantime, I suggest you allow me to show you some of the wonders my world contains."

The clouds cleared from Qala's face almost immediately, and she grinned, wiping at her eyes with the back of her hand. "Wonders? Really? I want to see!"

"Excellent," Rhas said, sitting back on his haunches. A shiver passed through him, and his body suddenly swelled to the size of a tiger.

Qala clapped her hands delightedly, then rushed forward to bury her face in his neck-fur.

"Climb up, child," Rhas said, pulling away so that he could crouch down low enough for her to clamber onto his back. Which she quickly did, giggling as the cat stood again with her legs now straddling him, her little hands clutching at his fur to keep herself from sliding off.

"That's it, then?" Zogrusz asked. "There's nothing else to be done?"

Rhas swung his head to him, the sadness in the world-spirit's eyes answering his question before he even spoke. "You heard the Wanderer. The attention of a Reaper is a death sentence for a world. But I do not intend to wallow in despair in my last moments – I would rather spend that time enjoying the things I love most." The cat slowly blinked his great golden eyes, then sighed deeply. "Perhaps a solution will present itself to one of us, Zog. Until then I will be wandering about with Qala here."

"Let's gooooo!" the girl cried, kicking her heels into Rhas's flanks.

The cat chuckled, shaking his head as he turned away. Zogrusz watched the world-spirit as he ambled down the slope, his tail flicking back and forth while the little girl bounced excitedly on his back. The sound of her chattering drifted to him long after they had vanished over a little swell, and then finally even that faded, and he was left atop the hill, alone except for the wind whispering through the dead grass.

ZOGRUSZ SAT on his throne and considered the nature of existence. He had seen in his wanderings that nearly the entirety of the cosmos was a vast emptiness, sprinkled here and there with spheres of superheated gases and rocks hurtling through the dark. Life in its desperate fragility had emerged in a few systems where dumb chance had created the perfect circumstances, but it was always fated to be brief, at least in relation to the age of the universe. A rogue comet or the death of a star or a ravenous cosmic monster would eventually destroy whatever had grown. It was inevitable.

He thought of the Old Ones, asleep while drifting in the deepest void. Of what did they dream? Great secrets perhaps, who or what had wound the cosmos up and set it in motion, or if there was indeed a plan that was unfolding with painstaking precision? Were they soldiers in a war to prevent the birth of a supreme being? Or were even the Old Ones just like all other beings in the universe, nothing more than accreted star dust that had achieved awareness and were now blundering along blindly?

Whatever the truth, Zogrusz realized on some level that he should not be concerned about the fate of this one insignificant world. It was a grain of sand in a desert that stretched almost to infinity. After the Reaper had come and gone and the Harvest had finished, it would be like it had never been . . . no, he amended, a shard of black crystal would remain, the history of a species locked within its faceted depths. And perhaps a godlike telepath would arrive in the far distant future and give form to what was contained within. Why should he care what happened to this world, when life here was always going to end, eventually?

But he did care.

So alone in his cavern, listening to the whir and click of the insects climbing the walls, Zogrusz grieved for everything that would someday be lost.

"Zog!"

Zogrusz roused himself, sitting up straighter on his throne. He'd been close to sinking into his deep slumber again, but the pull was not yet so insistent that he couldn't drag himself back to wakefulness.

From his perch atop his ziggurat, his gaze swept the cavern and quickly found the small girl staring about in wide-eyed wonder. It looked like she had come alone, as there was no sign of Rhas.

"It's wonderful in here!" Qala cried, her voice echoing. "I love these carvings . . . and the ceiling! Amazing!"

Zogrusz heaved himself to his feet and descended the tiered pyramid, flexing his wings to relieve their stiffness. "It's taken a long time," he said, savoring her praise.

She goggled at him. "*You* did this? All these carvings?"

He shrugged, as if to dismiss her reaction, but he couldn't keep his mouth-tendrils from twitching in satisfaction. "I saw what the humans had made and realized I wanted to learn how to create such things."

Qala drifted over to the wall and ran her fingers over a carving of one of the Great Old Ones. "And is this really what an adult Eldritch Horror looks like?"

"It's what I remember. That time for me is hazy. Like a dream half-remembered."

The girl glanced at him, then back to the carving, her brow furrowed. "It doesn't really resemble you, with all these mouths and tendrils and eyes. You're much more handsome."

Zogrusz couldn't hold back a surprised snort. He hadn't been expecting her to say *that*.

"I wonder if they once looked more like you," she mused, tracing his outline in the air. "You know, two arms, two legs, two eyes. But then when they grew up they changed. And left your more normal shape behind."

Zogrusz didn't want to think about that. The memory of Ixia telling him that the Reaper would excise his humanity had been weighing heavily, and she had reminded him of that.

"Where is Rhas?" he asked, gesturing for the girl to follow him over to the benches he'd placed beside the pool of water.

"He had stuff to do. He wanted to go talk to Annie, and I didn't." Her little face scrunched up when she mentioned the bird-goddess. "He really loves her."

Zogrusz settled onto a bench, picking with a claw at a crack in the slab of stone. "So you can see into his mind as well?"

Qala nodded. "You're all open books to me. Which is why I'm not worried about coming here, even though you're an Eldritch Horror living under a scary mountain. I can see your true self – and it's much nicer than Annie, even though she's so pretty." Qala suddenly gasped, pointing at the phosphorescent shapes flickering in the dark water. "Look! Fish!"

"Do they make you think of home?" Zogrusz asked, his mouth-tendrils twitching in amusement.

Qala made a face. "Ixia's pet wasn't my home."

Zogrusz leaned forward, suddenly interested to know more. He'd been curious about Qala ever since they'd stumbled across the little blonde girl in the city of the snake-men. "Oh? Where did you come from?"

"Don't know the world's name," Qala said, flicking away a many-legged insect that was undulating across the bench towards her. "Might not even have had one. My people were very primitive, still living in caves and hiding in fear every time it thundered outside. I don't remember much from back then, except that my parents were considered something like priests. There was a big skull everybody prayed to in our cavern, so big my mother could stand inside it and shout out what the spirit wanted everybody to do." Her voice was growing more distant as she talked, as if she was returning to that time. "One day I was just sitting in a field playing with the flowers while my mother gathered some berries, and I felt something . . . open inside me, and all these voices rushed into my head. I started crying because I didn't know what was going on. My mother ran to me, and I realized I could *see* her love and concern spilling forth . . . along with all those secret thoughts people have inside them. Pretty soon everyone in my tribe knew I was different. I guess I'm lucky they didn't declare me some kind of demon and throw me in a lake. Maybe it was because my parents were considered close to the spirit we worshipped, and my mother convinced them I had been blessed."

"Do you think that's what happened? That your god touched you?" Zogrusz found he had some trouble even saying that word, since he knew that 'gods' were nothing but cosmic beings – parasites, in truth – feeding off the emotions of mortals. Like him.

Qala shrugged. "I dunno. Ixia definitely didn't think so.

He said my gifts are bigger than any other creature he had met in the universe, cosmic or mortal." She twined a strand of her golden hair around a finger, her face clouding like she was thinking of something troubling. "It's not just the telepathy, you know. I stopped getting older that day in the field." Her face grew more somber. "I watched my mother and father grow old. Then my brothers and sisters. And then their children, but I always stayed exactly the same. If Ixia hadn't found me, I probably would still be there, sitting inside that skull getting sadder and sadder." She shook her head, her impish smile returning. "But I don't want to think about that. I'm happier now. I was happy on the fish too, for a while, but it's hard to stay around other people for so long when you always know what they're thinking. Ixia . . . he didn't really care for me. He was just obsessed with his project. When he realized I probably wouldn't be able to help him finish it, he lost a lot of interest in me."

Zogrusz tossed a pebble into the pool of dark water, and the glowing fish scattered. "You've mentioned this project a few times. What was it?"

Qala glanced at him sidelong. "It's supposed to be a secret . . . but just don't tell Ixia I said anything, okay?" She paused, waiting until Zogrusz nodded in agreement before continuing. "Do you remember all those strands from the fish that were going into his body? They were keeping him alive – he's very old, you see." That was exactly what Zogrusz had suspected – he couldn't imagine anyone connecting themselves to the innards of a fish unless the situation was extremely dire. "Anyway, Ixia wanted to find a way to . . . move his consciousness into another body. Not a copy – which is much easier – but his actual, original self. It's more complicated than you might think," she assured him hurriedly, as if he might be doubting her abilities.

Zogrusz certainly hadn't thought it would be easy. Even the simplest of minds he'd entered had been exceedingly complex.

"I'm surprised he let you go with us."

Qala rolled her eyes. "I wasn't his prisoner. When I first went with him, I told him I would only stay as long as I wanted to. And you all couldn't hear it, but I said a bit more to him just before we left." She tapped the side of her head. "I promised that if I ever . . . solved the biggest problem of his project, I'd come find him, and we'd finish what we started."

"What was this problem?"

"Well, you have to understand –" Her eyes suddenly widened, and she twisted around to stare at the entrance to his cavern. "Huh. She got here sooner than I thought she would."

"Who?" Zogrusz asked, craning his head to try and see down the tunnel.

"Anecoya. She just landed outside. And it doesn't seem like she's coming in, so I guess she wants us to go to her."

Zogrusz stood slowly as Qala slid from the bench. "Why is she here?"

"I asked her to come."

"All right . . . but why did you do that?"

Qala struck the side of her head, as if something had just occurred to her. "That's right, I hadn't told you yet." She brushed dirt from her hands, then smoothed down her rumpled tunic as Zogrusz waited with growing impatience.

"Told me what?"

"*Hm*? Oh, that another cosmic being just entered this system. Something quite powerful."

10

T hey slipped between the silent, tumbling rocks, alert to any sign of the intruder. Anecoya glided with effortless grace through the asteroid field, but Zogrusz kept having to twist and turn to avoid any collisions – it had been a long time since he had tried to move through the airless dark, especially when it was so cluttered with debris.

<You fly like a drunken chicken> Anecoya muttered in his mind, the words dripping with disdain.

<I'm just out of practice> Zogrusz replied defensively, briefly landing on a drifting chunk of pockmarked rock before gathering and leaping after her once more.

A telepathic snort sounded in his head. <I can't believe your kind was ever meant to exist out here. Wait, you did say you Horrors all looked different – did you perhaps choose a particularly awkward shape? Seems like something you'd do>

<Shouldn't we be focused right now?> Zogrusz asked, pushing another spinning asteroid from his path as he fought to keep her glimmering feathers in his sight.

*<I am focused, but I haven't felt anything strange. Can you? We're searching for one of **your** kind>*

<Not yet> he admitted, once again scouring the labyrinth of shifting rocks around them with his senses. Could Ycthitlig really conceal itself from him out here? This belt of asteroids at the fringes of their system would be the perfect place for a huge Eldritch Horror to hide from view, but surely he would feel its presence . . . right? Qala had been adamant that *something* had arrived around their sun, but even she couldn't tell what exactly, as its mind was draped with layers of obfuscating defenses. Indeed, if she was not so powerful and sensitive, she never would have even known it had come. And that was honestly what confused Zogrusz the most – he did not believe for a moment that a Reaper would bother moving stealthily. Which was why he did not share Anecoya's absolute conviction that they were about to finally confront the threat looming over their world.

<Wait> Anecoya hissed in his mind, and his attention sharpened once more on their surroundings. *<Can you feel that? There's something . . . odd up ahead on that rock>*

She had arrested her flight, her burning wings beating slowly as she hovered and her flashing beak pointing at a large asteroid. Zogrusz came up alongside her, struggling to keep from floating past where she had stopped. His claws scrabbled for a moment against a much smaller shard of space-stone, then slid away, and a sigh gusted through his head as a shimmering red and gold wing flashed out to press against his chest, bringing him to a halt.

<It's on the far side> she said, and now Zogrusz could perceive it as well, a presence heavy with coiled power. It didn't *feel* like another Eldritch Horror – but, then again, he had never been in the presence of a Reaper's true form.

<Do we attack immediately?> Anecoya asked, and Zogrusz

was surprised by her uncertainty. He had thought that violence was the unquestioned answer to all her problems.

<*We are not even certain it's Ycthitlig*> he cautioned. <*It could be something just passing through, like the Wanderer . . . or Qala*>

Through their mind link he could feel her roiling indecision. <*Then what do you suggest?*>

<*Perhaps we can approach cautiously*> Zogrusz suggested. <*And get a glimpse before it knows we're there. If it's the Reaper . . . we strike hard and fast, with everything we can muster*>

He hesitated, unsure if he should share his greatest fear about this confrontation.

<*What is it?*> Anecoya asked sharply, apparently aware that he was holding back.

<*It's just something Ixia told me. He claimed that the Reaper could have a way to . . . change me*>

<*Into what?*>

<*Something more like it. He said . . . he said it might be able to pluck the humanity from my soul like pulling a stray thread from a weave. The Old Ones could do such a thing . . . but I don't think Ixia was certain a Reaper was also capable of such a feat. He only suspected*>

<*You should have told me that before*> Anecoya growled in exasperation.

<*I know, I'm sorry. But perhaps we can overwhelm Ycthitlig before it thinks to attempt this. That sort of psychic surgery can't be easy*>

The annoyance radiating from Anecoya was palpable. <*I'll attack first, you follow behind. Hopefully this thing will focus on me, and it won't even realize you're its kin until it's too late*>

Zogrusz dispatched a mental affirmation, and Anecoya must have considered the discussion finished, because she surged towards the huge asteroid. He hurried to follow, keeping a few lengths behind her as she swooped around its edge and began gliding just above the cracked and broken rock.

The presence was now very near. Zogrusz could only hope that it was distracted, because there was little chance it hadn't noticed the approach of two other cosmic beings.

<In that crater> Anecoya said, angling towards a massive indentation on the surface.

Something was indeed there, but it was small, barely larger than a human. A cold rush of relief washed through Zogrusz that it was not a giant nest of writhing tendrils and madly staring eyes, or anything else like what he remembered.

The cosmic being was man-shaped, though strangely bulky. They settled on the scarred surface a hundred paces from where the creature stood with its back to them. Zogrusz studied it warily. It almost looked like a sculpture attempted by a novice stonemason – what flesh he could see was gray and rugged, like roughhewn rock, and its limbs were strangely proportioned, far too thick. Armor of smoky quartz covered much of its blocky body, all smooth surfaces and sharp angles without curves or ornamentation. A massive, scabbarded sword was slung across its back, the hilt a substance so black it looked like a piece of the void had been given substance. No helm adorned the creature's hairless head, which was also more of the same gray, lumpy flesh ... and webbed by cracks, as if it truly *was* stone.

Zogrusz and Anecoya shared a quick glance. He knew what she was wondering – should they ambush the cosmic being and seek to destroy it before it could prove itself a threat? Or approach it in peace and hope that it could be persuaded to leave this system without causing any trouble?

Before they could engage in a telepathic discussion about what course was best, the creature spoke, its voice like rocks grinding together.

"So thou hast finally found me."

Zogrusz's jaw fell open in surprise. His tongue flicked out, tasting air – yes, somehow a thin atmosphere wrapped this planetoid, allowing the entity's words to travel to them.

And it also knew they were there.

Slowly the creature turned to face them. Zogrusz's surprise deepened to shock – its eyes were yellow gems, its mouth a jagged fissure. What had looked like a statue from afar was indeed a man fashioned from rock, but there was intelligence glittering in the facets of the jewels sunk into its head.

"The hunt hath been long, but hither it ends." The stone-man reached up slowly and grasped the black hilt jutting over its shoulder.

Confusion gripped Zogrusz. Why was this thing acting like it knew them? What was it talking about? He opened his mouth to reason with the creature, but then his heart fell when he heard a sudden crackle of flame: Anecoya summoning her blazing sword. He gritted his fangs in annoyance – of course she would want to strike first and ask questions later . . . *if* anything remained that could provide answers.

"Long have I wished to draw the final weapon of mine people," the stone-man intoned in his gravelly voice. "And now that thou hast found me, there is no reason to keep it occulted. Vengeance shall finally be unsheathed."

A harsh rasping sounded as the creature drew forth his great sword. Its blade resembled malachite, a jadeite green inset with darker swirls, and the power seeping from it made Zogrusz's hide prickle. When the long sword finally cleared its scabbard a deep tolling shivered the air, as if somewhere far away a bell had been struck.

At the noise, the sharp edges of the stone-man's expression slackened into something that suggested surprise, and the brightness of his eyes dimmed for a moment. It truly looked like he had just blinked in confusion.

"Oh," he rumbled in what almost sounded like resignation. "I have made a mistake."

"What are you talking about?" Anecoya snapped, but the stone-man was no longer paying attention to them. He was turning slowly, his sword extended like he was expecting an attack, even though it seemed like there was no one else in the crater with them.

But there was.

With a wet tearing sound, the air suddenly ripped open, and through this ragged gash in reality stepped a hooded figure. In its pale, long-fingered hands it clutched the haft of a white-bladed scythe fashioned from a curving length of bone. Four other portals exactly like the first appeared, and through each emerged another robed figure, their features hidden deep within the recesses of their cowls. They were identical, save for the different weapons in their spidery hands: a long-handled ax, a scimitar, a two-handed greatsword, a pike. All the weapons gleamed dully in the faint light of the distant sun, seemingly made from the same substance.

The stone-man raised his massive sword into a guard position as the wraiths fanned out to encircle them all.

At long last dread Kalin'graeth slips free of its bonds. We knew if we waited long enough this time would come.

The words were strangely hollow, many voices spoken as one, emanating from everywhere and nowhere. Anecoya and Zogrusz shared another confused glance – they had clearly stumbled into something they had no business being a part of.

But what is this? Allies you have found? They must not know of your crimes. And you think to ambush us? Fools! Their corpses will adorn this rock for all eternity!

"Uh-oh," Zogrusz muttered as the shrouded creatures rushed forward in absolute silence, robes billowing and bone-weapons upraised.

He unsheathed his claws and set himself to meet their charge, but the asteroid spasmed as a circular wall of rock erupted from the ground, separating them from the wraiths. Zogrusz met Anecoya's shocked gaze, and then they looked to the stone-man, who had raised his hand, open palm turned upward. He clenched his fist, and the rampart high above them curved as it grew, eventually forming a dome that sealed them off utterly from the outside.

"Mine deepest apologies, strangers," he rumbled. "Thou hast stumbled into a rather perilous situation."

"Who are you?" Zogrusz asked, half-expecting the cowled creatures to teleport inside the sanctuary the stone-man had created.

To his surprise, the stone-man dipped into a stiff and very formal bow. "Mine name is Origenius Grex, and I am the last of the Sedimati. Mine people hast been hunted to extinction by the demons beyond these walls, and I fear I shall finally join them." He let out a deep sigh like an avalanche gathering strength. "I am sorry that I mistook thou for mine ancient enemies in disguise. And that by drawing mine sword, I drew their attention to this hiding spot."

The wall trembled, cracks fracturing its surface as dust sifted down from above. Zogrusz turned to Anecoya, who was staring at the buckling barrier in consternation.

"Your thoughts?" he asked her, and she shrugged without looking at him.

"I have no idea what's going on," she said, "but I have to admit I like the rock person more than the things outside."

"I agree."

"Also, he doesn't seem to want to fight us anymore," she said, glancing at the stone-man. "Is that right?"

His faceted yellow eyes dimmed before brightening again. "Aye. There is no quarrel twixt us."

"Good enough for me," Zogrusz said, flexing his claws as he rolled his shoulders. "Fight?"

"Fight," Anecoya agreed, the flames of her sword flaring higher.

The stone-man's rocky features contorted strangely, as if he was suddenly overcome with emotion. With a blocky finger he wiped something glittering from his eye, and it clinked and bounced when it struck the ground, coming to rest near Zogrusz's taloned feet. It certainly looked like a diamond. "Thou wouldst stand beside me in mine moment of need? To encounter such noble spirits quickens the magma in mine channels. 'Tis an honor to meet thee, mine new friends."

A curving shard of bone burst through the wall and then was violently wrenched back. Through this gap, Zogrusz glimpsed flowing dark robes and corpse-pale flesh, before the rock knit together like it was liquid flowing down to fill a hole.

"I canst not bear them back much longer," the stone-man grunted, his voice strained.

"You do not have to," Zogrusz said as he turned to Anecoya. "Let us show them whose realm they are intruding in."

The Phoenix crooked a smile, then plunged her burning

blade point-first into the ground. A great pillar of flame burst upwards to consume her, and the stone-man reeled back in shock.

"By Charox's heavy ingots!" he cried, raising a quartz-encased arm to shield his face from the fiery geyser. Within that roiling maelstrom, Anecoya's shadow was growing and twisting as her blazing wings unfurled.

Zogrusz also embraced his true form, power rushing through his veins as he swelled. The top of his head struck the dome, and it shattered, the walls toppling outwards as chunks of rock rained down, and the cowled creatures scurried away to avoid being crushed.

A surprised shriek rose up from below. *Horror!*

And then he heard Anecoya thrashing herself free of the rubble and the hollow voices came again. It might have been his imagination, but he thought they sounded almost panicked this time.

Phoenix!

Zogrusz stomped down on a wraith, mashing it into the stone. He tried to crush another, but it leapt away, though one of his curving talons caught the trailing edge of its robes. It fell flat on its back, losing its bone scimitar. Before he could finish it off, Anecoya's copper beak flashed out and plucked the wriggling creature up. Then with a shake of her great head, she tossed it into the air, so high it must have passed beyond the asteroid's weak gravity because it never came back down again.

He turned his attention to the remaining wraiths, but they had apparently decided they wanted no further part in this fight. With frantic haste they once more tore open holes to elsewhere, and then threw themselves through these portals, which immediately sealed shut behind them.

Anecoya made an explosive hacking sound, and he

turned to find her wiping at her beak with a crimson wing.
<Blech. That thing tasted terrible>

Her feathers blurred and grew hazy as she dwindled
back to human form, then immediately doubled over as she
tried to spit out whatever residue that creature had left in
her mouth. Zogrusz compressed his true form down to
about the same size and lifted his foot to examine the sticki-
ness he felt on its underside. There was a little bit of dark
ichor clinging to him, but thankfully nothing more disgust-
ing. Most of the pulped wraith must have sloughed off when
he shrank.

They turned as the stone-man's voice came from behind
them.

"Mighty warriors," Origenius rumbled, sounding awed.
He had slipped to one knee with his head bowed, his hand
resting on the hilt of his malachite sword. "Ne'r hast I seen
the Desiccated defeated with such ease. And thou hast
saved me. I must know thy names."

"I'm Zogrusz, and you're welcome," Zogrusz said, faintly
embarrassed by the stone-man's behavior.

"Origenius," the stone-man said quickly. "Please, call me
Origenius."

Anecoya paused her spluttering long enough to introduce herself. "And I'm Anecoya."

"Zogrusz and Anecoya," the stone warrior murmured. "I
am in thy debt, and I swear on mine blade I shall serve thee
till that debt is paid."

Zogrusz held up a scaled hand. "Oh, you know that's
really not –" he began, but Anecoya interrupted him by
clearing her throat loudly.

"We accept your service, Origenius," she said with the
cadence of a formal investiture, raising her eyebrows pointedly at Zogrusz.

Perhaps she had the right idea, he was forced to admit. "What were those things?" Zogrusz asked, nudging the bone-bladed scimitar with his foot. It hissed and crackled like coals doused with water.

Origenius rose stiffly and slid his malachite sword once more across his back. "The Desiccated are the remnants of a once-proud people. As am I. Long ago our races encountered each other, and I do not know the origins of our war, but it hath spanned countless aeons. I am the last of mine kind, and they are the last of theirs."

"You'd think they could finally let go of this grudge, then," Anecoya muttered, folding her arms across her chest.

Origenius shook his head slowly. "They live only for revenge. If live is the proper term – they long since changed their natures to be naught but avatars of vengeance. When I am gone from this universe, I believe they will soon follow me."

"What did your kind do?" Zogrusz asked, surprised by the intensity of the hate the stone-man was describing.

"I do not know," Origenius replied, turning his jeweled eyes to the robed body Zogrusz had crushed. "I was the last born of mine people, and they ne'er told me our history. Perhaps we are guilty of some terrible crime."

"Children do not inherit the sins of their parents," Anecoya muttered.

Zogrusz glanced around to make sure the ragged portals had stayed closed. "Should we expect those things to come back?"

"I do not think they will dare return so long as I am with thee," Origenius said. "They waited ten thousand years for me to draw mine sword and reveal where I hid – they can wait ten thousand more. Time means naught to them."

"Now I understand why you swore yourself to us," Anecoya said.

Origenius's gray face darkened slightly – was he blushing? Zogrusz wondered how that was even possible. Maybe there was indeed magma coursing beneath the surface of his stony skin.

"It is true, I will be safer with thee, beautiful and fierce Anecoya. But I also have a debt, and I swear on the molten souls of mine ancestors that I shall find a way to recompense it."

Zogrusz shared another meaningful glance with Anecoya. "Well, Origenius, about that . . . there is something we could use some assistance with . . ."

THEIR RETURN to Rhas's world was uneventful, though Zogrusz stayed on edge for much of the journey. He half-expected another ambush by those robed wraiths, despite Origenius's assurances that the creatures would bide their time and wait until he was no longer under their protection. Anecoya had offered to transport the stone warrior on her back, but Origenius had declined the offer, claiming that he was far heavier than he might appear. Instead, he had displayed his telekinetic control over rock once more by ripping away the chunk of asteroid he stood upon and then compelling it to follow them as they flew home through the frozen dark.

When they neared the world, Anecoya made to lead them towards the southern continent where she nested, but Zogrusz extended a mental tendril into her mind.

<No. We should return to my mountain>
<Why?>

<We should stay together, I think. At least until we're sure those Desiccated are not going to return. And Qala is back in my cavern. She'll want to know what happened>

Anecoya gave a mental sigh of resignation. *<Fine. But why did you leave her there?>*

<I couldn't think of anywhere safer> he told her. *<For if . . .>*

<If we failed> Anecoya finished for him bitterly. *<Which you think we will when that Reaper finally decides to show up. You've given up already>*

<I haven't> he replied forcefully, trying his best to convince her by letting her feel the emotion woven into this statement. *<I will sacrifice myself for this world if need be. But as I told you, I've felt the power of my kin before . . . I have no illusion about our chances>*

He could sense Anecoya's annoyance leeching across their link as she dove into the clouds shrouding their world. *<Well, at least it seems we have one more ally in the fight>*

<It would appear so> Zogrusz granted, twisting his head around to glance at the stone warrior in his quartz armor. He looked rather dashing, with his head held high and his chest thrust out as his shard of rock hurtled after the Phoenix, wisps of dust glimmering in its wake.

They descended and landed on his mountain near the collapsed entrance to his home. As usual, he felt a pang of sadness gazing at the ruin of his hard work, and he wondered if Anecoya had any guilt at all about what she had done.

Highly unlikely, knowing her.

A crunching thump reverberated as Origenius brought his rock down on the slope hard enough that for a moment Zogrusz feared the stone-man might have started an avalanche. Anecoya twisted around to stare at him with thinned lips, but Origenius was oblivious to her annoyance, moving past them with his attention fixed on the craggy peak clawing at the sky.

"By Terrax's glittering geodes! Is this truly thy home, friend Zogrusz?"

"Yes, I dwell within."

Origenius put his hands on his hips, his expression evoking something like satisfaction. "Thou hast chosen well," he said, crouching down to place his palm flat on the ground. The light in his faceted yellow eyes faded, and he seemed to be momentarily transported elsewhere. "The hallowed bones of this grandfather are strong, reaching deep into the earth. I would be grateful to shelter under his arms." Origenius's eyes brightened again as he stood, fixed on the destroyed entrance. "Yet what hast befallen here?"

"Ah," Zogrusz said, swiveling to face Anecoya. "*Someone* made a rather large mess."

Origenius picked his way over the scree to inspect the shattered masonry and broken statues. "Indeed," he said sadly, shaking his head. "They hath defaced this proud elder with gaudy ornamentation." He reached down and scooped up the half-obliterated graven head of an Eldritch Horror. "At least there was an attempt to destroy this travesty. Was that thee, friend Zogrusz? Didst thou try and restore this mountain to its former glory?"

Laughter burst from Anecoya, and it looked like she had to put her hands on her waist to keep from doubling over. Zogrusz tried to avoid glancing at her as he strode stiffly towards the passage leading into the mountain's depths, his mouth tendrils writhing in annoyance.

"Friend Zogrusz, is something the matter?"

∾

"Zog!"

Qala's excited shriek rebounded off the walls as he entered his cavern. She jumped up from where she had been sprawled on his throne, then lowered herself from the seat of the chair onto the topmost tier of his ziggurat. He couldn't help but wonder how she had climbed up in the first place, given that the base of the throne was higher than she was tall.

Over near his fish pond, Rhas uncurled from where he had been sleeping atop one of the benches, then stretched languidly before leaping down with the easy grace peculiar to cats.

"It's good to see you," he said as he padded over to Zogrusz. "I was quite worried when Qala told me about our visitor."

"You're not dead!" the little girl shouted as she careened down the steps with reckless abandon. Zogrusz winced, half-expecting her to lose her balance and fall the rest of the way. "Did you kill the Reaper? Was it dangerous?" She skidded to a halt when she reached the bottom, her eyes widening. "Wait – you brought it back! It's here, it's coming! And it's . . . not an Eldritch Horror. What an interesting mind! It feels like . . ." Her face twisted like she had just tasted something bitter. "It feels hard as iron!"

"Stone, actually," Zogrusz said, then gave a surprised grunt as the girl wrapped her arms around his scaled leg.

She turned her face to look up at him. "Did you bring me back a present?"

"What? A present?"

"Annie," Rhas said in relief as the Phoenix entered his cavern. "You're all right."

"Of course I'm all right," Anecoya said, then with a wave of her hand summoned a roiling ball of golden light. "I don't know how you all can stand this darkness," she muttered as it floated up to hover just below the mosaic covering the arched ceiling and drenched the cavern with a soft radiance.

"What entered my system?" the cat asked, his tail flicking in obvious agitation. "Is it a threat?"

"Rhas . . ." Zogrusz said as he heard a heavy tread approaching. "I'd like you to meet Origenius."

Qala gasped as the huge stone-man filled the entrance to the cavern, stooping slightly so that the hilt of his greatsword would not scrape against the top of the doorway. "Oh, wow! Are you really made of *rock*?"

Origenius took a few more steps into the cavern and then dropped to one knee, his head bowed. "Greetings and well met. Any friends of mine saviors are mine friends as well."

Rhas circled the motionless stone-man warily. "Are you a golem? Something created and then given the spark of life?"

"Nay, world-spirit," Origenius rumbled. "I come from an ancient and vanished people."

"I know why your mind is so different!" Qala suddenly yelled, clapping her hands together. "I can feel it's not tissue, but some kind of crystal! Oh, it's *beautiful*!"

Origenius's jeweled eyes focused on her with what looked to Zogrusz like respect. "Indeed, inside mine head is an element called silicon. 'Tis one of the few substances in the cosmos that can conduct thought, much like the fleshy ball in thy pate."

Qala giggled. "You talk funny. Is it because you've got crystal between your ears?"

"Nay, little princess," Origenius said, finally straightening as his gaze swept the cavern.

"He said I'm a princess!" Qala cried delightedly.

"What else could thee be, since we find thee in the

company of this world's spirit . . ." Origenius's words trailed away, and Zogrusz noticed that he was staring intently at the scenes carved into the walls, his fissure of a mouth slightly parted.

He almost looked aghast.

"Friend Zogrusz, who hath mutilated this beautiful realm with such crass imagery?"

Anecoya guffawed again, even louder than she had outside.

"All right, that's enough," Zogrusz said, sighing deeply. "There's something you have to know."

ORIGENIUS WAS contrite when told that it was Zogrusz who had carved the rock of this cavern, his face darkening with embarrassment. Anecoya kept chuckling through his stammered apologies, which annoyed Zogrusz even further, but in the end he simply waved away the stone-man's words.

"It's not important," Zogrusz said. "We have other things we must talk about."

And so they did. Rhas introduced himself and his world, describing how the other cosmic beings had found themselves on the planet and then the looming threat of the Reaper.

Origenius's gleaming eyes flickered at this, and he expressed his surprise over their belief that Anecoya and Zogrusz would be unable on their own to defeat the Eldritch Horror. He was apparently still very much impressed with how easily they had defeated the Desiccated.

"About that," Anecoya interjected before Rhas could respond. "This world does now have *three* powerful defenders – are we so sure this Reaper is still beyond our capabilities?"

"Four," Qala piped up, thrusting her hand out with the same number of fingers aggressively displayed.

Anecoya pursed her lips, and Zogrusz suspected she had just stopped herself from rolling her eyes. "You're just a fledgling."

Qala scowled. "I can help! I can do a lot of things!"

"And she can," Rhas said hurriedly, as if afraid the Phoenix's doubt would tip the little girl over into a full-blown tantrum. "However, I think we must hesitate before counting Origenius here as an ally. I do not mean to insult, good sir, but how do we know we can trust you? To stand against a Reaper is no small thing."

Origenius drew himself up taller, but it was Qala who answered first. "He will fight with us," she said confidently.

All eyes turned to her, but her certainty did not wilt under their attention. "I saw it in his mind. He considers the oath he swore to be worth his life, if it comes to that."

"I thought you said his mind was hard to read?" Zogrusz asked, to which Qala responded with a sly smile.

"It was pretty hard, but I figured it out."

Origenius reached up to tap his stony brow. "Are thou truly in hither, little princess?" he asked, his rocky features knitting together in concern.

"Yup!" she cried. "But don't worry, I won't tell anyone what else I found in there."

"Ah . . . mine thanks," the stone-man said haltingly, lowering his hand.

"I believe Qala," Rhas said, dipping his head in the girl's direction. "And so now I have confidence in our new ally. But that is not all I wanted to say at this moment."

Zogrusz frowned, surprised by the sudden change in

Rhas's tone. He noticed Anecoya shifting uncomfortably – she had also caught it.

The cat sat back on his haunches, lifting his head high. His golden eyes met each of their gazes, lingering longest on Anecoya. "You should leave," he declared solemnly. "All of you."

Anecoya snorted, folding her arms across her chest.

"You cannot understand how much I appreciate your loyalty," Rhas continued, ignoring her interruption. "Never could I imagine that I would have friends like you, willing to lay down your lives for my world. And I care for you like family and dearest friends. Annie . . . you have been my daughter since you emerged from your egg. And Zog, it warms my heart to see how much you appreciate my people. You are more human than many who inhabit this world. But now . . . now you must go. You must return to the stars where you belong. There is no reason for you to sacrifice yourselves here, to take some meaningless stand when the outcome is near certain. If I know you are out there, that the memory of my world persists somewhere in the cosmos . . . I can hold tight to that knowledge when the destroyer finally comes."

Rhas fell silent, the only sound in the cavern the clicking of insects as they scurried along the walls. Then Anecoya strode forward and crouched beside the world-mind.

"I will never abandon you," she said simply, reaching down to scratch affectionately behind the cat's ears. "Father."

Rhas's head jerked up as she said this. "But, Annie –"

"Enough, I will stay," she said sharply, glancing over at Zogrusz. "And you?"

"Of course," he said, a little hoarsely. He gestured

towards Qala and Origenius. "But this is not their fight. Perhaps it *is* best if they flee while there is still a chance."

Origenius's hand went to the hilt protruding over his shoulder. "I swore on mine sword I would repay the debt owed. I would not deserve to wield this blade if I proved myself so craven."

"And I'm not leaving, either," Qala said matter-of-factly, sticking out her tongue at them. "And none of you can make me."

Rhas lowered his head, his body sagging. Zogrusz couldn't tell if the cat felt relief or sadness – likely a little of both, he decided.

"Never has a world been luckier," he finally murmured.

"Take heart," Anecoya commanded, scooping up the cat and giving him an affectionate squeeze. "So long as we live, there is hope."

11

*Z*ogrusz woke with his cheek pressed against something scratchy, drool dampening his chin. He blinked blearily, raising his head to see it had rested upon a pile of rushes bound by twine. He reached up, extricating his arm from under a blanket of soft wool, and brushed away pieces of dried straw clinging to his soft fleshy face.

What was going on? Where was he?

Zogrusz sat up. He was in a wide bed, its frame intricately carved from dark wood, four posts wrapped by whittled vines supporting a canopy of gossamer cloth. Amber light spilled from an open window, gilding the other pieces of beautifully fashioned furniture in the large room – chairs surrounding a low table, a closet, a chest. Tiny motes of dust glittered like flurrying specks of golden snow.

He drew back his blanket. Nut-brown legs greeted him, and in confused wonder he wiggled his toes. Why could he not remember taking his human form? This body looked older than the one he usually assumed, which was strange.

And how had he gotten here, to find himself sleeping in a strange house?

Wait. Something was very wrong.

Zogrusz turned within himself, reaching for the cold core of cosmic power at the center of his being.

It wasn't there. In a surprised panic, he tried to shrug out of his man-cloak.

Nothing happened.

"Am I dreaming?" he mumbled, pinching the soft flesh of his forearm.

The pain was surprisingly sharp . . . and it did not wake him.

A tingling sense of unreality was spreading, his breathing becoming shorter and faster. Was he panicking? Was this what humans felt like when they were terrified and overwhelmed? The small part of him that was still detached to what was happening found this sensation interesting. The rest of him thought it was terrible. He ran his finger over his sweat-slicked skin, tracing raised bumps. Goose-pimples. He had goose-pimples.

Zogrusz slid from the bed, his feet settling on sun-warmed wood, and went over to the window. This room was on the ground floor, and just outside was a copse of gnarled white-barked trees, their branches heavy with golden fruit. Birds flitted from perch to perch, calling to each other in trilling song. Through the gaps in the foliage he could see a rolling meadow, and in the very great distance, a line of rugged mountains. His nose itched, and he sneezed loudly.

The sound of a door opening made him turn. A plump, gray-haired woman stood in the entrance to the room, staring at him with an open mouth and wide eyes.

"Oh, hello," Zogrusz said, unsettled by his inability to

delve into her mind. He felt isolated, adrift, confined to this fragile shell.

He felt like a mortal.

"Master Ahuatz! You're up and about this morning!"

Zogrusz swallowed, unsure how he should reply. "I suppose I am," he finally said.

The woman entered the room, her hands fluttering like she didn't know what to do with them. "You should be resting! Surely this is too much activity after so many days abed!"

He flinched back as she raised her arm at him, but it was only to gently place the back of her hand against his brow.

"Your fever has broken!" she exclaimed. "Still a bit of a chill, though. Back in bed with you, I must insist!"

Zogrusz slid away from her. "I'm quite well, I assure you. Never felt better." He paused, clearing his throat. "Though there is one thing . . . it seems my memory is hazy."

The woman folded her arms under her ample bosom, studying him with pursed lips. "Doctor Tochtlea said you might be a bit confused when you woke up. The fire in your head would cook your brain like an egg in a pan."

Zogrusz gestured broadly. "How did I get here?"

Her face creased in confusion. "Here as in your room? We carried you in after the wainwright's boys brought you home. They said you'd collapsed in the street – they first thought you must be drunk on pulque, but that would certainly be strange for the middle of the day, especially since everyone in town knows you never touch the stuff. They said you were mumbling all sorts of strange things, and your skin was burning hot. You've been sleeping for three days."

Zogrusz dredged up the last thing he remembered. He had been in his cavern, trying his best to resist the rising tide of exhaustion . . . His fear had been that Ycthitlig might arrive when he was asleep, and he would not be ready to challenge the Eldritch Horror, leaving his allies to face it alone. He raised his hand, examining the lines deeply scored into his palm. He used to be able to feel his blood flowing through his veins and make his heart stop beating with a flicker of will. Now . . . he felt powerless. This must be what it was like to be human.

Something occurred to him, and though he immediately he dismissed the thought, it lodged like a thorn in his skin. What if . . . what if his existence as an Eldritch Horror had been nothing but a bizarrely detailed dream? Already the memories were fading, growing blurred around the edges. Was his new human brain incapable of comprehending his previous life . . . or was Zogrusz a creation of the fever that had gripped him?

"I want some fresh air," he said, and the old woman's expression turned contemplative, as if she were weighing the benefits of going outside against more rest in bed.

"I suppose that's all right," she said, then nodded briskly before turning on her heel. "I'll go prepare some breakfast – Delia is still abed, and I've a mind to let her stay asleep a while yet. Poor thing has exhausted herself worrying about you."

"Delia?" Zogrusz asked, but the woman had already vanished. He stayed staring where she had gone for a few long moments, then slapped at his arm where some biting thing had alighted. If this was a dream, it was far more intricate than any he had experienced before.

Zogrusz shrugged on a shirt he found draped over the back of a chair and traded the light linen pants he'd awoken in for a sturdier pair he dug from a basket in the closet. After getting dressed, he glanced at the window again, and the soft morning light seemed to beckon him outside. He remembered the feeling of the sun on his skin in his borrowed man-form . . . Would it be the same in this body? Or had that memory been conjured by his recent sickness? He shook his head in frustration, then sneezed again – he had to hold tight to what he knew he was. He was an ancient cosmic being from the depths of the void, not a scrawny man in his middle years . . . with allergies.

Zogrusz left the bedroom and entered a corridor of dark wood. Low tables lined its length, interrupted here and there by closed doors, their surfaces covered by small statues of exquisite design. No two were alike, and Zogrusz only recognized some of the stone used – there was a stolid granite elephant, trunk waving; beside it ambled a white tiger carved of alabaster; and squatting next to that was a green soapstone frog. He hefted the tiger and turned it over in his hands, marveling at how well the sculptor had captured the flowing beauty of the beast. Then the clatter of crockery made him look to the right, and at the end of the long corridor he saw the old woman bustling back and forth in a large kitchen as she worked to prepare something. He turned to his left and saw that the corridor emptied into an outdoor space, though from the walls he saw rising across the way, he suspected it was some sort of enclosed area in the center of this complex.

Zogrusz left the sounds of cooking behind him and walked towards where the day was spilling into the house. He paused at the threshold, his hand on the door frame, and gazed out onto a scene of such tranquility he immediately felt the tumult in his mind subside. It was indeed a court-yard bounded by walls, filled with an artfully arranged garden that fairly glowed in the light from above. A path of red bricks wended towards a few gnarled banyan trees.

Crimson songbirds hopped between the branches as they called to each other, and from somewhere he heard the gentle trickle of running water.

Zogrusz followed the path, dazed by the strangeness of this place. It was too idyllic, too perfect, as if someone had tried to fashion the absolute opposite of his cavern and was trying to impress upon him how dreary his mountain home truly was. He passed between the banyans and realized that these trees had been hiding something. A great block of white stone had been placed within this grove, and emerging from its depths was the statue of a nymph, one arm raised like she was pulling aside a branch while slipping through the forest. Tools and shards of rock were scattered about the clearing, as if the sculptor had stepped away only moments ago. Zogrusz craned his head to peer through the foliage, hoping to glimpse this master stone carver, but a squirrel clinging to a trunk was his only companion in the garden.

His hands were aching. Zogrusz glanced down in surprise, flexing his fingers. But it wasn't a painful ache – no, his hands *yearned* to pick up the hammer lying in the grass by his feet. Swallowing back the dryness in his throat, Zogrusz bent down, his fingers closing around the handle and finding familiar grooves in the well-worn wood.

He'd used this hammer before, he was sure of it.

Zogrusz stepped closer to the statue. A chisel had been set where the nymph's torso vanished into still-uncarved stone, and he took that up as well. Feeling like he was wading through a dream, Zogrusz set the point of the chisel where he thought the sculptor had left off his labors and tapped the back of it lightly with the hammer.

A chip of stone sloughed away, revealing a little more of the nymph's shapely hips.

Zogrusz's heart was beating fast now. He could finish this statue, he was sure of it. All the years he had spent carving his mountain had well-prepared him for this moment. Taking a deep breath, he pressed the chisel once more to the stone and drew back the hammer.

"Papa!"

Startled, Zogrusz just stopped himself mid-swing – if he hadn't, he certainly would have miss-struck the stone and perhaps ruined the statue.

He turned, tingling with relief and surprise, and then was nearly knocked over as a small girl crashed into him. Her arms wrapped around his waist, and he had to grab hold of the nymph's raised elbow to keep from toppling over.

Dark eyes dancing with happiness stared up at him. Her hair was a mess of black curls, and her cinnamon skin glowed in the morning light. Zogrusz wasn't all that familiar with human ages, but he didn't think she could have seen more than five summers.

"Papa, you're awake!"

Zogrusz stared down at her in astonishment. "I . . ." he began, but then was interrupted as an almost ludicrously fat little dog bounded into the grove.

"Look, Waddles!" the girl cried, her breathless attention also drawn to this new intruder. "Papa is back! And he's sculpting again!"

She buried her head in his midsection. Unsure what else to do, Zogrusz began patting her on the head as he looked about in alarm. His gaze settled on the dog, who had plopped down on its pudgy haunches and was staring back at him with idiotic enthusiasm.

"It's good to see you, too . . . Delia," he ventured, finally pulling forth the name the old woman had mentioned earlier.

The girl jerked her head back, her face collapsing into either annoyance or a very mild anger. "Papa," she said sternly. "Are you really feeling better? You haven't called me that in a long time. I'm your little chick, remember?"

"Yes . . . yes, of course," Zogrusz said, his thoughts whirling. What was going on?

"You know, Papa," Delia said, pulling away from him. "I stayed by your bed while you were sick. You said the strangest things!" Her brow drew down, like she was concentrating hard to remember something. "You talked about a fish in the sky and a giant bird and something called a leaper."

Zogrusz blinked in surprise. 'Are you sure I didn't say 'reaper'?"

Delia hopped about in excitement. "You do remember! Oh, I want to know everything you dreamed about, Papa! It sounded so *interesting*." She rushed at him again, and this time he welcomed the embrace. He still felt like an imposter, but it just felt *good* when she clutched at him like this, the purity of her love obvious even though he could not see inside her mind.

What a perfect life this man had. A sculptor with rare skill, the master of this house with its sun-drenched garden, father to a little girl who clearly adored him . . . something twisted inside Zogrusz, and it took him a moment to realize that this was a pang of jealousy.

But why should he feel jealous? Perhaps this was his life, and what had come before nothing but an elaborate fever dream . . .

"*Meow*," said the dog.

"Oh!" Delia snapped crossly, whirling to face the dog with her fists on her hips. "Dogs say '*bark*'!"

The dog tilted its head to one side, staring at her in confusion.

"You had *one thing* to remember!" the girl cried, stamping her feet.

The dog glanced down at itself, inspecting its body like it was seeing it for the first time. "Apologies, little princess," the dog rumbled in a voice Zogrusz knew, its head hanging in shame.

"Origenius?" Zogrusz said numbly, squinting at the dog.

"*Gah*, and this took me *so long* to prepare!" the girl said, reaching up to wrap her tiny hand around his finger. Still not understanding what was going on, he let himself be pulled stumbling over to where the dog cowered. It raised its head, and he was struck by the contrition in its squashed little face. "Oh, don't look at me like that," the girl said crossly, then placed her other hand atop its head, grabbing some of its fur.

"What's going on?" he asked as the girl and the dog both turned to look at him expectantly.

"It's time to go back, Zog," the girl informed him, and her words sent him tumbling into darkness.

Zogrusz clawed awake gasping.

He lay on stone, staring up at the mosaic arching across the ceiling as a storm raged inside his head. Lightning flashes of pain pulsed, making him feel nauseous.

What a bizarre dream. Everything about it had been so real, the details etched as finely as stone carved by a master craftsman . . .

"Wow."

The voice was faint, barely more than a whisper.

Zogrusz sat up abruptly, glancing about in surprise. A small cloaked figure was slumped on the lowest tier of his ziggurat, scraggly strands of blonde hair escaping from within the cowl.

"Qala?" he slurred thickly, all moisture having evaporated from his mouth.

The girl slowly pulled back her hood, clearly exhausted. Her complexion was even paler than usual, but still she managed a shaky grin. "That was exciting, wasn't it?"

"What was?" Zogrusz asked, with some effort rising to his feet. His cavern briefly spun, then settled itself.

"Living another life!" she answered, sliding from the step. She also seemed unsteadied but kept from toppling over until she'd found her balance.

Zogrusz dragged himself across the cavern and collapsed where she had been a moment ago, putting his pounding head in his scaled hands. "You . . . you were in my dream?"

"That wasn't a dream, silly!" Qala cried. "I put our minds into other bodies, and it *worked*!"

Zogrusz kneaded his scalp with his claws. "You mean that 'great project' you told me about? How . . . how did you do it?"

Qala pulled the chunk of black crystal she'd found in the city of the snake-men from the folds of her robes and held it up triumphantly. "The Heart is the key!" she said. "I suspected it might help, but it worked better than I even thought possible!"

The implications of what Qala was telling him slowly filtered through the haze in Zogrusz's head. "That man . . . who was he?"

Qala ignored his question, still staring into the depths of the dark rock. "The problem was never the transfer of consciousnesses . . . it was what happened to the mind that was being pushed out. I was always afraid to try this because I knew it would dissipate like smoke in the wind . . . Ixia certainly wouldn't have cared, but I do! I didn't want to *kill* anyone! But the Heart is the answer." Her fingers stroked the gleaming facets lovingly. "It's capable of holding the memories of an entire race; there's a lattice inside of incredible density, which is also why it's so incredibly hard. What is one more mind? I put the consciousnesses of the sculptor and his daughter and their dog within while we were using their bodies."

"But they'll be all right?"

"Should be!" Qala said. "I suppose I'll have to go check up on them to make sure. But I can sense their minds are gone from the Heart, at least, so I believe I was successful in putting them back." She giggled. "Imagine their confusion when they returned to themselves in the garden standing around staring at the dog!"

The feeling of elephants stampeding through his skull had finally faded, and Zogrusz lifted his head from his hands. "You should be careful. Those were . . . good people." He could still remember the feel of the girl clinging to his waist . . . The memory was a little bittersweet.

"I know," Qala agreed. "I spent a long time looking for someone whose life I thought you would appreciate. And I did a good job, didn't I? If Ori hadn't messed up, I think I might have been able to convince you that *that* was your real life!"

Zogrusz sighed. "The man . . . his life seemed good."

"Thought you'd like it," she said, sounding very satisfied with herself. "Rhas is always going on about how much you like his humans . . . Now you know what it's like to truly be one."

The full understanding of what Qala had done was slowly coming clear to him. Her powers were staggering, far beyond anything he had imagined . . . and perhaps they could be his salvation.

"Qala, could you *protect* a mind from being altered?"

12

Over the following month, Zogrusz devoted himself to repairing the facade of his mountain abode. He dragged the remnants of shattered pillars and broken statues away from the entrance, and then heaved them over the side of a steep cliff. At first, he couldn't bear to watch his hard work explode into fragments far below, but as the cave mouth became clearer of debris, he found his excitement growing about the work he would soon undertake to replace what Anecoya had destroyed.

Zogrusz became so lost in his labors that he didn't realize that others had arrived until the ground suddenly trembled. He turned to find that a huge gnarl of rock and earth had appeared farther down the mountain. Origenius must have ripped off the top of a hill he'd found in a warmer clime, because it was covered in grass speckled with wildflowers, and the sides sloped down gently so that those atop could easily disembark. Which they were doing – Qala was first, of course, her little arms and legs flailing as she hurled herself through the long grass. Behind her came Origenius, keeping pace with his long strides despite not exhibiting nearly the same excitement, and draped around his neck was a familiar moon-colored feline. The stone-man held something long and thin that Zogrusz hadn't seen before, like a staff or a spear, and whatever was affixed to its end glittered darkly in the midday sun.

"Zog!" Qala yelled as she reached the mountain proper and began scrambling over the scree towards him. "Zog!"

Numbness washed through Zogrusz when she came close enough that he could hear the edge of panic in her voice. Something was very wrong.

"Qala, what is it?" he asked when she finally reached him.

She looked disheveled, her blonde hair hanging in scraggly clumps, and her eyes were wild. "It's here," she said between panting breaths, and it took him a moment to realize what she was talking about.

"Where?" he finally asked, a cold fist closing around his heart.

She lifted her face to the cloudless blue. "It's moving through our system – honestly, I don't know how it got so close without me noticing. It just . . . materialized."

Zogrusz took a deep breath, calming his suddenly thundering pulse. He needed to maintain absolute control in this moment . . . and for what was soon to come. "Then this is it. Have you told Anecoya?"

"She's on her way and will be here soon," Qala assured him. "Then we can leave this world and meet the monster before it arrives."

Zogrusz frowned. "You're not accompanying us," he said with finality, glancing at Origenius and Rhas as they came to loom over Qala. The cat and the stone warrior both looked somber, their faces hardened by the seriousness of the situation. "Tell her she's not coming," Zogrusz said, now addressing Rhas.

The cat gazed down at Qala, who had placed her hands on her hips and was staring up at them fiercely. "I've tried, but I can't command her," he said with a sigh.

"It's too dangerous," Zogrusz insisted.

"You need me," Qala countered, jabbing a finger at him and then turning it on herself. "I've been developing a way to protect your mind from the monster. I think I can keep it from transforming you into something terrible . . . but I have to be close by for it to work. Ori has promised to protect me. Won't you, Ori?"

The stone-man dipped his head stiffly. "I will protect you with my life, little princess."

Zogrusz scowled, annoyed that Origenius would support this madness. "Why can't you do this from afar?" he asked, feeling true fear for the first time. It was one thing for beings like Anecoya and Origenius to battle for the fate of this world . . . but not Qala. She was still a child in many ways.

"I can't," she said simply. "I'm not sure if I can explain it clearly. You see, the mind . . . it's like a house. There is a foundation that is permanent, created at the birth of every being, mortal or cosmic. As we grow, we build a structure atop this base through our experiences, which helps shape our personality . . . this is how we become who we are. You were different in that much of the materials for *your* house were taken from something else when you encountered the humans on this world for the first time. But since then, you have continued to grow and evolve into your own unique self. I believe this Reaper will tear down this structure and erect in its place something more similar to what exists in other Eldritch Horrors. Perhaps, if Ixia was right, what you should have been given long ago. When it tries to hit you with this . . . this storm, this hurricane, I have to be nearby so I can reinforce your walls and keep them from collapsing. I can't do something that complex from all the way down here."

Zogrusz flexed his claws in frustration. "But you're saying you think you can protect my mind?"

For the first time, Qala looked uncertain. "Truthfully, I don't know . . . but if anyone can, it's me."

A great weight settled on Zogrusz's shoulders, and he bowed his head. So much would be lost if they failed to turn away the Reaper – and now he had to add Qala to that tally. He had always thought she would use her great powers to avoid the fate of the rest of this world . . . but now he saw she was as willing as the rest of them to give her life to save it. The emotions twisting inside him at this moment were difficult to separate – gratitude and sadness, guilt and fear – although one loomed over everything else: anger that this Horror would destroy everything he cared for.

"Zog," Qala said, and with some effort, he pulled himself from his brooding. "I have something for you."

As if responding to an unspoken command, Origenius stepped forward and held out what he had carried here. It resembled a spear, with a long silvery haft, but its point was strangely warped and uneven. After a moment, Zogrusz realized that this glistening black object was the Heart of the world-mind that Qala had taken from the dead city of the snake-men.

"Ixia told me many times that it's the hardest material in the universe," Qala explained as Zogrusz's hand closed around the spear. The haft felt warm in his grip, and it might have been his imagination, but he felt a thrumming from within.

"I didn't think your claws would do very much against a bigger and stronger Horror, so I asked Ori to make this for you – if anything can hurt the Reaper, it's this."

Zogrusz turned the spear this way and that, watching the light slide along its silvery length and then vanish when it reached the Heart's perfect darkness. He imagined all those souls trapped within its bottomless depths, consigned there by the Reaper's scouring of their world . . . He supposed there was a certain poetic justice if he wielded it now against Ycthitlig.

He could understand why Qala had given him this weapon.

"I shouldn't take it," he told her, but he knew he sounded half-hearted. "When I grow to the full extent of my true form it will be like I'm holding a needle."

"A needle stabbed in the right spot is still very uncomfortable," Qala told him. "Ori and Annie have their blades. You needed a weapon."

His claws tightened around the haft, pulling the spear closer to his body. "Very well."

She grinned, her expression suddenly brightening like the sky after a summer storm. Then she glanced up, shielding her eyes against the sun. Zogrusz followed where she was looking and saw a blazing comet, etched against the blue.

"Ah, Annie's here. It's time."

~

THEY WAITED in the cold dark for the apocalypse to arrive.

Behind them, the world shimmered like a fresh-polished jewel, glistening azure wrapped by ribbons of white. Zogrusz remembered his first glimpse of this planet, wracked by hunger and exhausted after his long wanderings. The colors, so rich and vibrant, had awed him after standing upon so many dead wastelands of gray dust and pockmarked rock. He had hoped that his journey was finally over, that he had found whatever he had been searching for. And he had, but it had only been the beginning of his story.

He looked to his left, where Anecoya blazed in all her cosmic glory, her burning wings outspread. She looked to have been changed by their voyage to find the Wanderer, as if she'd fed and grown stronger on the light of that alien star. Zogrusz could feel the heat emanating from her, pushing back the freezing void, an aura of roiling energy that made his scales tingle. Her raptor gaze was fixed on the blackness, waiting for anything that might emerge.

On his right floated the same great chunk of earth that Origenius had brought to his mountain, but the grass and flowers that had covered its surface had long since succumbed to the cold. The stone warrior stood like a statue amid this withered vegetation, his malachite sword unsheathed, his faceted eyes reflecting the starlight. Between his legs, Qala sat cross-legged, plucking the petals of an ashen flower and letting them float away into the darkness.

Anecoya's voice drifted across the bridge linking their minds. *<Are you certain, child? I still see nothing>*

<It is coming> Qala responded with absolute certainty. *<I've never sensed anything so different . . . so cold. Like the emptiness between the stars>*

<I feel it as well> Zogrusz said. *<It feels like the void>* A

presence brushed his mind, heavy and vast, and he winced. Ycthitlig also knew he was here. That he meant to oppose it, and was willing to sacrifice his very existence if it meant this world would survive. The Reaper did not care. It was not worried, or surprised, or even amused. It felt nothing except the hunger that drove it on, the desire to consume the flickering consciousnesses that would bring it another step closer to becoming one of the dreamers in the darkness.

A frisson of surprise went through Zogrusz when he suddenly realized that a small patch of stars in the vast sweep of the cosmos had disappeared, winking out of existence like they had been extinguished. He adjusted his grip on the spear, trying to calm himself by exploring the fortifications Qala had erected in his mind. High ramparts and deep-sunk walls protecting his inner self, a bastion that surely Ycthitlig could not tear down.

At least before Zogrusz could shove the spear into him.

More stars vanished, as if somewhere out there an abyss was swelling larger, or a great maw was devouring the universe. Zogrusz knew what it was. The Horror was approaching, and its size must be immense if it was already occluding so many of the glimmering points of light. The others had seen it as well, and their minds seethed with the fear they no longer bothered to hide.

A world destroyer had come.

Ycthitlig emerged from the darkness. An eye appeared first, larger than Zogrusz at the fullest extent of his true form, a slitted black pupil set in a sea of sickly yellow. It was the color of jaundice, of infection, pus leaking from a festering wound. Surrounding this was a narrow ring of flesh set with gnashing mouths, each of these fanged orifices far smaller than the eye but still large enough to swallow any of them whole. These openings gnawed at the darkness idiotically, as if they could draw sustenance from the emptiness. Around these mouths was the bulk of Ycthitlig's form, though when set against the blackness of space, its dimensions were still not entirely clear – Zogrusz could apprehend a vast profusion of dark tentacles like the arms of a monstrous sea anemone, undulating madly.

<Ugly bastard>

Zogrusz's paralysis broke as Anecoya's words bloomed in his mind. He glanced over at the Phoenix and saw that her feathers were blazing brighter as she drew power into herself. He could sense her fear, but then she crushed this rogue emotion beneath iron determination, and he couldn't help but feel pride at her strength of will. He worked to match her, thrusting aside the terror that wanted to turn his insides to water and replacing it with anger about what this Horror had come to do to his world. He would fight for Rhas, for the humans and all the beauty they brought to the universe, for his friends who would stand so bravely against this emissary of the ravenous void.

Zogrusz surged forward brandishing the spear, his bellowed war cry swallowed by the airless dark.

Ycthitlig's great eye shifted, focusing on him, and the full power of its attention slammed into the mental defenses Qala had prepared . . . and tore through them like they were cobwebs. Zogrusz gasped as the Reaper's mind entered his own, reeling from the touch of its cold thoughts. His limbs spasmed, and he just managed to keep hold of the spear.

<THIS ONE COMES TO GREET US, BUT NOT THRUM-MING WITH GRATEFUL JOY. TAINTED THE SOWER OF THIS WORLD IS, POISONED BY THE WEAKNESSES OF LESSER BEINGS. A CLEANSING MUST BE DONE>

<No> Zogrusz croaked, barely able to form this telepathic objection as he fought to regain control over his juddering body. He felt another being enter his mind, something bright and sharp and brimming with righteous fury. Ycthitlig's vast presence recoiled for the briefest of moments, but then it descended like an avalanche upon this defender. It was Qala, he was sure of it, a tiny mote holding back the tide of darkness . . . and for a moment it seemed like she might do it, that she would shelter Zogrusz's inner self from the Reaper. But then the unexpected happened. Something deep in Zogrusz's subconscious answered Ycthitlig's call, a seed that had long been dormant in the soil of his mind. Racial memories spilled forth, bubbling up from below even as the older Eldritch Horror pressed down from above. Zogrusz felt Qala's anguished cry as she was crushed between these two implacable forces.

<Flee> Zogrusz begged her as she desperately fought to keep his sense of self from guttering out. He felt her refusal, but the power arrayed against her was simply overwhelming, and with a final raging cry she was forcibly ejected from his mind. The Reaper's will flooded into the sanctuary where she had tried to preserve him and

Zogrusz

FELT who

HE WAS

. . .

SHATTER.

AND YET.

AND YET.

When the tide of Ycthitlig receded, it left something behind that was unbroken. Seamless. Untroubled by doubts or any of the petty emotions that he knew had once concerned him.

He was reborn – no, he had finally emerged from the cocoon that had coddled and constrained him since his emergence in the dark beyond the stars.

He was pure. He was perfect. The void fashioned into flesh and given purpose.

\<REJOICE, SOWER, FOR YOU ARE WHOLE\>

FLOATING IN THE EMPTINESS, Zogrusz watched the battle unfold with detached curiosity. On the hilltop Origenius had compelled into space, Qala huddled among the dead vegetation with her head in her hands. The jagged face of the stone warrior looming over her was twisted into an expression of rage – he gestured sharply, and chunks of stone and earth tore free from around them and hurtled towards the Reaper. These newly-created comets could have knocked over a city's walls, but the massive Horror seemed not to even notice as they impacted against its flesh and broke apart.

Zogrusz shifted his attention to Anecoya. The blazing Phoenix was like a loosed arrow as she shot straight for

Ycthitlig, wings tucked into her sides, copper beak flashing. She meant to plunge into the great eye, Zogrusz knew, blinding the Horror as she ripped and tore at the jellied flesh.

He also knew this would never happen.

Serpents of glistening darkness twisted into existence, wrapping around Anecoya's body and wings. She broke off her attack, her flames swelling brighter as she thrashed, desperately trying to free herself from the constricting tendrils. Fire crawled along the oily lengths of these bonds but did not consume them, nor could she wrest herself from their clutches. Anecoya opened her beak to give a soundless shriek as she was dragged struggling towards the waiting Horror.

Zogrusz glanced down when he felt the thready pulses welling from the spear in his hand suddenly quicken. Ribbons of blackness like spilled ink were twisting in the depths of the jagged dark crystal affixed to the end of the haft. How interesting. A thought occurred to him, and he looked to the chunk of land floating nearby. As he suspected, Qala had raised her head and was staring at him intensely, her arm stretched out like she was trying to grasp something just out of reach. Another great throbbing passed down the length of the spear, and it almost felt like tiny worms were burrowing into his flesh where his hands touched the smooth metal . . .

Qala and Origenius disappeared as a vast tentacle smashed down on the stolen hilltop. It exploded in absolute silence into countless smaller pieces of spinning rock and earth, utterly obliterated.

The prickling sensation in his palms stopped.

Zogrusz turned from the rapidly expanding cloud of debris as Ycthitlig's great arm retracted trailing a glittering tail of ice and frozen dust. He wondered if the stone-man had survived this blow – the fragile, fleshy girl was certainly dead, but he supposed it was possible Origenius still clung to life.

It did not matter. Zogrusz knew the stone warrior did not have the power to threaten Ycthitlig – they were all insects before the terrible grandeur and beauty of the Reaper. So many of the lesser emotions that had poisoned Zogrusz had been excised when the Horror had revealed to him his true nature, but still he felt a thrill of excitement and anticipation gazing upon the glorious creature he would one day become.

Why had he once cared for these other beings? This world? The only thing that mattered in the universe was the progression from frail Sower to the divine glory of a Great Old One. Everything else was but a tool or an obstacle to be overcome on this path.

Anecoya's thrashing grew more frantic as she neared Ycthitlig's endlessly gnawing mouths. Zogrusz remembered how she had stood over him in the ruin of his temple façade, mocking his weakness. A voice in the back of his head whispered that he should feel shame for that moment and anger for all her insults and sneering rudeness. And yet he did not.

He felt nothing as she was dragged into a mouth and consumed.

Ycthitlig's great eye swiveled to focus on Zogrusz once more.

<COME, SOWER. THIS WORLD AWAITS ITS RECKONING>

∼

Wisps of white clung to the Reaper as it descended through the clouds. Below them spread a dun and sere landscape riven by great fissures. There was life in this place – as there was life everywhere on this world – but it was simple and sparse. Zogrusz turned to the Reaper in confusion.

<*Why here, Ancient One? Elsewhere, there are those that already fear and worship us*>

Great tendrils writhed, causing vast shadows to twist across the badlands.

<*WE SHALL SAVOR THIS WORLD. LONG HAS OUR JOURNEY BEEN, AND LONG WILL BE THE FEASTING. BEFORE WE GORGE ON THE SWEETEST FRUIT OUR APPETITES WE SHALL WHET. THIS ONE SHOULD EXTEND THEIR PERCEPTION AND REALIZE WHAT WE ALREADY KNOW*>

Zogrusz followed the Reaper's suggestion, sending his awareness over the land. He sensed insects stalked by lizards, snakes coiled in rocky crevices, birds cowering in cliff-side nests as they peered up at what had suddenly appeared in the sky.

<*I feel it*> Zogrusz said. At the very edge of his reach, he apprehended many, many minds. Not a herd of animals – no, this was an eddying swirl of dreams and desires that danced upon his tongue and made his mouth water in anticipation.

<*LEAD THE WAY, SOWER*> the Reaper commanded, and Zogrusz hurled himself towards this gathering of humans.

Reddish-brown wastes flowed beneath him, stark and empty. He knew that in the before-time he would have been curious how the humans had survived in such numbers in this harsh land, but now he was not interested in the slightest. All that mattered was the Harvest.

They arrived at a city within a canyon, built into its soaring walls. Countless holes pricked the rock, doors and windows that Zogrusz knew led into a hive of rooms and passageways. Huge rope bridges spanned the chasm, and as Ycthitlig's shadow plunged the city into darkness, the humans who had been caught crossing fled. Other consciousnesses watched them in terror from the openings in the canyon's walls . . . and then a torrent of panic struck Zogrusz, flooding the pathways sunk beneath his flesh. His body convulsed, disrupting the rhythm of his beating wings, and he nearly plummeted from the sky.

It was overwhelming.

Zogrusz struggled to form coherent thoughts as this searingly sweet nectar washed through him. He hovered there, dazed, as Ycthitlig descended towards the city and its tunnels filled with scurrying humans. Great tendrils thrust down, plunging into the rock on either side of the canyon – the Reaper was so large that it straddled the wide gap, hovering above the lattice of rope bridges. Fractures appeared in the walls, and then great chunks of stone sloughed away and plunged into the canyon's depths, tearing through the bridges as they fell. The terror welling up from the inhabitants of the city continued to strengthen, islands of white light dancing in Zogrusz's vision.

Black liquid poured from Ycthitlig's many mouths, thick and viscous. It flowed towards the tendrils that the Reaper had shoved into the ground and then slid down their glistening lengths to slip within the shattered stone.

The glimmering points of consciousness inside the canyon city began to go dark, like candles being snuffed. Zogrusz imagined the dark fluid pouring through the underground passages, seeping around the edges of hastily shut doors, seeking the humans as they cowered and begged their gods for salvation. Dissolving flesh and bones and minds. This flood swept through the warren, leaving utter silence in its wake. No whimpering thoughts, no stricken mewling.

Nothing.

And then the blackness returned. It welled from the cracks in the ground like blood from a wound, coursing along the surface until it arrived again at Ycthitlig's great arms. Rippling with a will of its own, it climbed up the tendrils until it reached the same gnashing mouths from which it had vomited forth and entered the Reaper once more.

Ycthitlig, the Crawling Dread.

All this Zogrusz watched with interest. He was sorry that the exquisite gushing of fear had ended so abruptly, but he knew this was the way of things. It was why the Reaper had come. During this time Zogrusz would nibble at the edges of this great feast, and it would push him farther along in his progression, and when this world was nothing but an empty husk he would depart. And if he was worthy, one day he would conduct his own Harvest, glutting himself on the dreams and fears of an entire species.

Zogrusz shivered at the thought, wracked by glorious anticipation.

Rending crashes sounded as Ycthitlig withdrew its arms from the stone, then ascended into the sky. To Zogrusz, it looked sated by what it had done here.

Bloated.

<WITH US, SOWER. WE CONTINUE>

~

THE CRACKED and stony ground of the tablelands eventually gave way to rolling sand dunes. Life was even rarer here – only once did Zogrusz sense anything more complex than desert mice, when they passed over a shimmering oasis fringed by palm trees and a few dust-stained tents. Ycthitlig proved disinterested in this paltry morsel, and it did not slow its progress to pluck the humans where they gaped from the water's edge. The Reaper was intent on their next destination – Zogrusz suspected that it knew far more about this world than he had realized. Perhaps its possession of the pilgrim Izel was not the only time Ycthitlig had visited.

Night fell, the swells of sand beneath them glowing silver in the moonlight. Dark patches of scrub eventually broke the monotony, and by the time a bloody dawn stained the horizon, they were drifting over an arid steppe. It was nowhere near as barren as the desert – great herds of animals bounded away from Ycthitlig's shadow, their curving horns glittering in the sun. There were more humans as well here, fighting to control panicked horses or huddled inside painted yurts. Again, Ycthitlig ignored them.

The climate slowly changed as they traveled. They reached a great sweep of jungle, the air trembling with an almost febrile thickness. Sweat sheathed Zogrusz's skin, glistening on his scales, and he was reminded of his first moments on this world when he'd encountered the People and absorbed some of their humanity. He also remembered that in that long-ago time he'd felt curiosity about what inhabited this world. He had deeply desired to meet others. Now those compulsions felt juvenile, even pathetic. Ycthitlig had torn away not just what had been imprinted in that forest clearing long ago but also the lingering remnants of the being that he had been ever since he'd first emerged from the void.

Zogrusz was grateful.

They flew over the trackless tangle until with jarring suddenness a city emerged. Most of it was comprised of low stone buildings of simple design, but rising from within this sprawl was a huge black ziggurat, so large it would have towered over even the great dome of Amotla. Each tier was taller than Zogrusz's true form, and a thousand steps climbed one of its four steep sides.

Terror rose from the humans here as Ycthitlig came to hover over the top of the ziggurat. Zogrusz was expecting the black liquid to spill from the Reaper's mouths and pour down the steps to the city below, so he was surprised when instead he heard Ycthitlig's telepathic command sweep out over the city.

Zogrusz wondered if the lords of this place would dare defy the Reaper, but he did not have to wait long before he had his answer. A large number of copper-skinned humans emerged from among the buildings, herded forward by warriors bearing spears. Behind this crowd, a man wearing a colorful headdress of iridescent feathers urged them on, gesturing empathically at the Eldritch Horror hanging over the city like a blackened sun.

Zogrusz's taloned feet settled on the top of the ziggurat, and he leaned upon his spear to wait, for he had seen in the images the Reaper had sent out that this was where the humans were coming. Some, of course, tried to flee and died by spearpoint. Most were driven to the base of the ziggurat, and after yet more threats, they began to climb the steep steps.

Ycthitlig had claimed in its message it only wanted adulation. That after the humans reached the top of the ziggurat and prostrated themselves in worship they would be spared.

But that, of course, was not what happened.

The first to finish the ascent was an old man with ancient battle scars slashing across his bare chest. He collapsed to his knees, raising his trembling arms in supplication to the Reaper that had plunged the city into darkness. And in response, a shadowy filament materialized, wrapping around the elder's waist and lifting him into the air.

The man's quavering wail abruptly ended as he was stuffed into one of Ycthitlig's gnashing mouths.

Chaos ensued. A ripple of panic went through the long line of humans climbing the steps. Most had seen the old man disappear into the Reaper's maw, and now they pushed and shoved in their frantic haste to descend the ziggurat. Bodies tumbled from the stairs to be dashed on the stone far below. And from where he stood at the edge of the highest tier, Zogrusz drank deep of the intoxicating fear. It had a sharper flavor, one he instinctively knew derived from their intense desperation, and it made him shiver with delight.

More serpents of darkness reached down to pluck the humans from the steps, and dozens were pulled screaming into Ycthitlig's mouths. The warriors in the streets below were also fleeing, scattering among the smaller buildings, but Zogrusz knew that in the end none would be spared.

For the Harvest was not yet complete.

THREE DAYS LATER, they departed the jungle city, leaving behind an empty, echoing ruin. They soared northward, over sea and veldt and mountains that scraped the sky, with this jagged range eventually subsiding into a plain that seemed familiar to Zogrusz. His memories of the time before the awakening of his new true self were hazy, as if they had happened to another being. But they proved accurate, for after a long journey across these grasslands, Zogrusz glimpsed white towers gleaming in the far distance, ringing a great dome that since last he'd seen it had been sheathed in copper. It flashed in the bright sun, drawing them onwards like moths to a flame.

Towards Amotla, the Queen of Cities.

13

Zogrusz basked in the river of dread flowing from the city. This was the wellspring for his worship; here the vintage had been aged the longest, its flavor deepening and becoming more complex. He suspected it would be the most delicious meal in the twilight of this world, and he was mildly surprised that Ycthitlig had come here so early in the feasting. But who was he to question the actions of an Old One? If now was when the Reaper decided to consume the city, then so be it.

<HOLD> Ycthitlig commanded, the unexpected message booming in Zogrusz's mind. He glanced in confusion at the Reaper and found that it had come to a halt hovering above the umber grass with its tendrils writhing and eye fixed on something ahead. Zogrusz saw immediately what had drawn its attention. A palanquin of white wood broke the monotony of the plains, its crimson curtains drawn closed. There was no sign of those who had carried it here, but the one who must have been its occupant was standing nearby. The woman was late in her middle years, her once fair hair now threaded with gray, twining flowers picked out in

colorful thread on her fine silken robes. A silver circlet rested on her brow, and in her arms she held a moon-colored cat.

Zogrusz extended a telepathic tendril and was surprised to realize he had felt her mind before. She had been a child then, afraid for the kitten lost in the priest-king's garden. Now she also felt fear, though it was far more muted than he would have expected, given the circumstances. And it was not fear for her own life, but for the lives of all who remained behind her in the city, those who had not yet taken to the ships and fled into the sea.

<That cat is the world-mind> he sent to Ycthitlig as the Reaper drifted slowly towards where the queen waited.

<WE KNOW> came its echoing answer. *<THIS VERMIN SURPRISES. IN PAST CULLINGS THEY SCURRY AND HIDE, EMERGING TO PLEAD FOR MERCY AS THE LAST ARE CONSUMED. NEVER HAVE THEY DARED TO CONFRONT US SO EARLY. IT IS BRAZEN>*

<It was close to me before you excised the corruption from my mind. Perhaps it believes some vestige of my old self remains>

<FOOLISH> Ycthitlig rumbled. *<BUT WE ADMIT TO CURIOSITY. LET US HEAR WHAT IT WOULD SAY>*

They descended, the wind created by the Reaper's writhing arms flattening the grass and making the queen's long hair dance. Zogrusz's taloned feet sank into the soft earth while Ycthitlig remained hovering, its pendulous body nearly brushing the ground.

"Zog." Rhas's voice cut through the wind like a knife.

"World-mind," Zogrusz replied, adjusting his clawed grip on the silver haft of his spear. "You are brave to meet us."

Rhas's tail lashed. "If there is any place where you might be swayed, it is here."

Zogrusz's mouth-tendrils fluttered in amusement. "Swayed?"

"To stop what you are doing," Rhas said. "I felt what has already happened elsewhere, the extinguishing of so many. Surely you do not want to see the same done to this city. You must remember your feelings about this place, how the beauty of its artisans stirred your soul."

Zogrusz shook his head slowly. "You speak of another. That one is dead, cast out. The Crawling Dread has poured the soul of an Eldritch Horror into the absence that was created. I am what I was always meant to be."

"Are you?" Rhas responded sharply. "I was there watching when you arrived on my world. I witnessed your first meeting with my humans – even then you sought companionship, Zog. That was your truest self."

Zogrusz tried to think back to that time, but his memories were muddled. He remembered being confused, uncertain, lost. He was none of those things now, and his purpose had been revealed to him with blinding clarity.

"Dark Lord."

The interruption surprised Zogrusz, and he looked to the woman holding Rhas. He heard only the slightest trembling in her voice, even though she stood in the shadow of Ycthitlig's dreadful majesty.

"Do you know me? We spoke in a garden long ago."

"I know you," Zogrusz replied.

"Then you must remember that you told me you had come to destroy my city, that we had displeased you. Something I said made you change your mind. Please, Dark Lord, we have exalted you, holding you as most high among all the gods and spreading your words to far-away lands. I beg you to show us mercy again, as you once did before."

Another memory emerged from the haze in his mind, of

standing in the priest-king's garden with a kitten in his hand. The girl beside him had contained a soul unsullied by even the smallest blemish, so pure it had made his heart ache.

Something stirred deep inside him, but Zogrusz brutally tamped it down. His claws tightened on the spear he held, scoring its metal.

<*ENOUGH*> Ycthitlig bellowed, and they all winced from the force. <*MY PATIENCE IS AT AN END*>

Serpents of shadow twisted into existence, slithering towards the woman standing beside the palanquin.

"To the abyss with you, monster!" hissed Rhas, baring his teeth at the looming Reaper. "You do not even have the courage to ask your Sower to destroy me, for you know he cannot! I sense his wavering!"

The strands of killing darkness hesitated, then dwindled into shreds of nothingness. Something Rhas had said must have struck true, because for the first time Zogrusz felt anger swelling in the Reaper.

<*YOU THINK THIS ONE IS STILL TAINTED? SUCH AUDACITY, VERMIN. AND YOU DARE CALL US MONSTER? WE ARE NO DIFFERENT FROM YOU*>

"Lies," Rhas snarled before leaping down from the queen's arms. His hackles were raised, as if such a display could somehow deter the Reaper's wrath. "We are life, and you are death."

<*WE ARE THE SAME*> Ycthitlig thundered. <*HOW MANY LESSER BEINGS DO EACH OF YOUR HUMANS EAT IN THEIR LIFETIME? COUNTLESS. THE STRONG CONSUME THE WEAK – THIS IS THE LAW OF THE UNIVERSE. YOU RAGE WHEN YOU BECOME THE PREY, BUT WHERE WAS YOUR INDIGNATION WHEN YOUR*

HUMANS WERE THE PREDATORS PERCHED ATOP THIS WORLD?>

"If you are so certain of your superiority, command the Sower to destroy me," Rhas retorted. "Let us see if he truly shares your nature."

<THERE IS NOTHING LEFT OF WHAT HE WAS> The Reaper's focus shifted to Zogrusz. *<SOWER! DESTROY THIS CREATURE>*

"Yes, Great One," Zogrusz muttered, shaking his head to clear it. Rhas darted away as he stalked forward, disappearing beneath the raised frame of the palanquin.

<WHERE IS YOUR CONFIDENCE, VERMIN?> Ycthitlig gloated as Zogrusz crouched down with his spear poised to stab the cat if it tried to run again.

Rhas growled at him from where he was hunkered behind one of the far poles supporting the litter. Zogrusz sneered, drawing back his spear.

Cloth rustled above him, and something emerged from within the palanquin's curtain to lightly brush the top of his head.

It was as if he'd been struck by lightning. Zogrusz jerked upright, but before he could see what had touched him he felt a powerful quiver travel through the haft of the spear, and the weapon jumped like it was trying to tear itself from his grip. It had started where the dark crystal was affixed, and then surged in the span of a heartbeat down its length until it reached his claws.

And

something

happened.

Zogrusz reeled back, stumbling upright as a crackling energy passed through him. He stared in shocked wonder at

the Heart . . . then without hesitating turned to the massive
Reaper and hurled the spear at it with all his strength.
Ycthitlig's great eye widened in surprise just before the weapon
pierced the very center of its pupil and vanished into its depths.

For a frozen moment, nothing happened.

And then, chaos.

A wave of force rippled out from the Reaper, every one
of its distended mouths opening to shriek at the same time.
Zogrusz was knocked backwards, tumbling into the palanquin as the frame shattered into wooden shards. He
bounced on the ground, and when he came to a rest he realized he couldn't see anything because one of the curtains
had somehow become wrapped about his head. Zogrusz
ripped the cloth away as he lurched to his feet, trying to
orient himself even as the world spun madly.

He had changed again. His old self had come rushing
back from somewhere else and collided with the identity
Ycthitlig had forced inside him. *That* dark Zogrusz had not
been completely destroyed, but now it was subordinated to
the being that he had been for centuries, and emotions that
had seemed so alien just moments ago were paramount
once more. He cared for this world and his friends . . . and
he despised the one who had hurt them.

Anger flooded Zogrusz as he focused on the Reaper.
Ycthitlig had crashed to the ground and was thrashing
madly, its vast tendrils drumming the earth. Black pus was
welling up from where the spear had entered its eye, sliding
over its surface like oil, and the keening from its many
mouths was drowning out all other sound. Zogrusz could
feel the pain radiating from the Reaper, a psychic battering
that made it difficult to order his own scattered thoughts.

Movement drew his attention. Something was extricating itself from the remnants of the palanquin, fighting to

be free of clinging silk. A small arm emerged, reaching up to pull aside an errant cloth, revealing matted golden curls . . .

Zogrusz's jaw fell open.

Qala grinned at him, then clapped her hands to her ears and winced as the screams spilling from Ycthitlig sharpened further.

Her voice slipped into his mind. *<Wow, that's annoying>*

Zogrusz could only gape at her. *<You're alive!>*

The sudden cessation of the unholy sounds made them both turn.

"Oh, no," Zogrusz murmured when he saw black bile pouring from the mouths surrounding the blinded eye.

"What *is* that stuff?" Qala asked, wrinkling her nose in disgust.

"It can eat flesh," Zogrusz told her as the liquid reached the ground and began moving in their direction, the grass it flowed over dissolving into wisps of smoke. He glanced around frantically, looking for something they could climb onto to escape the approaching tide, but there was only the destroyed remnants of the palanquin, and he was certain the bile would devour that as well.

"I'll have to carry you into the sky," Zogrusz told her, flexing his stunted wings.

"But what about Rhas?" the girl said in concern, her gaze searching for the world-mind.

"I'm here," came the cat's deep voice as he scurried out from beneath some debris. The queen followed close behind him, looking dazed.

"To me," Zogrusz commanded, nervously watching the black liquid creep closer. He supposed carrying two humans and a cat would be awkward, but not impossible.

The ground lurched, more violently than the shaking caused by Ycthitlig's flailing arms, and Zogrusz stumbled back a step as something erupted from beneath the grass in an explosion of soil.

"Well met, friend Zogrusz," Origenius rumbled, wiping a smear of mud from his rocky face. "I see thou hast returned to us."

Relief filled Zogrusz to see Origenius alive, but he also felt a sharp pang of dismay – there was no way he could carry the stone warrior away from the crawling darkness.

"I can't take you all," he said, unable to keep the edge of panic from his voice.

"Worry not," Origenius said as he drew forth his malachite sword. "This foulness will never reach us." He reversed his blade and thrust downwards, driving half its gleaming length into the earth. The trembling intensified again, and then a fissure opened where the sword pierced the ground. This crack spread rapidly, apparently guided by Origenius's will, widening as it formed a rough circle around where they stood. The black liquid reached this new-made moat almost immediately, pouring over its edges and disappearing.

<TRAITOR! ABOMINATION!> The agony in Ycthitlig's mental screams nearly drove Zogrusz to his knees. *<WE SHALL FEAST UPON YOUR BROKEN BODY AND SUCK THE MARROW FROM YOUR SOUL! YOUR BLOOD –>*

The bone-jarring proclamations abruptly vanished from Zogrusz's head, along with the splitting headache that had accompanied Ycthitlig's enraged presence.

"What –" he began, but before he could finish Qala cut him off.

"I've walled our minds off from the monster," she said with more than a little pride. "While you were doing awful things, I was using what I'd learned from our first encounter to figure out a way to protect us."

Zogrusz did find comfort in Ycthitlig's sudden absence

from his skull, but the Reaper was still very much alive – despite the injury to its eye, its arms continued to thrash about while its mouths spewed forth more of the dark sludge.

"Why are you not dead?" he asked Qala, taking advantage of the momentary reprieve Origenius had granted them.

The little girl nodded at where the stone warrior still knelt with his sword driven into the ground. "It was Ori."

"Rock is the great protector," Origenius said, clearly distracted by what he was doing. Zogrusz thought he must be continuously pushing the chasms deeper so that Ycthitlig's bile could not reach them.

"And how did you . . . bring my old self back?"

"You never went very far," Qala explained with an expression of smug satisfaction.

"But I felt what Ycthitlig did. It shoved the . . . the human part of my mind out of my head and replaced it with the identity of an Eldritch Horror."

"And it also released something deep within you," Qala added, "a fundamental essence that had been waiting a long time to be born. You're different than you were before that monster changed you. Luckily, you seem like the old Zog to me in the most important ways." She staggered as a massive tendril smashed into the earth, shaking the ground and sending up a geyser of dirt. "As to how I brought you back .. . the trick was not letting your personality dissolve as soon as Ycthitlig ejected you from your mind. The timing had to be perfect, and it was. I seized hold of you and pushed you into the Heart and then kept you there for safekeeping. I actually tried to reverse the process immediately so you could help us fight, but the monster disrupted that attempt. And that was when I learned it was really hard to do this from afar with such a powerful mind, so we had to come up with a way to get me close enough to make physical contact."

Zogrusz shook his head, awed by what Qala had done. "You're brilliant."

"Well, the idea was yours," Qala admitted, smacking him lightly on the scaled thigh. "You came up with the plan after I told you I could store minds within the structure of the Heart."

"I don't remember that at all."

"You wouldn't – it was too much of a risk that you'd keep enough of your memories after Ycthitlig altered you that you'd know to abandon the spear. So I cut away the memory of the plan from your mind, with your permission."

"Ah."

"I have to say," Rhas interjected, coming to rub against Zogrusz's leg, "things have gone better than any of us dared hope. But we still have a maddened, wounded Eldritch Horror. Does it need its sight to send out that blackness to cover this world? And how long until it heals itself?"

Zogrusz shrugged helplessly at the cat's questions.

"Friend Rhas," said Origenius, raising a hand from the dark hilt of his sword to point at where the Reaper writhed in agony. "Something is happening."

"What *is* that?" murmured the Amotlan queen, her voice heavy with dread.

Zogrusz peered at the wounded Horror, trying to see what had alarmed the others.

And then he saw it. Strange things were squirming from the ragged gash in the middle of Ycthitlig's eye – they resembled huge maggots, but their forms were strangely insubstantial, almost wraith-like. And after wriggling along the eye's broken membrane, they passed onto the Reaper's flesh, spreading out across its body.

"I don't think those things are part of Ycthitlig," Zogrusz said slowly as more and more of the long, ghostly shapes poured from where the spear had punctured the eye. The Reaper's movements had become more frantic, its limbs juddering madly, as if it was attempting to dislodge the swarming entities.

"Do you know what they look like?" Qala murmured, glancing at Rhas. The cat stood perfectly still, watching intently.

"The snake-men," Zogrusz realized, remembering the way the dead inhabitants of the underground city had moved. It did truly look like the same sort of slithering . . .

"S'skesspa's revenge," Rhas whispered. "That Heart is full of souls reaped by an Eldritch Horror . . . and we know the world-mind within remembers what happened."

"I wonder if transferring other minds in and out of the crystal allowed for this to happen," Qala said, running a hand through her snarled yellow hair.

"If only there was a giant snake skeleton buried under the ground here that the world-mind could possess," Zogrusz muttered, remembering the feeling of those sharp bones pressing into his flesh.

"It looks like they're doing well enough anyway," Rhas said, his tail lashing back and forth in excitement.

Zogrusz had to agree. The torrent of bile pouring from the Reaper's many mouths had stopped, and the movement of its arms had grown more sluggish. It was hard to tell from this great distance, but to Zogrusz it looked like the wraiths were worrying at Ycthitlig's flesh, rivulets of greenish ichor dripping from where they were fastened. The Reaper's massive body was visibly deflating, sagging into the grass-lands like a punctured bladder.

And then it was still.

"Oh, wow," Qala breathed, and he felt her little fingers tighten around one of his claws. "I think it's dead."

The ghost snakes certainly seemed to believe this as well. The edges of their hazy forms trembled, and then at the same time they began to dissipate like smoke in strong wind. In moments they were gone, leaving behind lacerated eldritch flesh and splotches of green ichor.

"Look!" Qala cried, releasing his claw to point emphatically at the ravaged Reaper. "It's still alive!"

It took Zogrusz a moment of closely examining the vast Horror to find what she had noticed. Most of Ycthitlig's mouths were still, trickles of bile leaking from slack jaws, but one down near where the body of the creature rested on the grasslands was moving strangely. The lipless maw twitched, then opened wider as something emerged.

Qala gasped, and Rhas made a strangled mewling sound.

The figure was almost completely coated in blackness, but patches of red were still visible beneath the gunk matting her hair. She placed one hand on the bottom of the mouth and another on the top, then wrenched it wider. This violent action was so angry that Zogrusz would have guessed who this was even if he hadn't seen her swallowed.

Anecoya clambered down from the mouth and dropped to the grass below. She wiped oily liquid from her face, then aimed a vicious kick at the rubbery flesh closest to her.

"Annie!" Rhas cried, and Zogrusz turned to see that the world-mind had swelled to the size of a large tiger and was gathering himself to leap across the crevice separating them.

He cleared it easily, and then the great cat was racing across the still-steaming swamp of sludgy grass.

"*Aw*," Qala murmured as Rhas reached Anecoya and nearly knocked her over with overly-exuberant nuzzling. She collapsed into him, wrapping her arms around his neck.

"Excuse my impertinence, Dread Lord," the Amotlan queen asked, her voice sounding strained. Which was understandable, he supposed, given everything she had just witnessed. "But who is *that*?"

"The goddess Anecoya," he replied.

"Oh," she said softly and then fainted.

EPILOGUE

"**P**ardon, child, but you want to do *what*?"

Qala set the greenstone statue of Zogrusz back down on the desk and smiled in sweet innocence at the Amotlan queen.

"I want to be a goddess," she said, running her finger along the edge of the intricately carved wooden surface in front of her. With her other hand she waved vaguely at the others standing behind her. "We all do," she continued, but then frowned. "No, wait, not Zog and Ori. They want to be gods."

One of the cats sprawled on the desk among the clutter of books and bric-a-brac lifted its head to stare at Qala, then stretched languidly and yawned. It did not seem nearly as surprised as her mistress.

The queen swallowed, raising her eyes to the dome arching over their heads. What had previously been displayed on its underside – a fiery bird emerging from a golden egg – had been painted over with an image of Zogrusz in his true form dictating the Book of Zog to a kneeling Cozotl. He suspected Anecoya had already noticed this and was silently seething.

The queen tugged at the hem of her beautifully embroidered robes. "But, child . . . *are* you a goddess?"

"Does it matter?" Qala replied without hesitation, tracing a flower that had been engraved into the desk.

The queen coughed nervously. "The official position of my royal house is that our Dark Lord Zogrusz"— she dipped her head respectfully towards him with her hands pressed together—"is the only true god, although we still of course allow for the worship of the Reborn Goddess."

Anecoya snorted, and the queen winced like she expected to be struck down for her insolence.

Zogrusz was glad his mouth-tendrils hid his smile, as he didn't want to provoke the Phoenix any further. The last few days had been hard enough on her. Anecoya had somehow survived inside Ycthitlig without suffering any permanent damage, but every time he had seen her since they had moved into the palace of Amotla, she looked to have come straight from the bath. Her once-pale skin was now pink from scrubbing, and her red curls were perpetually damp.

He couldn't blame her, honestly.

Zogrusz realized the queen was staring at him almost pleadingly. For a moment he was confused as to why, and then it dawned on him. Of course. She would never agree to any changes in the foundations of her faith with her god standing a dozen paces away.

He stepped forward, resting a claw on the copy of his scriptures lying open on her desk. "A new era has dawned," he intoned, trying to infuse his words with as much gravitas as possible. "Now the people of this world will have a pantheon. They may worship whichever divinity most appeals to them."

"A pantheon," the queen murmured.

"Yes!" Qala cried, clapping her hands together. "And we shall all represent different things. Ori can be the god of the earth and warriors and making boring old oaths."

"I would perform mine duties honorably if granted such a place," rumbled the hulking stone warrior. "This I swear."

"See?" the little girl said. "He's perfect. And Zog, since he needs to be feared, I suppose he has to be the god of night or death or something like that. Even though he's actually very sweet."

"Sweet?" the queen gasped, her eyes widening before she quickly controlled herself.

"Yeah, in all honesty, Anecoya would be a better dark lord," Qala continued, jerking a thumb at the glowering goddess. "She can be really scary."

"Unlike the Eldritch Horror, I need my worshippers to love me," Anecoya said through gritted teeth. "So I suppose I'll have to try to be more . . . friendly."

"And what will you be?" Zogrusz asked Qala, now not bothering to hide his amusement.

"I'll be a trickster!" the little girl exclaimed, puffing out her chest. "Goddess of mischief and being sneaky. I tricked that Reaper, didn't I?"

"That you did," Zogrusz agreed. "Although I suppose in truth it was *my* plan, even if I'd been made to forget it."

"I shouldn't have told you that," Qala said with a sigh. "Then you'd all think I was brilliant."

"Methinks thou are brilliant, little princess," Origenius interjected solemnly.

"Why, thank you," Qala said, turning to him and dropping into a curtsy.

"Goddess of mischief makes sense to me," Anecoya

agreed. "Since that would also be the goddess of being annoying."

Qala replied to this by sticking out her tongue.

The Amotlan queen looked dazed by the banter, though Zogrusz had to admit she was handling the events of the last few days with remarkable aplomb, better even than her late father. Cozotl had only had to deal with one cosmic being, not a veritable cavalcade.

"We will need to codify this . . . pantheon," the queen said slowly, gesturing at the open book on her desk. "Nothing helps spread the word like a sacred text. My father wrote the Book of Zog, and before that we had the Burning Scrolls"—she swallowed as Anecoya coughed pointedly— "so I believe if you truly wish to promulgate a new faith, we will need to write down its founding myths."

"Wonderful!" Qala cried, bouncing up and down in excitement. "Oh, I have all sorts of stories to put in our book! First, we need to set the scene." She cleared her throat loudly, and when next she spoke her voice was an octave lower. "It was a black and formless void. There was no light, because light hadn't been made yet. And into this darkness swam a fish." She paused, frowning at the queen. "Are you writing this down? I might forget it if I have to repeat myself."

"Uh, yes, divine child," the queen murmured, scrabbling amongst the mess on her desk for a quill and a sheet of blank parchment. "I'm ready now."

As Qala resumed her babbling, Zogrusz wandered across the royal study to where a table had been set in front of an open window. Several more cats were lazing here in the late afternoon sun, including Rhas. The world-mind looked as peaceful as Zogrusz had ever seen him, his eyes closed and a satisfied smile on his face. His good mood might have been because a calico cat was curled beside him, licking the top of his head vigorously.

Zogrusz folded his arms across his chest, staring out the window at the fading day. Through Amotla's forest of minarets he could glimpse patches of dark flesh, the vast corpse of Ycthitlig rising like a mountain on the plains beyond the city walls.

"Do you think another will come?"

Zogrusz glanced at Rhas, who had spoken without opening his eyes. "I don't know," he replied. "Are you worried? You don't look worried."

"Perhaps I should be, but at this moment I simply want to enjoy our victory." Rhas's golden eyes slid open. "It was your victory, Zog. You struck the killing blow."

Zogrusz shrugged. "We all played a part. And Ycthitlig never would have even come here if it wasn't for me. The blood of many are on my claws."

Rhas's tail flicked back and forth. "Don't dwell on that. It wasn't you."

"That monster was what I should have been."

A low rumbling issued from the world-mind, which Zogrusz interpreted as vehement disagreement. The cat beside Rhas paused in its cleaning and stared at him, as if affronted by the sound.

"I was not lying to you out there on the plains – I remember what you were like when you arrived, before you met my humans. You were never callous and cruel. You came to my world because you wanted companionship, not to consume. Ycthitlig remade you in its image, but that was not what you truly are."

Zogrusz fell silent, watching the amber light gild the city's white towers. He wanted to tell Rhas how much comfort his words gave him, but he was certain the world-mind already knew.

"Whatever comes next, we will be ready to protect this world," Zogrusz finally said, running a curving claw through Rhas's fur. This elicited a pleased purring, and the cat closed his eyes again in contentment.

The calico cat who had been cleaning Rhas still looked mildly perturbed, its gaze flicking from Zogrusz to Rhas and back again.

"Rhas, old boy," it suddenly said, causing Zogrusz's mouth tendrils to go slack with surprise. "Is this the chap you've been telling our secrets?"

AUTHOR'S NOTE

Thank you so much for reading Zog's story! I had a tremendous amount of fun writing this book, and I truly hope you enjoyed your reading. Reviews are of incredible importance to authors, so if you have the time and the inclination I would be very pleased to receive a review on Amazon or Goodreads.

Again, thank you so much, and happy reading.

Alec

ABOUT THE AUTHOR

Alec Hutson grew up in a geodesic dome and a bookstore and he currently lives in Shanghai, China. If you would like to keep current with his writing, please sign up for his newsletter at www.authoralechutson.com.

ALSO BY ALEC HUTSON

The Raveling (Epic Fantasy)

The Crimson Queen

The Silver Sorceress

The Shadow King

Swords & Saints (Sword & Sorcery)

The Cleansing Flame

The Twilight Empire

The Hollow God

The Sharded Few (Epic Progression Fantasy)

The Umbral Storm

The Shadows of Dust (Space Fantasy)

The Manticore's Soiree (Short Stories)